TRANSLATED BY NANDAKUMAR K.

YOU

A NOVEL

M. MUKUNDAN

eka

eka

First published in Malayalam as *Ningal* by DC Books in 2023

Published in English as *You* in 2024 by Eka, an imprint of Westland Books, a division of Nasadiya Technologies Private Limited

No. 269/2B, First Floor, 'Irai Arul', Vimalraj Street, Nethaji Nagar, Alapakkam Main Road, Maduravoyal, Chennai 600095

Westland, the Westland logo, Eka and the Eka logo are the trademarks of Nasadiya Technologies Private Limited, or its affiliates.

ISBN: 9789360455750

10 9 8 7 6 5 4 3 2 1

Typeset by Jojy Philip, New Delhi

Printed at Thomson Press (India) Ltd

YOU

M. Mukundan was born and brought up in Mahe. He rose to critical acclaim and popularity with *Mayyazhippuzhayude Theerangalil* (1974). His stories and novels have been widely translated into various Indian languages as well as English and French. He has been awarded the Ezhuthachan Puraskaram, the highest literary honour given by the Government of Kerala, the Crossword Book Award twice, in 1999 for *On the Banks of the Mayyazhi* and in 2006 for *Kesavan's Lamentations*, and the Sahitya Akademi award and N.V. Puraskaram for *Daivathinte Vikrithikal* (*God's Mischief*). His other major works include *Prasavam* (2008) and *Kesavante Vilapangal* (2009). He was presented with the insignia of Chevalier in the Order of Arts and Letters by the French government in 1998. He also served as the president of the Kerala Sahitya Akademi from 2006 to 2010. Four of his books have been adapted into award-winning films. *Delhi Gadhakal* (2011), translated as *Delhi: A Soliloquy*, based on his experiences of living and working in Delhi for forty years as a cultural attaché at the French embassy, won the JCB Literature Prize in 2021. In 2004, he retired from that position and now lives in Mahé.

After completing his master's degree in economics, **Nandakumar K.** started his career as a sub-editor at *Financial Express*, followed by stints in international marketing and general management in India and abroad. His co-translation of M. Mukundan's *Delhi Gadhakal, Delhi: A Soliloquy*, won the JCB Prize for Literature in 2021. His other translations are: *A Thousand Cuts*, the autobiography of Professor T.J. Joseph; *The Lesbian Cow and Other Stories* by Indu Menon; *In the Name of the Lord*, the autobiography of Sr Lucy Kalappura (*Karthavinte Namathil*); *Anthill* (*Puttu*); *Elephantam Misophantam* (*Aanaththam Piriyaththam*) and *Blackened* (*Karikkottakkary*) by Vinoy Thomas; and *Zin* by Haritha Savithri. Nandakumar is the grandson of Mahakavi Vallathol Narayana Menon. He lives in Dubai and works for a shipping line as a business analyst.

CONTENTS

BOOK TWO

'None of us choose to be born, but we should have the right to choose when and how we die.'

Dr Heidi Henson

BOOK ONE

1

YOUR DEATH

Your name is Unnikrishnan.

Your mother is Lakshmikutty and your father Goyindan, document-writer and stamp-paper vendor. You, Unnikrishnan, erstwhile movie-house manager, are the fourth of their five children. The oldest one, Ramakrishnan, runs a grocery store, the second son, Shivaraman, is a tailor, and the third, Vasudevan, is a clerk in a company owned by a Gujarati. Chubby, mischievous Kausalya, your baby sister, completes the family.

Although you are now over seventy, the muscles on your chest and thighs are still supple. Your age shows more in your hair; occasional dark strands peep from between the dominant grey, like distant memories of a youth long gone. As with everyone else, there was a time when you were a young man; before that, an adolescent; a child. And before that . . .

Why have you come to the city now, taking a bus from Kundachira?

Rare are the occasions when you leave home these days. Your house remains hushed, like nature during an eclipse. There's a sticky darkness everywhere. A little light may still be milked from it, but you have no intention of doing so. You've become one with the darkness. You're also aware that this universe has more darkness than it has light.

On Friday, 14 November 2019, you left for the city to give the 'public' a piece of news. The public for you is the common person. As you often say, 'There are a few people around me who live an uncelebrated life, like me.' You need to get the news to them. And you thought long and hard about how to do this.

The easiest way to reach out to people is through social media, you know that of course. But you also know that fish sellers, headload workers, coconut-tree climbers, construction workers, employees at restaurants, they are not all on Twitter and Facebook. You are certain in your belief that, even now, the easiest way to reach the ordinary person is through the newspapers. And that's why you decided to hold a press conference.

You know that if it's held at your house, no one will turn up. So you chose the Press Club as the venue. There can be no better place to hold a press conference, right?

The Press Club is located on the first floor of Century Buildings in the heart of the city. On the ground floor is Kottoor Krishnan Bakery. The bakery, established by Kottoor Krishnan in the month of Chingam in the Malayalam year 1117, that is, August 1942, is now run by Kottoor Thazath Divakaran. During Krishnan's time, it sold salted and sweet banana chips, laddoos, breads, buns, biscuits and lotta kach, a sweet-and-sour snack. These days, you'll also find cutlets, puffs and samosas. Divakaran has been speaking of introducing burgers too, very soon.

Whenever you are in town, you go and stand in front of the bakery for a while. 'I like the smell of onion vada being fried,' you've been heard to say. Their laddoos are famous too. They don't contain artificial colours and you enjoy crunching on the bits of rock candy. Banana chips are another speciality of the bakery. The ever-present aroma of thinly sliced chips being fried emanates from the back of the building and wafts into the narrow lane in front.

The press meet is scheduled for 10.30 a.m. At 10 a.m., you slowly climb the steps behind the bakery to the Press Club, your feet hurting. The pain comes from deep inside your bones, not just the muscles.

The Press Club has a dais large enough to accommodate seven or eight chairs. The hall itself can seat thirty. On the back wall of the hall hangs a framed portrait of Mahatma Gandhi.

When you reach the door, the first person you see is a woman sweeping the floor.

'My name is Rajalakshmi, but my parents call me Raji. So, everyone calls me that,' is her usual mode of self-introduction. She is the Press Club's sweeper.

'No one here?' you enquire without entering. You are favouring your right leg, which hurts even more than the other.

She straightens up and appraises you, holding up the broom like a flaming brand. For a moment, you wonder if she is a member of the Aam Aadmi Party.

You look at yourself through her eyes: you are wearing a starched white shirt and mundu. Your shirt sleeves are folded just below the elbow. Your greying hair is combed back neatly. Your shirt pocket holds a fountain pen and a piece of paper folded in four. You never leave your house without those two things in your pocket.

'Secretary sir is inside.'

She is referring to Moosakutty.

As you try to step inside, Rajalakshmi stops you. 'What, you don't have eyes on your face? Stay out till I finish sweeping!'

You do as she says, not uttering a word. You will not be able to stand for long; the pain is crippling.

You watch as Rajalakshmi sweeps up the paper plates and cups and squishy banana peels from under the moulded chairs—leftovers from the refreshments served at the press conference last evening. You've made no such arrangement for yours. You didn't know it was expected, and it's too late now.

The Aam Aadmi Party member enters the secretary's room, her broom held high, and immediately, Moosakutty emerges from inside. He is a short man and wears thick, black-rimmed glasses. His shirt is tucked neatly into his trousers and a belt is strapped over his generous waist and protruding belly. 'I'm a biryani lover, this belly is the result,' is his usual apology.

He smells strongly of cigarette smoke.

'Who? What do you want?'

The look on his face—as if he has consumed something bitter—tells you that, for some reason, he is not happy to see you standing there. You are aware, however, that despite his gruff behaviour he has the reputation of being a good man.

'There's a press conference at ten-thirty.' Hesitantly, you continue, 'May I sit down here for a bit? My legs are hurting.'

'Did anyone tell you not to sit down?'

You walk in and take a seat in the back row. Moosakutty stands in the veranda, puffing on his cigarette and blowing out smoke. When Rajalakshmi is done with her cleaning, he steps back into the President's room with its attached toilet.

It's past 10.30 a.m. now. No one has turned up. Inside you, anxiety raises its head like a gangly earthworm.

Some more time passes. A young man with a bulging shoulder bag hurries in. Vasavan sir is the publisher, editor, reporter and owner of *The Evening News*, a local city paper. He says with apparent relief, 'Thank God it hasn't started yet! I thought it would be over by now.'

Close to 11 a.m., one more person turns up. Tall and middle-aged, stick thin, with greying stubble on his face. This is Achutty Gurukkal, a reporter for a local daily. Everyone knows that he gave up the family occupation of kalarippayattu to get into journalism. Vasavan sir and Gurukkal shake hands with each other.

You sit there impatiently, looking at your watch. After five minutes, Moosakutty comes back in and announces, 'We may as well begin. You aren't the only one to have a press conference here, you know. Others will turn up soon.'

'Aiyyo, but no journalists have come,' you protest.

'And that's my fault? Uncle, climb up to the dais. If someone else comes, they can join.'

You go up to the dais and choose to sit in the chair next to the secretary. By that time, one more person arrives and seats himself in the back row.

Moosakutty stands up, clears his throat and, gazing indifferently at the empty chairs, welcomes the audience. Then he turns to look at you. 'Start now, Uncle. First, introduce yourself.'

With that, as if exhausted after a long discourse, he collapses into his chair. You stand up and address Vasavan sir, Achutty Gurukkal and the stranger in the back row. 'My name is C.V. Unnikrishnan. C.V. stands for Chapparath Veetil. I live in Kundachira.'

Vasavan sir leans over and whispers in Gurukkal's ear, and both laugh silently. You feel like a deaf man watching someone's raucous laughter. You can guess what triggered it. If the syllable 'ee' were added to the second syllable of Kundachira, what would that make it? Ugh . . . you cannot bear to think of such vulgarisms now.

You continue softly, 'I have something to say to the public, to my people. Please help me carry my news to them. I would have preferred to say it directly to them, but that is impossible, so I decided to hold a press conference. Sadly, I don't see any reporters from the main dailies or TV channels. Possibly because I am a poor man who leads a poor life, invisible to all.'

You gaze at Vasavan sir and Gurukkal, who are seated in front of you, and realise they are not paying attention. The secretary throws you a dirty look, as if telling you to hurry up and be done with it. You raise your voice a little and say, 'I know you are in a hurry to leave, so I'll say what I have to in four sentences. Let me not waste your valuable time.'

Vasavan sir and Achutty Gurukkal seem to be waiting for your next words. The stranger at the back also looks interested.

You say to them, 'I shall die on the sixteenth of next month, a Monday.'

Vasavan sir and Achutty Gurukkal look back at you, uncomprehending, then alarmed. Moosakutty guffaws and lapses into silence. For the first time, they all give you dark looks. You are an old man, past seventy. It's not surprising that death is closing in on you. But your announcement has clearly thrown them.

'This is all I have to tell you. Please inform your readers of my impending death. This is my request. Thank you. Namaskaram.'

You have no desire to say anything more. You may have spoken at length if the hall were full and there were representatives from all the local dailies and TV channels. What is the point of holding forth to this apology of an audience?

Moosakutty says to himself, 'The man is mad. Absolutely no doubt about it.' He looks at Vasavan sir and Achutty Gurukkal and asks, 'Do you have any questions for him? If not, let's go. I have a lot of work to do.'

'No tea?' Gurukkal enquires anxiously.

Vasavan sir says, 'Why do you need to let the public know about your death? Who do you think you are? The chief minister?'

'How are you going to die? Dangle from the end of a rope or throw yourself in front of a running train?' Gurukkal asks listlessly.

'Neither.'

'How else do you plan to commit suicide? Poison?'

'I don't plan to die by suicide.'

'Is someone going to murder you? If so, how do you have advance information?'

'No. When the time comes, you'll get to know.'

'He's mad. Let's not waste any more time,' Vasavan sir tells Gurukkal.

'Don't ask me anything more. I can assure you of one thing. I'll die on the sixteenth, and it won't be by suicide. I'll tell you more later. That is, if you are interested.'

You nod to the three men in the audience as a mark of your gratitude and walk out.

'Not even a glass of tea,' grumbles Achutty Gurukkal.

'He's a lunatic, have no doubt,' Moosakutty says.

Press conferences are a daily occurrence here. Political parties, religious groups, NGOs, they all hold them, either to complain or to protest. Cultural organisations use them to announce awards. This is the first time someone has held a press conference to announce his imminent death.

'So, how are you going to die?' Moosakutty mumbles to himself as he pulls up his trousers, which keep slipping down despite the belt.

You leave the Press Club and walk towards the bakery. You have a craving for hot onion vada. The thin attendance at the press meet was disappointing, but you console yourself that at least Vasavan sir and Achutty Gurukkal showed up. There was also the stranger at the back.

'What'll you have, Uncle?'

'Onion vada, piping hot.'

'How much?'

'Hundred grams.'

'Hundred grams?' Divakaran is scornful. People come to his bakery to buy laddoo, mysore pak, vada in kilograms. 'Get lost, old man,' he mutters under his breath.

'The onion vada has not been delivered yet. Will you have medu vada instead?'

'That's not the same.'

'Then come back after half an hour. We should have the onion vada and bonda by then.'

'All right.'

You walk past the Municipal Office to the auditorium where an exhibition-cum-sale of handloom fabrics is going on. The breeze blowing in from the sea is salt-laden. You go around the exhibition and inspect the khaddar mundu, thorthu and sarees on display. A man of your age with a large umbrella tucked under his arm peers at you and asks, 'Who are you? You look so familiar. I've seen you somewhere . . .'

'Must be your imagination,' you reply.

'No, I know you. I've seen a photo.'

'Impossible.'

After loitering around the exhibition for some more time, you head out to the bus station. A bus has just arrived, its signboard announcing its destination: Moozhikkara. You wait while two men finish unloading plantains and elephant yams from the top.

'Does this bus go to Moozhikkara?' An old woman in a thakka, her head covered, shuffles up to you and asks in a loud voice.

'Yes, it goes to Moozhikkara,' a passenger confirms.

You are happy to have the company of the old woman on your return journey. You notice her sagging, ptosis-affected breasts, flat on top and with the nipples visible below the fold of her thakka. The seat next to her is vacant, but you take one that is two rows behind—men do not sit on seats reserved for women. The bus fills up quickly, the passengers packed together like sardines.

'Where are you headed?' enquires the passenger sitting next to you. His right ear is smaller than his left one, you notice.

'Kundachira.'

'Do you live there?'

'Umm . . . yes. What else do you want to know?'

The man says no more and, with his hands tucked between his thighs, sits staring into the distance.

You return home despondent from the failed press conference and the onion vada you didn't get to have.

Two days later, a girl comes in search of you.

2

YOUR MEMORIES

'My name is Parvathi. My pet name is Paru. My friends call me Kunjimookki. My nose is rather small, you see. You can call me what you like—even Tiny Nose. What's in a name, after all?'

You nod, thinking about a day when no one would have names.

'Why are you silent? Do you not like it that I am here?'

'I dislike no one.'

The truth is that, in this moment that crawls along like a sloth, you don't feel like talking to anyone. If you say anything at all, it will be about your death, your luminous, radiant death. But whatever you had to say, you said at the press conference. You have no desire to repeat it all over again. You also don't want to reveal anything more than you already have.

She is watching your mouth keenly, as though ready to jot down everything that comes out of it. Her mind is her notebook.

You feel increasingly uneasy.

'It was really hard, locating your house. No one knew your address. And not even your neighbours know you.'

'They shouldn't. That's why I live in this isolated place, where there's no one else.'

'Don't you feel bored?'

'What's boredom for someone who's going to die soon?'

In your seventy-odd years, you've never felt bored with anyone or anything. You've always looked at the world with affection, almost a paternal indulgence. You've held life close to your chest, sung lullabies and gently put it to sleep. You fall asleep listening to your own lullabies.

You want to go in now and lie down on the bed by the window. An armchair is placed near it. When the window is open, the breeze comes in, carrying the fragrance of the laburnum flowers it had caressed on its way here. The rustle of leaves can be heard. The trees need the breeze to be able to talk.

Who is this Paru who has come to you in your last days? You are unable to understand why she has taken the trouble to find her way to your tiny, insignificant home, reaching even before the sun had climbed into the sky.

She had taken the direct bus, 'Shabari', to Kundachira, not the one that went to Moozhikkara. She had asked all the people she met along the way, but no one seemed to know the man she was looking for. So she stopped at each house and asked, 'Do you know where Unnikrishnan stays?'

'Which Unnikrishnan?'

'The one who's going to die . . .'

'There's no Unnikrishnan here. And no one's going to die.'

'Do you have a police station here? Maybe the policemen would know him?'

'The nearest police station is in Moozhikkara. Go check with them.' The shirtless elderly man dressed only in an ochre-coloured mundu shut the door in her face.

Finally, after drawing a blank with everyone she asked and every house she stopped at, a disappointed Paru knocked on the door of a tiny house with flower pots hanging in the patio.

It was your house.

You rarely have visitors. The only visitor—and he too comes only occasionally— is Balan, your childhood friend and the doctor who treats you when you have any minor ailments.

Unlike other doctors, Balan always wears a shirt and a mundu, not trousers. Because of this, people used to find it hard to believe he was a doctor. 'He's no doctor, he's a compounder,' they would say. 'He's a quack,' Velukutty would say loudly, to make sure that everyone heard him.

You were then the manager of Velukutty's cinema theatre, and Balan used to visit you often. You were of the same age, and young, bursting with vim and vigour.

Nowadays, when he comes to your house, Balan brings chicken curry cooked in roasted coconut paste and appam, or idiyappam and mutton stew, or something like that, and you eat together. You've always enjoyed good food.

After Balan leaves, you wipe the dining table with a damp cloth. Although you've had your share of setbacks in life, you've always ensured that your house is clean, and you always wear freshly washed and ironed clothes. It was Sree Narayana Guru who taught you to prioritise personal hygiene and keep your surroundings clean. Gurudevan had passed through Kundachira once, long before you were born. Later, along the route he had taken, schools started to sprout.

You were born in 1945, though your school-leaving certificate shows the date as 1944.

'Achcha, did you forget the year I was born in?'

'It's only a difference of one year . . . no big deal,' Vendor Goyindan said carelessly. He wasn't one to take things lightly. But to justify his own actions, he would go to any length.

Vendor Goyindan is no longer alive. But when you left home on leave, he was still alert and sprightly. He used to hold one corner of his mundu and stride ahead rather than walk. You could never catch up with him. When he had to go to the eye hospital at Vadakara for treatment, he would take you along. You were a child at the time, and it was a struggle to keep up with him; you were running all the time. Passersby used to look curiously at this man walking briskly by, arms swinging, with a child running behind him.

Your father died while you were away on leave. You had no idea he had died; no one told you because you were living in a place without an address. Only when you returned home did you learn of his passing. By then, your mother had died too.

'Unnikrishnan sir . . .' Paru says softly, reminding you that she is still here. She can tell from your faraway expression that you are in danger of getting submerged in a swamp of memories. These are your last days and there is a lot to remember.

Seated on the chair in the patio, Paru looks around.

'Why haven't you put curtains on your window? Your bedroom is fully visible from the road.'

Your unease is turning into irritation.

'You can see only if you look. Who asked you to look?'

You always leave the curtain-less windows open. You need the light and air to come in. Your house is in the middle of a large plot of land, and isolated. There are no houses or other buildings in the vicinity. You chose to rent this house precisely for that reason. Your tharavad is in Karikkat village, twenty miles away from Kundachira, but you prefer this house and its environs.

'What do you want? I'm in no mood for socialising or chatting with anyone. Say what you have to and be done with it.'

'All right, don't get so irritable. I'll tell you why I'm here. Two days ago, you held a press conference. I've come to talk to you about that.'

'I've got nothing to tell you. I said what I had to at the press conference.'

'I wasn't there.'

'No one was there.'

'I didn't know that.'

You remain silent. You have no wish to continue the conversation. If only she would leave.

She seems to sense this from your expression, but she has not come of her own volition.

'My editor has told me to get all the information I can from you and report to him.'

She is working as a trainee at a newspaper called *Aagolam* or Global, started by a newly affluent man called Konnath Pappan. *Aagolam*'s rival is a daily that was part of—and grew with—the freedom struggle, as well as Sree Narayana Guru's reformation movement. Pappan is constantly devising strategies to try and eclipse its circulation numbers.

Paru is sincere in her desire to not trouble you. Once you realise that, you feel some sympathy for her.

'I'll give you five minutes. Be brief. And please leave immediately after that. Do you understand?'

'Yes, boss.' She sticks out her tongue and licks her lips. 'Vasavan sir and Achutty Gurukkal reported your story in detail. Those who read it have two questions for you.'

'Ask then.'

'You've announced the date of your death in advance. Only someone who has decided to kill himself could do that. But you say you are not planning on suicide. Can you please explain?'

'I'll die on the sixteenth of next month. I'll explain everything before I die. Hold on till then.'

'Will you be holding another press conference on the day of your death?'

'I haven't yet decided.'

The girl's face falls.

'Why are you going to die? Can you at least tell me that? If I go back empty-handed, the editor will . . . Sir, I am a trainee.'

'Not just you. Everyone is a trainee.'

She looks at you with folded hands. You are not unsympathetic to this girl who is young enough to be your granddaughter.

'Listen,' you say, 'life is like a detective novel. If the end is revealed at the beginning, who will read it? Where's the fun in reading it?'

Desperately clutching at this thread, she says, 'At the end of the detective novel, the culprit is caught. That's how it always ends. Sir, are you a culprit? What crime have you committed? At least answer this one question. Please.'

'I'll give you the answer on the sixteenth. You should come then.'

'Even my dog won't come!' she snaps. She gets up hurriedly, picks up her bag and notebook, and walks off without saying goodbye. Then she stops, turns around and says loudly, 'You're a crackpot.'

'It's your lover who's a crackpot.'

'Bugger off.'

You stand there and watch until she vanishes from sight. You expect her to turn and look back at least once, but she does not. A deep sigh escapes you. A young girl telling someone older than her father to bugger off!

'Bad luck will dog you,' you mutter, 'for you were born out of wedlock.'

Crackpot.

You would never admit that you are a crackpot. You do like the word, however. And it's not like you haven't been called names before. Mad fellow. Nutcase. Loony. Insane. And these are the milder ones. Scoundrel, wacko, lunatic, sex maniac, you've been called these and worse.

Paru will come again to see you. She'll come for sure. You are certain about that.

You had announced unequivocally that on Monday, 16 December, you would die. You also said that it would not be by suicide. How are you able to predict your own death so accurately?

That is the question troubling not only Paru but also Vasavan sir and Achutty Gurukkal, and all those who read about it. You don't know it yet, but you have become the subject of a great deal of speculation.

3

YOUR CHILDHOOD, YOUR HOME

Your earliest childhood memories are of shame and humiliation. When you were a third standard student, the entire class was witness. The perpetrator was Raman Kutty Master.

Raman Kutty Master wore a half-sleeve khaddar shirt, with a broad-bordered khaddar veshti twisted around his neck. He was constantly chewing paan, and would spit out a red stream before entering the classroom.

Although a Gandhian, Raman Kutty Master did not believe in non-violence. As soon as he entered the classroom, even before taking attendance, he would pick up the cane that lay on the windowsill. Without a stick in hand, he seemed incapable of doing anything.

'This master is something else! If he had a gun in his hand instead of a cane, he would shoot and kill me,' you had said to yourself more than once.

Raman Kutty Master would enter the classroom the instant the school bell rang. Cane in hand, he would do a quick survey of the class. As soon as he noticed that your place on the bench was vacant, his face would redden; the veins on his neck would swell and throb; his agitation would be reflected on every student's face.

'Hasn't that boy come yet? Where the hell is he?'

He would look at each student slowly, terrifyingly. This was a boys' school. If there had been girls in the class, they too would have been at the receiving end of that look. You would shudder at the thought.

While Raman Kutty Master stood there fuming, his cane-wielding hand upraised, his eyes burning holes into your place on the bench, you would streak into the classroom as if shot from a bow. You would put your books down on the bench and stand quietly, terrified even to look up.

Raman Kutty Master did not know that you got to school after negotiating two miles of slippery ridges between fields, narrow lanes where you had to squeeze past grazing cattle and goats, and rutted, dusty paths used by bullock carts. Even if you ran all the way and at your fastest, it would have been impossible to reach before the bell rang.

Your mother had to take the blame for this. You could not leave for school before finishing your breakfast of kanji with grated coconut and coconut chutney.

'Amma, please give it to me quickly. Raman Kutty Master will cane me.'

By then, you would be ready to leave, dressed in shorts and a shirt, your oiled hair combed neatly, Cuticura talcum powder on your face. Your mother would say calmly, 'The kanji will be ready soon. Meanwhile, let me grind some chutney.'

She would start to grind the roasted coconut pieces, shallots and bird's eye chillies. Pale and fretting, you would look on, wondering if you should forego breakfast and start the long run to school. The school did provide lunch—rice, sambar and fish curry. Some days there would be plain dal instead of sambar. However, you would have to stay hungry all morning. You couldn't bear the thought of that.

After having your fill of the kanji, you would set off for school, clutching your books, knowing that Raman Kutty Master would be lying in wait, cane in hand.

'Come, eda, come, I'll whip your ass into a pulp,' he would say, looking like a fox about to catch a chicken. 'Come here, you rascal. I'll teach you a lesson today. After this, you'll never be late to school again.'

Still panting, you would squeeze past Balan, who was seated to your right, and stand in front of Raman Kutty Master.

He would move closer, cane in hand, and say, 'Take off your shorts.'

As the other children struggled to control their laughter, Balan would give you sympathetic looks, as though it was his bottom that was about to be whipped.

'Didn't I tell you to take off your shorts, you moron?'

You refused to comply.

'Such impudence! Take it off, you mule!'

Raman Kutty Master would forcefully pull your shorts down, while you held on and tried to pull them back up. A mere child, you did not have the strength to wrestle with the master. He would lower your shorts to your knees and make you stand facing the class.

'Bend over.'

You would try to pull down the front of your shirt to hide your privates. But as the first stinging blow landed on your buttocks, the pain would make you howl and leap in the air, exposing everything.

Once, while bathing you beside the well, in the shade thrown by a plantain leaf, your mother asked you, 'What's this on your buttocks?'

She used a piece of husk to clean the caked mud on your legs. 'I asked you a question. What is this?'

'Raman Kutty Master beat me with a cane.'

'Because you didn't do your lessons. You deserve it.'

She moved on to your heels and said unsympathetically, 'So much mud. What kind of muck have you been rolling in? It's easier to give an elephant a bath.'

Your mother started to rub the husk over your buttocks. You thought she spent more time than was necessary on the task, as though secretly enjoying it. 'In my next life, let me be born without buttocks,' you prayed to Karikkat Bhagawathy. She was the favourite deity of your people.

Your childhood passed thus, in a jumble of thrashings, pain and humiliation.

Your parents, Vendor Goyindan and Lakshmikuttyamma, had five children—four boys and a girl: Ramakrishnan, Shivaraman, Vasudevan, Unnikrishnan and Kausalya. They had fervently hoped that their fourth child would be a girl. But though they made offerings to Karikkat Bhagawathy, she did not bless them. You, Unnikrishnan, were born as a boy.

When the midwife Kunjanni pulled out your bloody, slippery head from your mother's womb, she screamed. The old woman held you upside down by your ankles and slapped you gently on your bum until you let out your first cry. It was a half-hearted cry, as if you were crying for someone else's sake.

Your mother's eyes, tired after hours of labour, first went to where your tiny legs joined your torso. Through her tears, she could see nothing there. Her eyes filled with happiness. When the blurring reduced and her eyes cleared up, she was shocked. There, below your navel, was a small hibiscus bud.

Your mother turned her face away. You came as a great disappointment to your parents, your birth entirely unwelcome. However, you loved and nurtured your own life as you might a hatchling. You were determined to love life dearly until your last breath. You surprised yourself with this lifelong ambition.

*

Your father was left-handed. Brushing his teeth, eating, everything was done with his left hand. He was also a disciplinarian, and honest. He never earned money through dubious means, although there was no dearth of opportunities for doing so.

Your part of the world was full of paddy fields, banana plantations and coconut groves. There were streams and canals and ponds that overflowed during the monsoons. To the east was a river with mangroves proliferating along its banks.

Your village had no post office or school or library. It only had a few shops and a Bhagawathy temple. A fifteen-minute walk through the coconut groves and an open trail beyond would take you to Koman Chettiar's pottery shop. The junction was called Paathimukku.

If you took the path through the fields, a mile or so due east, you would reach the kiosk run by Kungkar, from which he sold paan and confectionaries. Your father used to despatch you to the shop to fetch a cheroot and tobacco. The cheroot, he would smoke; the tobacco was massaged and softened in the hollow of his palm, and parked between his molars. Everyone has a smell that you associate with them—your mother's was that of breast milk and your father's, tobacco.

Velayudhan's teashop stood by the side of the ferry landing. Because of his stammer, almost everyone called him Ve . . . Ve . . . Velayudhan. Water boiled constantly in the samovar in Velayudhan's shop. People waiting for the ferry would drink tea to kill time. If they had an additional anna, a banana fritter or parippu vada would accompany the tea.

The single trail through the banana plantation led to Choyi vaidyar's dispensary. You would cut through the temple grounds to get there. The air in the dispensary was heavy with the odour of herbs and various concoctions, decoctions and liniments. You can still remember the time your father carried you on his shoulders to the vaidyar when you developed symptoms of scabies on both your legs. You enjoyed that trip. You imagined you were riding an elephant, and it made you forget the itching and burning from the oozing scabs.

On the way to your school was a thatched shed with one room. A woman from somewhere farther north lived there alone. She was dark and voluptous, and wore a nose stud. Her name was Pankajakshi. Although your mother warned you not to look towards the shed on your way to school, you could not look away. You would ask yourself, 'If I look at her, is the sky going to fall?' You had a tendeny to do things that were banned, to focus on what was proscribed.

Your brother Shivaraman's tailoring shop was located in Paathimukku and Ramakrishnan's grocery store was not far from there either. Karikkat was like an island beneath a green blanket and Paathimukku was its nerve centre. There were houses on both sides of the junction, but there were no other buildings.

*

When you were promoted to the fourth standard, you had only one period a day with Raman Kutty Master. In the fifth standard, he stopped coming to your class altogether. However, the humiliation that he had put you through remained like a raw wound in your mind. Some of your classmates would poke fun at you and say hurtful things, but you bore that stoically. For an eleven-year-old, you were remarkably mature.

Eventually, Raman Kutty Master retired from service. You were so relieved, you thanked Karikkat Bhagawathy for saving you.

Then, one day, he arrived at your house, veshti, cane and all. Your father was away at work and your mother was having a bath. You were lounging on the veranda, daydreaming.

'Achchan is not here.'

'I didn't come to meet Vendor, I came to meet you. Take off your shorts.'

He climbed onto the veranda. Hearing his voice, your sister Kausalya peeped through the window and was horrified to see the master.

'Why are you beating me now? I've done nothing,' you said.

'Are you arguing with me? Take off your shorts.'

When he bent to pull down your shorts, you snatched the cane from his hand, broke it in two and threw it away.

'Who's that, Unni'shna?' asked your mother, stepping into the house through the kitchen door, her clothes still damp.

'Our Raman Kutty Master.'

'Aiyyo, its you, Master. Please sit down. I'll be with you in a minute.'

Raman Kutty Master, seething from the ignominy of the battle lost to his student, stepped out as if he had not heard the invitation. He cast a pitiful look at his cane, which lay with its spine broken. Then he lifted his foot and stomped on it.

You were not a brilliant student, but you never failed an exam. You would always get just enough marks to be promoted to the next class. Eventually, you got through high school and passed the tenth standard exam. At that point, your father said peremptorily, 'Enough of studies. You aren't going to become a magistrate. Work for a living now. I'm getting old and can't keep supporting you all.'

Your oldest brother, Ramakrishnan, had failed the ninth standard and started a grocery store. He was reasonably successful. Among the things he sold was a kind of sweet jaggery made by boiling and reducing fresh toddy. The liquid was poured into small rings made with coconut leaves and solidified. It melted in the mouth.

Your third brother, Vasudevan, learnt typewriting after school and left for Bombay. Although he found employment in an office, he never sent home any money. Some time later, he married a Gujarati woman and stopped coming to Kerala altogether.

'What arrogance! Did you give birth to him, suffer all that pain for this? Did I educate him for this? He doesn't need his father and mother any longer. He only needs his Gujarati wench,' Vendor Goyindan would say, his lower jaw trembling with rage.

Your other brother, Shivaraman, left school after the seventh standard and was at a loose end for a while before starting a tailoring shop. Since he never delivered on the promised date, people stopped giving him work. Every day, he would turn up at his shop and wait for someone to come and bring him cloth to stitch a shirt or a blouse. But no one ever did.

People had started talking about it. 'You know Vendor Goyindan's son, Shivaraman? His life is finished.'

'Why are you going to the shop to sleep? Isn't there a place at home for that?' your father used to mock him when he left in the morning carrying a torch and the key to the shop.

'I always wished someone in the family would become an officer. But my children have all turned out to be duds. Now only you are left, Unni'shna. You should study and become an officer.'

This same father was now telling you, 'Enough studying! Are you planning to become a magistrate?' You were in college by then, studying for a degree. No one in your family had gone beyond the tenth standard.

A room of your own, that was what you dreamed of all the time. You were a thinker. Why had Shivaraman become so lazy? Why did Vasudevan, after marrying the Gujarati woman, stop coming home? Why was Kausalya, though of marriageable age, not receiving proposals from any good families? Why did Raman Kutty Master lash you with the cane on your buttocks and never on the palms of your hands or your calves? You needed the privacy of a room to reflect on these things.

As the sun skimmed the tree tops and dropped and dimmed, and the petals of crape jasmine turned reddish in the dusk, your thoughts started to deepen. As the night progressed and the lamps that bathed the walls with yellowish light were extinguished, they became more profound and you needed your own private space, to think rather than to sleep. Later, when you started to scribble down your thoughts, you needed the solitude of a private room.

But Vendor Goyindan was a skinflint. Your house did not suit his status as a document-writer. It was thatched, with a small veranda running around it, and had four small rooms as well as an office room. The floor was coated with cow dung. Even in the day, the rooms were dark and cave-like. Goyindan slept in one of the ground-floor rooms; Kausalya and your mother in the other. The two rooms on the first floor were shared by you and your three brothers.

In the beginning, you shared a room with Kausalya. Then, one day, when you were in the ninth standard, your mother saw a red patch spreading on the back of Kausalya's skirt and chucked you out of the room. 'I don't want to see you here, ever again. Go and sleep in Vasudevan's room.'

When Vasudevan left for Bombay, you found yourself alone in the room. You would be able to do all your thinking without any disturbance, you thought. However, Shivaraman soft-soaped your mother and took over the room, and you had to start sharing the lumpy, bed-bug-infested cotton mattress with your grocer brother Ramakrishnan, who smelled of coriander and turmeric.

Why were you so adamant about having a room of your own?

Because, in order to think independently, one needs to be shorn not only of prejudices but also of clothes. Only when you are a digambara can your mind be pure and untainted. At least, that was what you believed. And if there was someone else in the room with you, how could you do this?

4

YOU AND HIDDEN THINGS

All through your childhood, you were attracted to hidden things. You liked to uncover and gaze upon concealed objects. It was a habit that brought disrepute to you and your family. Once, you were even beaten black and blue for it.

Later, when you stepped past adolescence and into your youth, you discovered that all your friends had a love interest; a few had multiple love interests. You alone had no romantic inclinations. You were friendly with a few girls, but none of these matured into romantic love. You were responsible for this—your disinterest and your lackadaisical attitude.

'Unni'shna, try falling in love. Then this black-and-white life will turn into Eastman colour,' Balan said to you once.

Balan was your classmate through school and college. Short, and with dishevelled hair, he was saved by his milk-white skin. 'Whatever else your failings, if you are fair-skinned, girls will be ready to elope with you.' It was this thought that gave Balan self-confidence. Anyway, he was not the sort of person who wept over what he did not have.

'Falling in love is not my ultimate aim,' you told him.

'Then what is it?'

'I want to be a writer.'

'A document writer? What's the problem with that? Your own father is one. He'll teach you. And don't document writers also fall in love and marry? I'll tell you what, Unni'shna, I'll point out a girl and you start pursuing her.'

'Who do you have in mind?'

You were keen to see this unknown girl. Was she also hidden from view?

'The bus stop where we take our bus from. You know the house with the patio, on the northern end of that road? There's a stunning looking girl there, waiting for you to fall in love with her.'

Were there brokers who found one girls to romance, just like there were marriage brokers? Listening to Balan that day, you thought so.

'You can see her on the patio, brushing her hair. As if she's waiting for someone. Maybe she's waiting for you, who knows? Let's go and take a look. We'll stand on the road and check her out. We've got be careful, though. She has thugs for brothers.'

You went with him only out of curiosity. She was standing in the patio, combing her hair, just as he had said. You waited by the roadside, but she did not turn her gaze towards you.

'What do you think? Do you like her?' the date-broker enquired.

'No.'

'What's wrong with her?'

'Nothing's wrong with her. I just didn't like her. End of story.'

'Fine, then! You're such a strange fellow, even God can't set you right.'

Balan walked away, his rage propelling him along. He never broached the subject again. For all you knew, she could still be standing there combing her hair, as if waiting for someone. But you knew that someone was not you. You continued to live your life in black and white.

Your first brush with femininity was in the form of long, wet hair left untied after a bath. You were in the sixth standard and Kausalya in the fourth, and you slept on the same bed, the one made with the timber of a hundred-year-old jackfruit tree. This bed that had witnessed many deaths and births was still firm and strong, although it had grown so black and discoloured with time that it was hard to tell it was made of wood. Even when you both jumped up and down on it, it did not so much as creak.

One day, when you returned to the room after gathering ripe mangoes that had fallen to the ground, you saw Kausalya sitting on the bed and sewing. Her hair was still wet from her bath. You went closer to her and asked, 'What are you sewing?'

'Are you blind or what? I'm embroidering a rose on my handkerchief.'

As you sat down next to her, saying 'Let me take a look,' the damp smell of bathing soap and oil infused with peppercorns rushed into your nostrils. You wanted more of the fragrance that hid beneath her hair. You inclined your head until your face rested on her wet hair, closed your eyes and inhaled deeply.

'You degenerate fellow, what are you doing?' Your mother rushed inside, her arm raised to slap you. 'If you do such vile things, I'll kill you.'

Her hands, toughened by hours of grinding coconut, pounding rice and beating clothes on the washing stone, rained blows on your face and shoulders.

'Aiyyo, I didn't do anything . . . don't thrash me.'

Your cries reached Vendor Goyindan just as he was entering the house. He wiped the sweat off his face with the towel over his shoulder and scraped his feet against the steps to rid them of mud. Then he braced himself on the umbrella he had just closed and jabbed its pointed end on the floor.

'Did you see what your darling son has done?'

'Eda, what did you do?'

'I only smelled her hair. I didn't do anything else.'

'Oh, is that his great crime? Lakshmikutty, bring me a glass of kanji vellam.'

Your father didn't think twice about what you had done. After his walk in the hot sun, his throat was parched. He only wanted some warm rice water with salt to slake his thirst. Your mother paid no heed to his request and declared, 'Enough! From now on, you won't sleep on the same bed. You, Kausalya, spread a mat on the floor and sleep on it. If this boy gets up to any mischief, just let me know. I'll flay the skin off his bum.'

From that day onwards, you slept on the bed while Kausalya lay on a mat spread on the floor layered with cow dung. On cold, rainy nights, the sight of your baby sister curled up on the mat was painful. You would take a sheet and cover her with it. A few times, you saw a shadow moving in the darkness and guessed it was your mother snooping around, playing secret police. She had lost faith in you. What a shame!

Around that time, your neighbour Kelu Asan died. Old age had made him blind and deaf. His family had been yearning for him to pass on peacefully. In spite of that, you could hear them bellowing like cattle. His pale, yellowing corpse was cremated in the compound of the house.

One day, during the school holidays, you were walking home past Kelu Asan's house when you noticed an earthen pot suspended from the rafters. Its mouth was tied with a piece of white cloth. Suddenly, you were filled with curiosity; you wanted to see what was inside that pot. You stepped onto the veranda and pulled up a footstool, then climbed on it and took the pot in your hands. You got down, untied the string around the cloth and peered into the pot. All you could see were ashes and a few small, scorched bones.

Just then, Kunjiraman, the oldest son of Kelu Asan, came towards you, asking, 'Who is that?'

When he saw the pot in your hands, he shrieked, 'Give that to me!'

You stared at him.

'That's my father inside the pot.'

You peered in once more, but you couldn't see Kelu Asan; only ashes and bones.

Kunjiraman tried to snatch the pot from your hands. In the scuffle, it fell with a thud and shattered.

'Aiyyo, my father,' Kunjiraman shouted. He tried to grab you by the neck and strangle you, but you managed to run away.

Your father broke off two branches from the chandada tree and whipped you with them. Most of the strokes fell on your buttocks. This did not surprise you in the least. Raman Kutty Master had taught you that buttocks not only house the conduit for excretion but are also the site for beatings. He was an excellent teacher.

'You know that son of Vendor Goyindan? Because of him, my father will never get moksha,' Kunjiraman went around lamenting to anyone who would listen.

Another time, you were seized with curiosity about an old, termite-eaten wooden trunk with a metal handle that lay in the darkness under your father's bed. You combed the room looking for the key, but couldn't figure out where your father had hidden it.

One day, you found the key. On a shelf above your father's bed were arrayed his medicines and bottles of herbal massage oils, most of them empty. Among them was a dark bottle of Waterbury's Compound, with its red label and cap. Your father had hidden the key in it.

When your father was away from home, you crawled on your tummy under the bed and, without making a sound, opened the box and looked inside. It was very dark, so at first you could see nothing. When your eyes adjusted to the darkness, you saw a stack of documents and neat bundles of one-, five- and ten-rupee notes.

'Who has opened my trunk, Lakshmikutty?'

Vendor Goyindan had just returned in the evening with his collection of stamp papers from the village office. Hearing his roar, your mother came running.

'Who has opened my box?'

'God himself must have come down and opened it.'

'Are you talking back at me? I'll smash your face in!'

'Shouldn't there be a key to open it? Isn't that key with you? Aren't you the one who hid it?'

'Then who has opened it?'

'Your children, who else?'

His fearsome look fell on Kausalya, who was hiding behind the door. She thought she would pee her pants in fright.

'Edi, come here. Tell me, who has opened my box? Tell me the truth or I'll kill you and bury you deep underground.'

When she reluctantly pointed at you, you felt as if arrows had been shot into your eyes from the tip of her fair little finger. Your father went outside to break a couple of prickly twigs from the Indian coral tree to whip you with.

There were other such incidents. One day, you were walking along the road when you happened to meet Varunni, the ten-year-old son of Kunjukuttan, the goldsmith. Suddenly, you were filled with an irrepressible desire to see what he was hiding in his shorts. When you asked the dark, thin boy to drop his shorts, he exclaimed in shock.

'Drop them or I'll strangle you and throw you into the village pond.'

Trembling, the terrified Varunni dropped his shorts.

'I'll tell my father.'

'You can tell your mother too.'

This curiosity to look at all things hidden reached its peak when you were in the eighth standard. That's when you ended up in the single-room abode of Pankajakshi, the dark lady with the nose stud. Although your mother had forbidden you many times from even looking in that direction, you arrived at her doorstep, school books in hand. The front door lay open. You scraped your soles clean against the stone that served as a step and peeped inside.

'Who's that?'

Pankajakshi was cooking rice in the room at the back. She wiped her wet hands on her mundu and came out and stood in front of you.

'What do you want?'

Looking at the books in your hands, she understood that you were headed to school.

'Tell me quickly, son, the rice is on the stove.'

'I want to see.'

'See what?'

'You.'

'That's funny! I'm standing right in front of you. Are you blind?'

Pankajakshi had met all sorts of men in the course of her life, some old, some young. But no one had made such a demand of her. She wondered whether you were a bit soft in the head, but she couldn't help feeling amused.

'My sweet boy, here, look as much as you want.'

She posed for you, head thrown back, her curves generous enough to arouse anyone who set eyes on her. The single mundu was tucked in just below her navel; she wore a tight red blouse. When grown men came to meet her, she would cover her chest with a towel. But in her eyes, you were a school kid.

'Have you had enough of looking?'

'This isn't enough.'

'Then how else do you want to see me?'

You wanted to see things that were hidden from you. You had used your nose to draw out the fragrance your sister hid under her hair. The key that your father hid away allowed you to look at the objects that were secreted inside the trunk. You saw what Varunni had hidden in his shorts. You were used to pulling out all that was hidden from you, looking at them with your eyes or nose. One day, you would pull out death itself from its hiding place and gaze upon it.

'Tell me, boy, how else do you want to see me?'

'Without a stitch of clothing on you.'

'You rascal, you are something else!'

Astonished, Pankajakshi looked at you, index finger on her nose. You waited anxiously for her next move.

'If you don't want to, it's okay. I'm leaving.'

She fell for the bluff.

'Come here, kid. Why the hurry?'

You turned around and gave her a once-over.

'Do you have any money?'

'No. What's the money for?'

'You oaf, does anyone come to me without money?'

Does one need money to see someone? This was news to you. You had been to see Choyi vaidyar. You had met Ve . . . Ve . . . Velayudhan. You had met Koman Chettiar. You saw your parents and siblings every day. No one had demanded a single paisa from you. Once again, you made as if to leave.

'Hey, where are you going? I'll show you as much as you want. But first hand over ten rupees.'

You could not believe your ears. If you had ten rupees, you would have bought yourself a new shirt and a pair of trousers.

'I don't have a single paisa.'

'Okay, then give me at least five rupees.'

'No, I'm leaving.'

You had no desire to look at anything that money could unveil.

'Get lost then, you fool!'

Pankajakshi slammed the door in your face.

'You get lost,' you swore as you walked away.

Many days later, it happened that you were strolling along behind a bullock cart loaded with rice bags, its shadow stretching behind you. It was late November and the sun was not very warm. At Paathimukku, when the cart changed direction, you lost its shade.

That's when you saw Khadar musaliyar coming towards you, the customary white turban on his head. Your heart quickened with an intense desire to see what was under it. Although you were strangers to each other, the musaliyar smiled at you as if you were acquainted. He was tall. In the eighth standard then, you did not even even come up to his shoulder. When he passed by, you ran after him and leaped up and knocked the turban off his head. It came loose, unfurled and fell to the ground.

'You idiot, are you mad?'

The musaliyar lifted his leg and aimed a kick at you, but you managed to evade it.

The skin on his scalp was pale from wearing the turban; his hair had turned grey in some places and stuck to his head; there was a lump in one place. Other than that, you could see nothing hidden there.

Gradually, your predilection for uncovering things turned into an obsession. If a vessel or pan or milk pot was kept covered in the kitchen, you would remove the lid and peek into it. There was a rice chest in the room on the southern side of the house. You lifted its lid and groped inside even though you could see nothing. Then you stepped inside the dark chest, lit a match and explored it in detail.

You would pull out every closed drawer and look inside. During a bus journey, you were overcome with a desire to look inside the conductor's bag. What could be hidden in it? You squirmed your way through the crowded bus until you were behind the conductor. While he was issuing tickets to the passengers, you hurriedly opened the flap and peeped in. The man slapped your hand away and shouted, 'Thief! Catch him.'

You stood dazed as the passengers encircled you.

'He's not even old enough to have a moustache. You scoundrel, have you started stealing already? Driver, let's go to the police station. He should not be allowed to go free,' one of them shouted.

'Aiyyo, I'm not a thief.'

'Are you the police then?'

The conductor grabbed you by the collar and raised his hand to slap you.

An old man who was watching the spectacle spoke up. 'Conductor, this is our Vendor Goyindan's son. He doesn't steal. Leave him be.'

You managed to get away unscathed.

Another time, while visiting one of your relatives with your mother, you noticed that the door of their bathroom was shut. What was hidden behind that door? You forced it open. A middle-aged woman who was bathing inside screamed in terror, covering her nakedness with whatever she could lay her hands on.

Your mother scolded you, your father used the stick on you and Kausalya teased you non-stop, but you persisted.

Until, finally, there came a change. When you became a young man, you stopped trying to look at concealed objects. Instead, you began to examine and unravel any hidden ideas or beliefs that you encountered. This proved to be far more dangerous.

5

YOU AND WOMEN

If your childhood and adolescence were a time of reckless curiosity and wonderment, youth became a time for creativity and femininity. For you, these qualities were inseparable, like Siamese twins with their heads congenitally joined. And both heads gazed in the same direction: creativity followed femininity.

You liked to think you were the product of a politics embedded in your creative and feminine selves. In your old age, you believe that it was the fallout of this politics that compelled you to flee to a distant land.

'What is a woman to you?' Paru asks you on one of her now regular visits.

You are lolling in the easy chair, stroking your flabby arms and thinking about your imminent death. If everything goes to plan, on the night of the sixteenth of the following month, you will cease to exist. This makes you alternately happy and sad, one emotion chasing after the other.

'Why're you silent?'

'I'm past seventy. Is that a question you should be asking me?'

'To me, you are still young. Even now.'

You know she is trying to flatter you. By putting you in a good mood, she is trying to get you to tell her how and why you are going to die. She has to gather as much information as possible. She is, after all, a journalist. Any fool can understand her motive, and you, whatever people may think, are nobody's fool.

'Why are you so quiet? Say something, Handsome!'

She calls an old man handsome. 'Keep your tricks to yourself. I've seen enough of this world,' you think.

'So, in your view, when will I become old? Once you are born as a human being, ageing is inevitable.'

'It's not mandatory. Some people never age.'

You agree. The woman you first loved and desired has not aged despite the passage of years. Even after two World Wars, the Bolshevik Revolution in Russia, the Spanish flu that killed forty million people, she remains thirty-eight. That was her age when you met her for the first time.

'You haven't answered my question. What is a woman to you?'

'Sagacious.'

'Or gorgeous?'

'Let's say, shrewd.'

'Which dictionary would have that definition? It's not in the *Shabdatharavali*. I know that for sure. I have a copy at home.'

You don't respond. You have no desire to continue this conversation with her. You know she is trying to ingratiate herself with you. All morning, you have been feeling tired. You just want to lie down.

'You can leave now, you bootlicker.'

'Bootlicker? Whose boots have I been licking? Not yours!'

She sounds wary and indignant.

'I'm tired, let me lie down for some time.'

Leaving her on the veranda, you go inside and shut the door behind you.

Having the door shut in one's face has to be the ultimate humiliation. She does not betray her feelings, however, either in her expression or in her voice.

She knocks on the door and asks loudly, 'Will you die by suicide? Say yes or no. I'll leave you in peace after that.'

You sit behind the closed door as if you have not heard the question. Like an idol floating on the sea.

You don't know how long she waits or when she finally leaves. Of one thing you are sure—she will come again. Her visits have become as regular as the rising and setting of the sun.

You will die on the sixteenth of the following month. Not many days remain now. You have little to put in order—no possessions, or even a will. A few things, however, remain to be done. You are, after all, preparing for a journey of no return. You are determined that no one should suffer the slightest inconvenience because of your passing.

Hordes of memories follow you around. Sometimes they show up as if a dark cave has opened in the far distance; sometimes they flow like the waters of a stream. At other times, they arrive like a pack of howling wolves. You are aware that this is natural. Alone and on the cusp of death, only memories can keep one company. Once, when Paru asked you, what is life, you answered without any hesitation: an old man's life is his memories.

You recall the first woman you ever wanted to be with. Her name was Charlotte. The name suggests she was a Christian, and she was indeed a Christian. But you were never concerned with her religion or sect. You had no complaints about her faith or what she chose to believe in. It was enough that she was there.

She entered your life around the time that you stepped out of adolescence and into youth. Sometimes, it felt like it was you who had entered her life, not the other way round. Charlotte arrived silently; even her footsteps were inaudible. It was the same with you. Without knocking or ringing the bell, you silently opened the door that had been left ajar and walked into her life.

'I never liked long walks,' Charlotte wrote on the first page of the book. You were the opposite. You enjoyed long walks. That was what led you to Charlotte.

You had to give up your long strolls when the pain started in your legs. You walk with difficulty these days. Today, you feel like you may not be able to walk at all without a hand on someone's shoulder. Although Charlotte is not by your side when dusk falls, you imagine that your arm is around her shoulder as you walk from your house to the temple surrounded by flaming lamps. You stand in front of the temple for a little while, leaning your head against Charlotte's imaginary shoulder, your palms joined worshipfully as you pray to Devi.

'Who's this Charlotte?' Paru asks on her fifth visit. Perhaps she is aware that you carry Charlotte within you.

She had found some words you had scribbled about her four decades ago. All her waking hours are spent now in the hunt for your life's secrets. She dusts off a book that you had closed over thirty-five years ago and starts to look through it. 'No, girl, no, don't do it,' you say in your head.

You had borrowed the book from the library during your first year in college. After everyone had dinner and your mother had cleaned up, locked the front door and gone to bed, you switched on the light in your room and started to read Charlotte's novel. You read through the early hours of the morning, lying down, sitting up, pacing up and down. You realised then that being awake and reading was the same as being asleep and dreaming.

While the others woke up and got busy with their chores, you fell asleep in your room with the mottled sunlight on the floor. In your sleep, you kept reading Charlotte's novel. A novel that could be read when awake and asleep had to be the greatest of them all.

'Who's she?'

'Haven't you read *Jane Eyre?*'

'No.'

'You don't know Charlotte Brontë?'

'I've heard of her. Who's she?'

'She's a writer.'

'Like you?'

'Like me? When did I become a writer? What kind of silliness is this?'

'Don't try to fool me. I know everything.'

She extracts a package from her bag and places it in front of you.

'What's this?'

'Oh, nothing, some breakfast for you.'

Four idlis. Some chutney. A splash of sambar.

'I ground it myself. I know you're very fond of coconut chutney, Unni'shna, now eat.'

You are old enough to be her grandfather, yet she calls you by your name.

'Girl, what are you up to?' you think to yourself. Each time she comes, she has something up her sleeve. Idli with coconut chutney is your favourite breakfast. How does she know that? You answer the question yourself. 'If she has discovered Charlotte, whom I carry inside me, how difficult could it have been for her to discover the chutney in my belly?'

Secretly, you have begun to look forward to her visits. You are anxious to know what she will come up with next.

You have never met Charlotte. And there is no photograph of her on the front or back cover of her book. You've tried to visualise her hair, her cheeks, teeth, chin, shoulders, eyes, breasts, navel, hands, fingers, the curve of her back, but you failed each time.

You've sketched humans and animals on paper purely from your imagination. Yet, you are incapable of creating a picture of Charlotte, who lives inside you. She is disembodied. She is intelligence, femininity and creativity personified.

Just once, you managed to give shape to an image in your head. It was the image of a pale-faced and frightened girl reflected in a mirror. It was, in fact, the reflection that Jane Eyre, Charlotte's heroine, sees of herself in the mirror. You were visualising the heroine as the author.

While reading *Jane Eyre*, you felt an uncontrollable attraction to Charlotte Brontë. 'I hear the wind blowing:

I will go out of doors and feel it,' she wrote. When you looked out through the casement window, you observed that the breeze blowing in your direction was born among the branches of the laburnum trees.

Charlotte, who died in 1855, appeared as a breeze a hundred years later to one of her readers, young Unni'shan. You read *Jane Eyre* over and over again. You could not separate Charlotte Brontë and Jane Eyre, the novelist and her heroine, from each other. When Jane married Rochester, who was blind and old enough to be her father, you forgot yourself and asked aloud, 'Jane Eyre, why? Why Rochester? Why couldn't you come to me? Although I may not have the wealth of Rochester, I have youth on my side. I would have given you everlasting pleasure.'

That night, lying in bed with Jane on one side and Charlotte on the other, you indulged in passionate lovemaking all night long. Orgiastic, mind-blowing love that the author, the heroine and the reader experienced together. You had never felt such intense pleasure in your life. Like aftershocks following an earthquake, the waves surged and washed over you until dawn broke.

Paru comes over again and asks, 'How are you going to kill yourself?'

You repeat, 'I don't intend to kill myself.'

'Then how are you going to die?'

'Let the sixteenth of next month arrive. You'll know then.'

Life is a detective novel, the end should never be disclosed. You remind her of this once more.

Will she give up? No, not at all.

'Some readers are able to guess the ending.'

'Can you?'

'If I could, would I be here now? Would I hassle you with my questions?' She has switched to the informal 'you' when she speaks to you now. The formal, respectful form of address has been shelved.

You give her a sympathetic look. Immediately, she asks, 'Unni'shna, why do you want to die? Can't you at least tell me that? I'm ready to do anything to keep you from dying. I'm ready even to die for you.'

'Go away! Try buttering up someone else.'

She leaves then, grumbling, disappointed.

She'll come again. There's no way she won't.

6

YOUR STUDENT DAYS

You were a proud graduate when you left college. Although your tharavad could boast of illustrious kalarippayattu practitioners and temple oracles, patriarchs with four or five mistresses in addition to their legally wedded wives, and even recipients of freedom-fighter pensions, there was not a single graduate among them. You filled that lacuna.

'Edi, Lachmikutty, didn't I tell you that our Unni'shnan will become a big man? You didn't believe me then. Now see, he's become a BA degree holder. How could he not? He's my son, after all,' Vendor Goyindan gloated. He could find no good words for Unni'shnan in the past, but here he was now, lionising him. Lakshmikuttyamma ignored her husband. Unlike him, she was never boastful.

'Unni'shna, come here.'

In your childhood, your father had only ever summoned you for a caning with the stick of a vattayila plant, which he always kept ready. Until you were fourteen years old, you carried the marks of those beatings on your buttocks, extensions of the marks left by Raman Kutty Master's cane. There were times when you wondered if your father would continue to beat you his entire life.

One day, your father took the stick lying on the veranda, broke it in two and flung it into the yard. 'You're incorrigible. You're not going to improve however much I beat you. I'm fed up!'

Maybe he was ruing those words now.

'Come here, Unni'shna,' he called again.

You watched as he pulled out the trunk from under the bed and extracted its key from the Waterbury's Compound bottle. He opened the trunk and took out five one-rupee notes, which he handed to you. 'Here, go and watch a movie. Get bread and mutton chops from Janata Hotel. And a glass of hot tea afterwards.'

'No, Achcha.'

'Why not? I've beaten you a lot, may God forgive me. But you have made our family proud. I can walk with my head held high, be proud that my son has passed out of college with a BA degree. That's not a small thing, is it?'

You were hesitant to accept the money. You liked uncovering hidden things, but there was a secret behind your graduation that only you knew. You had to reveal it now to your father; you were not capable of hiding things too long.

When Kausalya had her first period, she and your mother had tried their best to hide it from you, but you found out very easily. If you could discover other people's secrets so easily, you felt you had an obligation to reveal your own. So you confessed.

'Father, I passed . . .'

Your father looked at your face and thought it resembled that of a woman going into labour. You were embarrassed when it came to revealing your own secrets. 'Why is that so, Unni'shna,' you asked yourself.

'I passed by copying the answers,' you blurted out.

You had thought your father would be shocked. But his big face with bags under the eyes showed no change of expression. For a moment, you wondered if he had not heard you. But he wasn't hard of hearing, was he?

In the examination hall, the person who sat next to you was none other than Satyanarayanan, Raman Kutty Master's son. From the corner of your eye, you read all that he wrote on his answer sheet before reproducing it on your own. You could see clearly from the corner of your eyes, a talent that only you possessed. When you had confided this to Satyanarayanan some years ago, his response was, 'Which means you can ogle girls as much as you like and they won't know. Lucky guy!'

Satyanarayanan was aware that you were copying his answers. After the exams were over, he asked for two rupees as remuneration. You did not even have fifty paise with you. Whatever you had, you gladly handed over to him.

You waited for your father to fetch the stick he had broken and flung away. To your surprise, he said, 'Eda, these days, who doesn't cheat? Whatever it is, you have passed. That's enough.' After a moment, he continued, 'What you've just confessed to is gross stupidity. You would have passed the examination even without copying. You are an intelligent boy.'

It was as if your father had read your mind. You knew that you could have passed the examination without copying.

The answers to all the questions were at your fingertips. Then why did you feel the need to copy? You had always felt that certain things were beyond logic; this confirmed it.

Vendor Goyindan thrust the money into your hand. You closed your fist over it and decided that you would spend three-and-a-half rupees on yourself, setting aside the rest for Satyanarayanan.

'Now you have really become my son,' Vendor Goyindan concluded.

'What did Achchan give you? Money?' Kausalya asked as you left for your bath, oil glistening in your hair,

'Nothing,' you said, to provoke her.

'It was money, I saw it. He hasn't given me even twenty-five paise.'

'Have you passed your BA exam?'

'Is that my fault? I was forced to stop studying, wasn't I? So how can I pass anything?'

'Who asked you to start having your periods? You had to stop going to school after that . . .'

'That's not my fault. It's because I'm a girl,' Kausalya said, shooting you a fiery look. It was only the good deeds from your past life that prevented you from being turned to ashes instantly.

You knew the decision to stop her schooling had been taken by your mother. Your father supported it, and you did not intervene.

'Molu, you keep this.'

You took pity on her. She pushed the one-rupee note into her blouse surreptitiously.

'Don't tell Amma. I have to buy bangles during the festival at Karikkat Bhagawathy temple.'

If you were to hand over one-and-a-half rupees to Satyanarayanan, you would be left with two-and-a-half rupees. Is that what you had swotted and passed the exams for?

You changed your mundu and were halfway out of the house when Kausalya shocked you by saying, 'I'll tell everyone.'

'What?'

'About you sleeping naked.'

You were stunned.

'It's dark when I lie like that. Can you see in the darkness, you cat?'

Cats can see in the dark, right? Bats can too.

'Call me anything you want, cat, dog, anything. But I'll tell everyone.'

'Everyone meaning . . .?'

'Achchan, Amma, Sathiyechi . . .'

'Aiyyo!'

'Give me one more rupee. Then I won't tell anyone.'

You took one of the notes tucked into your rolled-up shirt sleeve and offered it to her.

You were embarrassed that Kausalya had seen you in such a state. But it was unavoidable. You had to become a digambara in the dark in order to think deeply about things. Last night, it was the weighty subject of religious conflict. To immerse oneself in unbiased cogitation, not only should the mind be free, but also the body; this was the reason you had been demanding a room for yourself. To contemplate in total freedom.

You had heard about the novelist Honoré de Balzac, who consumed fifty cups of coffee in a day. That much coffee would cost a lot of money, and you were too poor to afford it. To lie naked and contemplate, or even to write in the buff, cost you nothing. You were like Victor Hugo in this matter. You had heard that he used to write in the nude.

For a short while after Vasudevan left for Bombay, you had a room to yourself. Your parents slept in one room; Ramakrishnan and Shivaraman in another. Kausalya and you had a room each.

Why should she come and peep into your room while you lay there lost in your thoughts? When Victor Hugo was writing *The Hunchback of Notre-Dame*, did his sister peek at him on the sly?

At some point, you had realised that clothes were an impediment to the free flow of thoughts. You believed that superstitions as well as impropriety travel with one, just like clothes do. As you grew up, you were increasingly inclined to ponder over ideas like this. Already, you were becoming very different from others in your thoughts and actions.

They say patients with amnesia do not know they suffer from the condition. All through your adolescence, you were constantly trying to uncover hidden things. Yet, you remained unaware of this twitch in your own personality.

The harshest punishment you received for it was when you were in the tenth standard.

One Sunday, you went into town with no particular plan in mind. You had four annas tucked into the folded sleeve of your shirt. You were waiting at the bus stop after enjoying an onion vada and a glass of hot tea. You had also bought a laddoo for Kausalya from Kottoor Krishnan Bakery. Just then, a woman came by, wearing a burkha that covered her from head to toe. You felt a strong desire to look at her face that was hidden behind the fabric. When you went up to her and lifted her veil, you were dazzled—her face was like moonlight on a river's surface. You had never seen such a beautiful face. You stood there worshipping her beauty. And in that instant, you realised that truth and beauty could be found only in things that were hidden from sight.

The woman you had touched began to scream, and people rushed to her aid. You have no further recollection of what happened. When you came to, you were lying on a hospital bed, your face swollen and your limbs bandaged. Your mother was by your side. Your father was present too.

'Look, he has opened his eyes,' your mother said.

'Why has he opened them? So he can lift the naqab of a woman and look at her? Rascal! Let him not open his eyes. Let him die.'

His words made your mother's heart writhe in agony.

'He's only a kid. Everything will be all right once he grows up.'

'How much more growing up does he have to do? He's in the tenth standard already.'

'I'm sure he'll mend his ways.'

At that moment, a tall, handsome man with cropped hair and a long beard appeared at the door.

'May I come in?' he asked, looking uncertain.

'Who are you?'

'I'm the husband of Jameela, from the Malikapuram family. I only reached this morning from Dubai. I've come to apologise to you.'

'No, I must ask for your forgiveness. My son did this out of ignorance, please forgive him.'

'It wasn't Jameela's fault, you know. She didn't say anything. It was the public who thrashed your son. Hooligans!'

'What is your name?'

'Mohammad Sarfaraz.'

'Mohammad, you can leave now if you like. At least you came to meet my son. That's more than enough.'

'Please say you've forgiven Jameela and me.' The man's face lost its nervous expression.

'No one has to apologise to anyone. It happened. My son was in the wrong. Let's all forget that it ever happened.'

A look of relief spread over Mohammad Sarfaraz's face. He stood for a moment looking at you, then came closer and placed his hand on your forehead.

In those days, men from Kerala had just started to leave for the Gulf countries. Many of them travelled in dhows and jumped into the sea to swim the last bit to the shore. Mohammad Sarfaraz was one of them. You listened to the conversation between your father and him, but it was beyond your comprehension. Your brain was simply not working.

'All right, then, I'll take your leave.'

Your father watched his retreating back and said to himself, 'Son, you are the real God.'

Sarfaraz had left behind a large carrier bag.

'Edi, what has he left . . . ?'

Before he could finish the sentence, Kausalya picked up the bag and looked inside. Dates, almonds, perfumed soaps, Yardley talcum powder, deodorants, pearly hairpins . . .

'Achcha, look at all this . . .'

Kausalya could not believe her eyes.

'Etta, you should lift more veils to see what lies behind them.'

You mother aimed a mock slap at her.

All this happened when you were a schoolchild. By the time you became a graduate, you had stopped trying to uncover hidden things. Instead, you took the cover off every hidden belief or concept you encountered and studied it.

Some nights, you woke up from nightmares. In one that recurred frequently, a Jewish man was shot repeatedly by German soldiers. *Sterben*! *Sterben*! Die! Die! they screamed. They killed that old man with the big nose again and again. You could see the blood flowing from beliefs that had long been lidded up.

You wanted to continue your studies and apply for a postgraduation in philosophy. But you quickly discovered how expensive that would be, since it would mean moving to the city. So you gave up the idea. You had started to write by then. You decided to go down that path.

A few decades later, Paru has discovered this about you.

'You are a writer, I know. Whatever you try to hide from me, I'll find out,' she says.

She has the same knack that you possessed for uncovering hidden things.

7

YOUR MOTHER

You loved your mother very much. But then, who does not love their mother?

'When I see you loafing around like this, it breaks my heart,' your mother would say, looking at you sadly.

Those were the days when educated young men hung around like zombies, unable to find employment. You became one of them; in fact, one of the youngest among them. You were desperate to land a job, any job, and continue with your writing on the side. That's what you dreamed of. Vendor Goyindan's grouse was that you were not trying hard enough. He could never understand your aspirations. And when a father cannot read his son's mind, disaster awaits.

'Unni'shna, get out of the house and try to meet people. The whole day, you shut yourself in your room. Who will give you a job? Will someone come to you offering a job? Will someone come and say, "Here is the post of a clerk" or "Join us as a typist"? What a fool you are!'

Your father had been pressing you to learn typewriting. In the town, across from the carpentry shop, was a typewriting institute. Its students were mostly young men who had passed their tenth standard exams. Many of them left for one of the big Indian cities after mastering basic typewriting skills. If they could reach Bombay or Madras, they would be able to find some job or other. They would be saved.

'Look at Vasu, learn from him,' Vendor Goyindan would remind you regularly. Your brother was a smart cookie. As soon as he passed out of school, he joined the typewriting institute. No one had asked him to; no one had to persuade him. He knew his salvation lay in escaping the place of his birth, and he had set his sights on Bombay. Once, when he saw a photograph in a magazine of a smoke-emitting factory in Bombay, he joined his hands worshipfully to express his devotion to the city.

'Why don't you go to Bombay too? I'll write to Vasu. You'll never do well if you continue to stay here. You'll get into bad company and destroy your future.'

It was commonplace to see young men of your age frequenting the arrack shops in Karikkat. They sat in the company of men old enough to be their fathers and grandfathers, gulping down alcohol.

The elders would counsel them, 'Eat a bit of the mackerel or some peanuts. If you drink the arrack neat, it'll burn through your intestines.'

Your mother did not like the idea of you going to Bombay. 'You shan't go anywhere. One is enough. He has forgotten his own mother, the scoundrel,' she said.

As soon as he reached Bombay, Vasu had found employment with a Gujarati businessman, eventually married a Gujarati girl and fathered a child. Lakshmikuttyamma was happy about all of that. But why couldn't he come home once a year and meet his parents and siblings? Or, at least, write them a letter every month? Maybe send an occasional money order? Your parents had not even seen photos of Vasu's wife and child. Your mother feared that if you went to Bombay, you would turn into another Vasu. Who could say that you would not marry a Gujarati girl and forget your parents and siblings?

Your other brother, Ramakrishnan, loved his family and was a hard worker. Every morning, he would have a bath, get dressed, have kanji for breakfast and leave before 8 a.m. for the store, keys and a flashlight in hand. Even during the monsoons, he kept the shop open and rarely got home before 10 p.m. Every week, he would make a trip to the Vadakara market and return with banana stalks loaded on the top of a private bus with the unlikely name of Punchiri. At the Orkatteri market he would buy coir ropes and jute strings at bargain prices. He would make occasional visits to Wayanad and come back with jackfruit, mangoes and bamboo containers filled with honey. Vendor Goyindan's only regret was that Ramakrishnan had no children even after three years of marriage.

Your mother would say caustically, 'Where does he have time to make babies? He's out early and returns only at midnight. As soon as he's back, he falls asleep like a buffalo. How can he father a child?'

Sathi had no complaints about Ramakrishnan's timings. However late he returned at night, she would be by his side when he sat down to dinner, her eyes filled with sleep. She would then clear the table, wash all the dishes and switch off the lights before lying down beside Ramakrishnan, by which time he would be snoring loudly. They had got married to lie beside each other and snore.

Three years passed in this fashion.

'Da, Unni'shna, come here. Let me tell you something.'

'What do you want to tell me? To go to Bombay? Don't bother.'

'It's not that. Come and sit beside me.'

When you obeyed and sat down next to her, you got an unpleasant whiff of turmeric paste. The villagers who came to buy stamp paper often brought yam and turmeric as payment. Vendor Goyindan brought these home in his cloth bag. Your mother would dry the organically grown turmeric fingers and powder them in the mortar. She needed it to make fish curry and dal.

'What is it, Amma? Why are you silent?'

Your mother's uncharacteristic behaviour made you anxious. You thought that she wanted to discuss something of grave importance. For someone who never hesitated before speaking her mind, why this reluctance, you wondered.

'Unni'shna, it's been three years since your brother got married. Everyone is asking why Sathi hasn't delivered yet.'

'What can I do about that?'

You were surprised and disturbed that your mother saw fit to discuss such matters with you.

'Sathi says your brother is impotent.'

'Why are you telling me this?'

'Sathi should have a child. Otherwise, how will your parents face the world? We won't even be able to step out of the house!'

Were these things that a mother should be telling her son? You wanted to get up and leave.

Your mother said, without further prevarication and with startling directness, 'If your brother can't do it, then you do it. Sathi will agree. If she doesn't, I'll make her.'

You stared at your mother as though she was some untamed creature that had stepped out of the wilderness. Until then, you had only seen her as a fount of affection. You felt as if your heart was being split wide open.

'Why're you silent? You're loafing around doing nothing. At least let the family benefit from your existence!'

You felt a deep sense of dread, as if you were readying to face a charging, trumpeting rogue elephant.

'Is this something a mother should be telling her son?'

'Who else will tell you this? If you can't do it, then tell me that. I'll send a telegram to Bombay and get Vasu to come down. He'll do it for me if I tell him.'

'How can you even say such things?'

'What's wrong with what I said? Didn't Kunti give birth to five sons? And didn't those five sons marry the same woman?'

You had only respect for your elder brother's wife, Sathiyechi. She was beautiful, with long, lustrous hair and was as tall as you. You sat with your head bowed, trembling within.

'If you can't do it, tell me. I'll find other ways.'

'Amma, don't speak like that, it's depraved. I'll leave this house.'

'You've got your BA degree but you still haven't found a job. You're good for nothing. Go away, leave, get out of my sight!'

You walked away even before your mother had finished speaking. After that, you could never look Sathiyechi in the eye. You would look away whenever you happened to see her.

'Unni'shna, why don't you look at me any more? Are you angry with me? What have I done?'

'Nothing like that, Sathiyechi.'

You could not find the words to say more.

Your mother remained lost in thought. She was thinking up ways to get Sathi pregnant and make Ramakrishnan a father. Had she tried her luck with Shivaraman too, and demanded that he give your sister-in-law a baby? Who could say?

While the mother was looking for ways to get her daughter-in-law pregnant, the father was seeking a job for his son. The mother failed; the father succeeded.

You were not overly worried about being unemployed, you were busy mapping out your life. So far, you had only managed to sketch the outlines. There were so many hindrances. You had a definite view on life and you knew how your life should be lived. But it was slow going. You were like someone who had leaped into the middle of a pond without knowing how to swim. Life was turning out to be as slippery as a snakehead murrel. It slipped through your hands every time you thought you had a grip on it.

You wanted to be a writer, but was writing an occupation? You thought it wasn't yet time to think about that. You hadn't written a story or a poem so far. Did you even have the talent to write? You had to establish that first.

Around this time, your father found you a job.

'I'll educate my sons,' he declared. 'I'll find them jobs. I'll marry my only daughter into a good family. As long as I'm alive, you won't have to worry.'

'If you're such a great man, give Sathi a baby,' your mother said.

Sparks flew out of Vendor Goyindan's eyes.

Your mother was obsessed with this one thing. Every day, she prayed to Karikkat Bhagawathy. She begged every god and goddess. On the eve of the Malayalam new year, after making the ritual offerings at the temple, she beseeched, 'I'll pay for the chuttuvilakku; I'll feed the poor during the Sabarimala season. Please just give Sathi a baby.'

She beseeched the god, the treasurer of all religions, 'Give my Sathi a baby.'

'That's not my job. That's Ramakrishnan's,' said the overlord of all religions.

Your mother stood there with her eyes closed as the god appeared in front of her in the darkness. He wore a white khaddar mundu with a green border and a white shirt that reached his knees. On his nose was perched a pair of bifocals. But this god did not answer her prayers. Neither did your mother hear his words.

When your mother realised that even God had forsaken her, it tore her up. She came out of the temple, her eyes brimming with tears. In the days that followed, she stopped going out of the house, claiming that she was unable to face people.

'If you can't get pregnant, at least go someplace and bring home a child,' she told Sathi, who probably didn't hear her, for she nodded in response.

Several times, you found your mother crying on the veranda, wiping her eyes and fretting about Sathi.

'Amma . . .'

'My heart is breaking . . .'

You sat by her side and hugged her. You tried to console her, 'Nothing has happened to her for you to grieve like this. One day Ramakrishnettan will become a father. Karikkat Bhagawathy is with us. You shouldn't be sad, Amma. You are our beloved mother . . .'

Sathi had no regrets; Ramakrishnan felt no heartache. Nor did Vendor Goyindan. Why, then, was your mother pining away? You couldn't understand it. Like Karikkat Bhagawathy, you were helpless.

8

YOUR OCCUPATION

During the seventies, you were in the prime of your youth. You recall the alienation of those days like a particularly bad case of toothache. Although you've lost most of your teeth, you still occasionally feel the shooting pain that tunnels through to your temple from the side of your face.

Many of your friends who had embraced silence during those days later turned voluble, almost garrulous. You could have become like them, but you chose the path of silence.

Now, in your old age, it can be said that you are not friends with anyone but Balan. When life started to bloom again, when some of your old friends wanted to make their way back to you, you did not welcome them. The only friend you have is Balan.

Once, when you pulled a muscle in your back, Balan took leave to stay with you and apply hot compresses to relieve the discomfort. As you lay on your stomach, a fiery tongue of pain shot through your spine. Like the taste of extra-spicy tender mango pickle.

Vendor Goyindan kept his promise and found his son a job—at Kalyani Talkies, the cinema theatre owned by Erattu Velukutty. Your father, although himself a man of integrity, had helped Velukutty with a few dubious land dealings. You could never fathom why. Vendor Goyindan himself could not understand why he had done it. Whenever he thought about it, he was deeply troubled. But then, why did you resort to copying when you knew the answers to all the questions in your examination? Mysteries, both.

While your father was waiting for the ferry in front of Ve . . . Ve . . . Velayudhan's teashop, Erattu Velukutty came by. He had made a turban of his thorthu as there was no shade on the river and the scorching sun would have heated up his head like a flat iron by the time the boat reached the far bank.

'How are you, Vendor? Why are you waiting here?' Velukutty asked your father.

'Sha . . . shaa . . . shall I may . . . may . . . I make a cup of str . . . stro . . . strong tea?' Ve . . . Ve . . . Velayudhan offered.

'Edo Velukutty, I heard you are starting a silima talkies?'

'Yes, Vendor, I'd like to. I'm trying to find the money for it.'

'Why don't you start some other business? Does it have to be a theatre?'

'When our people want to watch a movie, they have to take a bus or a ferry into town. By the time the movie is over, there's neither bus nor ferry to bring them back. They have to walk all the way home. Now, imagine if there was a theatre here. They could all watch movies without any hassle. That's why I'm starting this business.'

Velukutty spoke as if he was doing it solely for the benefit of the villagers. Scoundrel! Politician-like, he pretended that anything he did for himself or his family was actually for the sake of the public. Flecks of paan and juice sprayed from his mouth as he spoke.

Goyindan thought the cinema theatre was a good idea. He had watched only a few movies—the last one was *Jeevitha Nouka* featuring Thikkurissi Sukumaran Nair and B.S. Saroja. *Madhumati* had been released some seven years later. Those who went to see it spoke endlessly about it. Goyindan never understook how they, with no knowledge of Hindi, figured out the ghost story at all.

When he heard that a cinema theatre in town was on sale, Velukutty took the boat and headed to Valapattanam with a sackful of money. The boat was packed with workers headed to the plywood factory.

The roof of the dilapidated talkies leaked; a part of the gallery had collapsed; the majority of the chairs had broken legs. Velukutty closed the deal and had everything transported to your village.

And so, a thatched movie hall came up in your village. An old generator was repaired and installed. A projector was leased. The theatre was named after Velukutty's wife— thus, Kalyani Talkies. The maiden screening was of a new movie, *Nairu Pidicha Pulivalu.*

'Are we fools to grab a tiger by its tail?'

The Nair men threatened to disrupt the showing. But their wives wanted to watch the movie. When the husbands sidled up to them in the night hoping for some action, they turned to the other side. That was the end of the Nairs' protest. Old and young thronged the talkies.

The men were bewitched by the film's heroine, Ragini, while the women fell for the hero, Sathyan. Having brought the talkies to the village, Erattu Velukutty strutted about like he was the real hero. As he went by, one corner of his mundu held in his hand, his mouth dribbling betel juice, women gazed at him from behind half-open doors with unconcealed admiration. For them, he was God incarnate.

Your father arranged for you to be employed at the talkies.

You would reach the theatre by 7.30 a.m. By that time the sweeper would have started her work, and you supervised. There were galleries on either side of the screen and benches in the middle, facing it. Behind the benches were chairs, for which one had to pay considerably more. The rich men and women of the locality chose to sit there.

The unpaved floor of the hall was usually littered with beedi butts and chewed betel leaves. The floor of the galleries was damp and reeked of urine. There was vomit in the corners. Drunks, sloshed to the gills, would buy tickets only so they could have a place to puke in and a bench on which to sleep off their drunkenness. Some even shat in the talkies.

'I can't clean up all this shit and piss. I may be poor, but I too was born in a tharavad,' Nani would protest, and you would thrust a twenty-five paise coin into her hand to mollify her.

Only after satisfying yourself that the cleaning was complete did you leave for home. After a bath and a change of clothes, you would have a glass of tea. At 11 a.m., you would be back at the talkies to check the accounts.

Occasionally, Velukutty would come by. He would look around as if trying to unearth an interloper.

'Edo Unni'shna, how were yesterday's collections?'

'Not too bad, boss.'

'The chairs were sold out?'

'No, boss, the benches were—for both shows.'

'How many song books sold?'

'Twenty-seven.'

'Ummm . . .' Velukutty would grunt, spit out a stream of betel juice and leave. He had no time to tarry anywhere. Even when he wasn't busy, he acted busy.

Your office was a small room with a tin-sheet roof. The tickets were sold from here, and this was where you sat and wrote out the notices and checked the accounts. There were two square holes in the wall; through these you handed out tickets—the one on the left was for women, the one on the right for men. Ticket sales were also your responsibility. No one bothered to queue up, and there would be pushing and shoving, especially for the new releases. But everyone got in, as long as they had the money for a ticket. They would sit or stand, depending on the availability of seats.

If the start of the movie was delayed, people would start whistling. 'Son of a whore, start the silima,' they would shriek at Kunjiramettan. But he would only start the projector after you sounded the bell. When the screen lit up, there would be loud cheers.

There was no second show during the monsoons. When you did run a night show, it ended past midnight. By that time, you would have calculated the revenue from ticket sales that day, mostly in 25- and 50-paise coins, all bundled together in a thorthu.

The generator and the projector were manned by Kunjiramettan. After locking up the projection cabin, he would come up to you and ask, 'Shall we switch off the generator, what do you say?'

Without waiting for your reply, he would go and switch it off anyway, silencing its rumbling. Soon, the lights would be turned off, and the building and the trees around it would be enveloped in darkness.

You would then leave for Velukutty's house with a flashlight and a bundle of cash in your hand. He would be waiting for you. The accounts could be submitted the following day, but the cash could not wait. Kalyani would feel sorry for you as you approached through the darkness shining your flashlight.

'Rohini's father, can't you wait and collect the cash in the morning?'

'Our money should be in our hands. No one should walk around with it.'

'Will Unni'shnan run away with the money?'

'Who knows?'

Where money was concerned, Velukutty trusted no one, not even his wife.

By the time you reached home, the early rooster would have crowed. Tired of waiting, your mother would have got into bed beside your father and fallen asleep. Kausalya would be dozing next to the food kept for you. When she heard the sound of the door opening, she would snap out of sleep and open her eyes.

'Which movie was on tonight?' she would ask as she served you rice and curry.

'*Kaattu Mynah.*'

'Aiyyo, that's a new release! Doesn't P. Susheela sing *Kaattu kurinji kaattu kurinji* in it? Tell me the story, please?'

'You read the notice, didn't you? The story was in it.'

'That's not enough.'

The notice never revealed the end. It always closed with 'The rest on the silver screen . . .' Also, she knew you would narrate the story better than any notice could. There was a writer within you, suffocated and waiting for release.

'I'll tell you tomorrow.'

'No! I want it now.'

After dinner, in the dim light of the veranda, with Kausalya sitting close to you, a light breeze playing, you narrated the story of *Kaattu Mynah*. The early rooster was still crowing. The moon was on the wane in the sky, occasionally slipping behind a patina of rain clouds. Your father's snores reached you from inside.

Still seated on the veranda, talking and listening, you and she would fall asleep.

You had a busy life at Kalyani Talkies. You worked from morning till night. You had to sell the tickets and song books. For the generator to work, you needed to arrange diesel, of which there was a severe shortage. Sometimes you would have to go into town to arrange for some. For every release, you had to write up the notice, then travel to town and get it printed. The notice brought by the film distributor's representative never appealed to you. You always rewrote it. After reading your synopsis, people landed up at the talkies to watch even bad movies. Velukutty recognised this talent of yours.

'Achcha, did you read this notice? It's like an S.K. Pottekkat short story.'

This was high praise, coming from Rohini, Velukutty's daughter. Even if the father was uninterested in books, the daughter was an avid reader. She was enamoured of Pottekkat, though she had never seen seen a photograph of him.

When she brought to his notice your skill in converting a mere synopsis into a short story, Velukutty increased your pay from Rs 60 to Rs 65. That same day, you bought a pair of slippers for yourself. You would no longer go around barefoot. You also bought a mundu for your mother and a skirt and half-saree for your sister.

'I need nothing; whatever I have is enough,' Vendor Goyindan said. 'Spend your money carefully. Kausalya needs to be married off. Don't forget that.'

You kept Rs 15 and gave the balance to your father. Your father took out the key from the Waterbury's Compound bottle, opened the trunk and placed the money inside. It was your maiden contribution to Kausalya's wedding fund. Every month, without fail, you gave your father some money towards it.

Whenever a hit movie played at the talkies, you ran matinee shows. Kausalya would come for one of these. She would sit in your pigsty-like office and say, 'Today I'll sell the tickets, Etta.'

She accepted the money thrust through the square holes in the wall and tore out and issued tickets in return. She was very keen to do the job. But the first time she did it, they ended up short by fifty paise. And that wasn't the only time. Each time she issued the tickets, they ended up with a deficit. Once, when she was handing over a ticket, a man grabbed her hand; she could not shake him off. Two of the glass bangles on her wrist broke and cut into her skin. When the news reached Vendor, he was furious.

'If you so much as step into the talkies again, I'll break your leg,' he warned her.

Lots of people were envious of your job at the talkies. Women wished they were your mother or sister, so they could watch as many movies as they wanted. You had found a place in some girls' hearts too. When a proposal came for Sharada, mason Shanku's eldest daughter, from a boy who worked as a booking clerk in the Railways, she refused it. 'I won't go with him.'

'What's wrong with him? He has a government job and an income on the side from all the bribes. He's awash with money.'

'Let him adorn his own cash box with it! I want to marry the boy who works in the talkies.'

You were in her heart. If she became your life partner, she could watch movies unhindered all her life. Instead of finding a place in the gallery or among the benches, she could sit regally on a chair. What more did one need from life?

It was different for you. Once you started working at Kalyani Talkies, you lost interest in watching movies. Eventually, you started to hate them.

When your sister realised this, she got worried. She feared that you would give up your job. She said to you, 'Swear upon me that you will not quit.'

'Find someone else to swear on you.'

Although you refused to take the oath, you continued to issue tickets, sell song books, rewrite synopses and print notices, and arrived punctually at Velukutty's house at midnight to hand over the day's collections, thus gladdening the hearts of your parents and siblings.

Only Balan was unhappy about it.

'You've screwed up your life. You're not the kind of person who should be issuing tickets at a movie theatre, you're a reader of Charlotte Brontë,' he would tell you.

It was not that you disliked the talkies. You had grown links to the benches and galleries that reeked of urine, the generators that growled and spat, the projector that snapped the reels now and again, causing the audience to whistle shrilly. Your eyes had a glint when you thought of the talkies. It was to you what the hospital was to Balan.

But you did not remain in that job for long.

Life had other plans for you.

9

YOUR READING

To you, reading was everything. Birth, death, eating, sleeping, praying, loving, yearning—everything was about reading. In the dictionary, reading as verb and noun are equally pregnant with meaning. You lived to read. There was no way to keep track of all that you read until the time of your sabbatical. After that, your reading tapered off, like your thoughts. You were not a vegetarian, but you had entered a vegetative state.

The village where you were born had a toddy shop but no library. Although there were women like Pankajakshi, who rented out their bodies, no books were loaned out. While many men had two or three common-law wives, their homes had no bookshelves. Chaste women who read Ezhuthachan's *Adhyathmaramayanam Kilippattu* could be found, but none who had read Thakazhi's *Thyagathinu Prathiphalam*. You said to yourself, 'It's a pity that everyone reads about the gods but there's no one here who reads about human beings.'

You read every kind of book there was. In college, you transitioned from reading in Malayalam to reading in English. Worlds of beauty, bliss and sorrow surfaced in front of you. You devoured books by Gandhi, a Hindu; Rumi, a Muslim; and Kafka, a Jew. You realised that reading had no religion, sect or caste. Your reading was catholic and secular. As a result, thoughts that others might have eschewed would crowd into your mind. They became the reason that your life turned into a tragedy.

You were the first person in Karikkat village to read about human beings and understand them. Your thoughts always centred on people. You thought about them with humility, aware that you were one among many.

Once, you were to undertake a train journey to Vadakara. You reached the station, but instead of boarding the train, you returned home. You were in the eighth standard then, and the welts on your buttocks from Raman Kutty Master's caning had vanished.

You were accompanying your father, who was headed to the eye hospital. It was your mother who had told him, 'Your sight is blurred, don't go alone. Take Unni'shnan with you.'

'He's no longer a child. I'll have to buy a full ticket. Why waste money?'

'Is money more important than your well-being? You miss a step and fall, then you'll know!'

Your father did not argue any more. He took you along. You were fond of trains and got ready with high expectations. You had a blue shirt on and, like your father, you were barefoot. In Karikkat, there were more bare feet than slippered ones.

You had to walk to the railway station. Your father surged ahead with his giant strides; it was tough keeping up with him. That day, you realised how well regarded your father was in the village. Some people showed their deference by holding their palm over their mouth, a sign of mute servility. Others let down their mundu, which had been folded up and tucked in. Yet others invited him to stop and have tea with them. You had no idea that a stamp vendor was a VIP.

As you left a bylane for the main road leading to the railway station, your eyes fell on a signboard on top of a line of shops—P. Krishna Pillai Library and Reading Room. A majority of the shops there flew the red flag of the Communist Party. For a moment, you wondered whether this was a reading room or a flag store.

You looked back as you tried to keep up with your father, imagining all those books inside, hidden from your view. Stacked books touching one another, arrayed on endless shelves.

Outside the station, the same red flags flew from the branches of tall trees, covered in dust and bird shit. As you walked on, the library disappeared behind one of the spreading trees.

Your father bought two tickets for the passenger train terminating at Kozhikode. It was a small station and the platform was full of people. The morning's passenger train was always crowded. Most of the passengers were traders headed to Vadakara or office workers going to Kozhikode. Your father kept swabbing his eyes using the edge of the towel that was twisted around his neck. Both his eyes were bloodshot. He had been suffering for about a month now.

Choyi vaidyar's treatment brought no relief, so he had decided to go to the hospital in Vadakara.

The bell sounded, indicating that the train had reached the outer signal before the station. It would arrive soon, huffing and puffing, and in a hurry as always.

'Achcha, I'm not coming.'

'Not coming? Where?'

'To Vadakara.'

'Then why did I buy this ticket?'

'I have a stomach ache.'

'Didn't you shit in the morning?'

Afraid to look at your father, you remained silent, staring into the distance where the rail lines seemed to extend into infinity.

'The stomach ache will go away,' your father said. An acquaintance of your father came up just then, and they started to chat. The studs in the man's ears gleamed.

In the distance, grey smoke hung like rain clouds over the twisting rail tracks. The coal-powered train rolled in, spewing smoke and steam and making the platform tremble. A few passengers disembarked; there were many more waiting to board.

'Go on, get in.'

'I'm not coming.'

The next instant, you saw stars and flashing lights. You staggered from the blow. You had been caned and beaten, but this was the first time you were experiencing such pain, as if your head was being torn from your neck. Your father had swung his fist hard.

Your father boarded the train. You could see that several of the seats were vacant. You saw him use the towel to mop his eyes and wipe his nose and face.

As the train chugged away, shuddering, you started to walk back. You could see the library building through the branches of the mango tree. You saw the train speed up and disappear into the distance, huffing and screeching. Dark smoke hovered above the tracks. Dark smoke lingered in your mind too—the regret of sending your father alone to Vadakara.

You walked quickly towards the library. Would it be open? It was only a few minutes past 8 a.m. The staircase to the left of Komala Vilasam restaurant led to the library. The handrail was covered in soot. You could see puttu wrapped in plantain leaves inside a glass-paned almirah. The aroma of kadala curry rose from an aluminium vessel placed on the table near the cash counter. Normally, you would have salivated at the sight of the puttu and curry, but not today.

You were consumed by thoughts of the library and the books it contained. That was what made you salivate. If you could, you would have swallowed books like puttu and kadala curry and washed the meal down with a cup of hot tea.

Having taken the stairs up, you found yourself in front of the library door, which lay open as if waiting for you. A signboard informed you that it was open from 7 a.m. to 11 a.m. in the morning and 4 p.m to 8 p.m in the evening.

You hesitated at the door. Five or six men were seated inside, reading newspapers. One of them raised his head and asked, 'What do you want?'

You were hesitant.

'Where are you from? Who are you?'

'I'm Vendor Goyindan's son, Unni'shnan.'

'Why have you come here?'

'I want to read books.'

'You'll get books only in the evening. If you like, you can read the newspapers. There are weeklies too.'

You noticed then that all the six almirahs were locked. You went closer and tried to read the titles of the books stacked inside. Thakazhi's *Chemmeen*; Kesavadev's *Odayil Ninnu*; Uroob's *Kunjammayum Koottukaarum*; S.K. Pottekkat's *Vishakanyaka*. You were hooked. You felt like a famished man in front of whom a full plate of rice and mackerel curry had been placed. A craving for books started to grow inside you.

When he saw you standing there lost to the world, a man in a long kurta who had just entered the library came towards you. He had a thick moustache. This was Kunjampu, the library secretary.

'What do you want?'

'I'm looking at the books.'

'Do you want books to read?'

'Aiyyo, yes, of course.'

'For that you need to become a member. Only then can you borrow books and magazines to take home. If you are not a member, you can sit and read the newspapers. But not books. For that you have to be a member.'

'What should I do to become a member?'

'A quarter rupee per month. Two rupees as deposit. Do you have the money now? If not, go home and come back later.'

Your face darkened as if you had been walking in the heat of March. The disappointed look on your face went unnoticed by Kunjampu. But someone else was watching. As you walked out, trying to conceal your dismay and tamping down the craving for books, he called out to you.

'Wait!'

You turned and looked back at the unshaven man in his crumpled shirt and mundu. He was reading the *Deshabhimani* newspaper, a publication of the Communist Party. He looked older than your father. His name was Kunhikannan, you would find out later. Those close to him called him Kunhi. To others he was Comrade Kunhi.

'Where are you from? I haven't seen you around.'

'My house is in Karikkat.'

'You study in . . .?'

'Eighth standard.'

'Will you be able to understand these books if you read them?'

'Perhaps . . . possibly . . .'

Comrade Kunhi took your hand and led you back to the bookshelves.

'Take whichever one you like.'

You raised your head, uncomprehending, and looked at him. His shirt was wrongly buttoned. He had no body hair; his chest looked shaven.

'Edo Kunjampu, make this kid a member.'

'I don't have the money,' you said.

'Kunjampu, I'll pay his membership fee and deposit.'

You stood there, stunned.

'Don't worry, take a book.'

You chose Thakazhi's *Chemmeen*. Two days later, you returned it and took Kesavadev's *Odayil Ninnu*.

After that, you became a member of many libraries, borrowed many books. You read and evolved. While still a teenager, you read the Malayalam translation of Maxim Gorky's *Mother*. Not long after that, you read Mikhail

Sholokov's *And Quiet Flows the Don*. As a young man working at Kalyani Talkies, you read Dostoevsky's *Crime and Punishment*. Also, Albert Camus's *Happy Death*.

Countless books; a reading marathon.

You took a sabbatical once, a break from life itself. Did you read during that time? No one knows. Or perhaps Paru does. She knows things about you that no one else has an inkling of. She is obsessed with sniffing out the truth about you. With all that sniffing, has her tiny nose become even tinier?

You would like to die while lying in the easy chair placed by the window, reading a book. But you know this wish of yours will remain unfulfilled. You'll die lying on a bed, like most people.

In all these years, you have never seen a person breathing their last while still on their feet. You have only heard of Benkei, the mythical Japanese warrior who died on his feet, though his body was shot full of arrows. He is your hero.

By late evening, your father returned from the eye hospital. There was a lump on his forehead that had not been there when he left in the morning.

'Aiyyo, what happened?' your mother asked.

'I had a fall, Lachmikutty,' your father said casually.

Your mother rushed towards you with her hand raised to strike.

'You let him go alone to Vadakara with these poor eyes of his? You may be as big as a full-grown buffalo but you are of no use to anyone. What a waste!' your mother cursed you.

You knew you were in the wrong. Your father was at fault too. Despite his blurred vision, he walked as briskly as ever. You should have gone with him. If you had been with him, this would not have happened. The lump stared at you accusingly from your father's forehead. It was a full week before it went away.

While your father was busy selling stamp paper in the village office and writing deeds, you got busy becoming a member of different libraries, borrowing books and reading them late into the night while the household slept and Karikkat fell silent.

That reading was, for you, life itself, is already on record. But the truth is, reading cannot give anyone deliverance. There are many who do not read at all, yet lead happy lives.

The villagers of Karikkat were of the opinion that your brother Shivaraman's life was blighted. But it was your life that was becoming blighted. Exactly how blighted was yet to be revealed.

10

YOU AND KAMADEVA

Sex hit you one day like a bolt of lightning. You were a student in the ninth standard; fine hairs were beginning to sprout reluctantly above your upper lip. The sexual awakening that descended on you was entirely the doing of Kamadeva. When you think about it now, it no longer surprises you. You are aware that it's not just humans but also the gods who can play mischief. Like they have with your life.

As a child, the carvings of Khajuraho had introduced you to the idea of sex. On the way to school, you had watched animals mating by the roadside. But no one would allow you to study them for a more intimate understanding of the subject. Like a moral police squad, passersby would shout, 'What are you staring at? Scoot!'

They would drive you away as if you had done something wrong. And you would run without really knowing why. So many of your actions stemmed from a lack of awareness.

'He's not yet out of his nappies, but he wants to watch!'

No one would allow you to complete your education. Every bit of knowledge you gained was half-baked, and you tried to fill the gaps with reading. Like a spider, you started to weave sticky webs that connected and grew into fingers of knowledge.

You had never visited Khajuraho, nor did you particularly want to go there. There were so many places to see in the world. But the P. Krishna Pillai Library had a book on Khajuraho. Your eyes fell on it quite by accident. It was a glossy coffee-table edition donated by an NRI comrade. When he first received it, Kunjampu had started leafing through it casually, then dropped it as if it had singed him. His communist values would not allow him to accept it. But the NRI comrade persisted and, finally, the secretary agreed to a compromise. The book would be locked up in a steel cabinet in his room, along with some important documents he kept there. The cabinet was always under lock and key, so nobody would see the book, let alone lay hands on it.

Inevitably, you became fixated on that book which had been sentenced to life imprisonment. You already had a knack for uncovering hidden things. You knew that a request to borrow the book would be futile, so you bided your time. You borrowed more books than anyone else from the library. Even the obscure tomes that others shied away from, you would borrow and take home.

'How can you understand all this stuff? Are you borrowing them to read or to show off?' demanded Lakshmanan, who was reading a newspaper as you walked off with Victor Hugo's *Les Misérables*. It was a weighty tome, but there were several other, slimmer books you could think of that felt just as heavy. Herman Hesse's *Siddhartha* for one.

You returned the books long before the return-by date marked on the sticker on the inside of the book cover. The secretary was astonished. That you were Vendor Goyindan's youngest son made him fonder of you. He started to buy you tea whenever you came to borrow books.

'Come Unni'shna, let's go down and share a chai and bonda.'

You were trying to find something that you had not yet read. You had been burning through the shelves so rapidly that you were worried you would run out of books to read. You didn't know then that the world has more books than human beings.

'Maybe later,' you said.

'Come on, you can't keep reading all the time. You have to eat something too, or your health will suffer.'

You believed you could survive on a diet of books alone. Secretary Kunjampu had other ideas. He believed in the primacy of the belly over the mind. He dreamed of a country that provided tea and bonda free to all its citizens.

When he saw that you would not budge, Kunjampu gave up and went down to Komala Vilasam restaurant on the ground floor. The place was famous for the tea and meals it served.

Kunjampu had left the key dangling from the door of the cabinet. You opened it and quickly leafed through the book on Khajuraho. Your eyes photographed every erotic image; every caption was memorised. By the time Kunjampu returned with his paan after a round of tea and gossip with the restaurant's owner, half an hour had passed.

'You should have come with me. The bondas were sizzling hot and fresh.'

'I'll have tea when I'm here next, Kunjampu'etta. I'll go now.'

Did Secretary Kunjampu offer tea and bonda to everyone? Was he as loaded as that?

You left the library with two books—a copy of Parappurath's *Ninamaninja Kaalppadukal* tucked in your armpit and *Khajuraho* ensconced in your mind.

Everyone knows that the education one receives in school is not adequate, but it's not possible to enrol in two schools at once. One can, however, become a member of two libraries at the same time. That was how you became a member of Thunjan Library. On school holidays, you would walk four miles to reach the library, which was located in an old house with two rooms and a small veranda in the front. Moss and fungus covered the chipped, old tiles on the floor.

When it rained, the water fell directly on the veranda. In the summer, people would sit on the benches placed there, smoking beedis and chatting. You would be the first to arrive. The library allowed you to borrow two books at a time, to be returned within a week. A late return attracted a fine of a quarter anna per day. You never had to pay it.

On your first visit, your eyes fell on Nalapat Narayana Menon's *Rathi Samrajyam*. When he saw you leafing through its pages, the librarian Venukuttan frowned. He was the antithesis of Kunjampu—clean-shaven and lean, in a shirt rather than a kurta.

Venukuttan took the book out of your hands and said gently, 'Edo, don't read this book. It's not for kids.'

'I'm in the ninth standard. I'm not a kid.'

The previous year, on Onam, you had given up wearing shorts in favour of a mundu. It made you feel more self-confident. You had always answered your teachers' questions confidently and held your head high; it went up higher now. You took to wearing a mundu as if it was the most natural thing to do. With it folded up and tucked in jauntily, you strode ahead swinging your arms. When you passed an older person, you let down the hem to show respect.

'What if I read it?' you asked Venukuttan.

'It's a dirty book.'

'Then why do you keep it here?'

'For the grown-ups to read.'

'Why should grown-ups read dirty books?'

'Unni'shna, you're the limit! I can't argue with you. But I won't issue this book to you. Pick something else. Or you can cancel your membership and go home.'

Venukuttan placed *Rathi Samrajyam* back on the shelf.

Sometime later, Venukuttan fell ill with a cold, congestion and fever. When you got to the library, you found that Bhargavan was standing in for him. Although he was a regular at the library, you had never seen Bhargavan reading a newspaper, or anything else for that matter. He was younger than Venukuttan and had a thick moustache like Kunjampu. You knew that as long as Venukuttan was alive, he would not let you so much as touch *Rathi Samrajyam*, let alone read it. But chances were Bhargavan had not read it. He probably didn't know what kind of book it was. Nevertheless, you decided to put him to the test.

'Bhargavetta, who's this Nalapat Narayana Menon?'

'He's a Kathakali artiste. He specialises in kaththi roles.'

That was enough for a kind of happiness to froth inside you. To be doubly sure, you asked, 'Have you read *Rathi Samrajyam?*'

'Who hasn't read it? It's the story of an army nurse. I read it while I was still in school. I used to be a voracious reader then. It's only now that my reading has come down. Although I still read enough to keep in touch. I've read *Padatha Painkili* too.'

There was nothing to fear anymore. You picked up *Rathi Samrajyam* and the latest *Kaumudi* and placed them before Lakshmanan.

'Do you mind making the entry? My handwriting's not very good.'

You took *Rathi Samrajyam* home. Avoiding the eyes of others, you sat in your room and devoured the book. That's when Kamadeva's arrows started to find their target in your heart.

At school, you were already enamoured of Janaki Teacher's English classes—learning a new language was thrilling. Teacher had got married recently, and these days, her eyes had a newfound sparkle in them and her cheeks were flushed. Just as class was about to begin that day, you were distracted by a sound from outside. Kamadeva, who happened to be lurking there, shot one of his floral arrows straight into your heart. From that moment, you had eyes only for Janaki Teacher. You dropped your pen on the floor and groped for it while gazing at her feet and ankles under the table.

Kamadeva now began to pursue you everywhere with his arrows.

It was your sister who first noticed the change in you. The lecherous look on your face annoyed her. You stared at every woman as though you were seeing one for the first time. Even if the shadow of a female form drifted into view, your eyes latched on to it. None of this escaped your sister's attention.

You began to tail women who were headed to the fields to plant seedlings and teachers headed to school. You made up excuses to cadge money from your mother and took the bus to the town. You roamed the bus terminal, clothing stores and movie theatres, ogling women. Short-statured and moon-faced young women; women with hair and cheeks that were shiny after generous oil baths; wheat-complexioned, long-legged beauties; nervous-eyed ones with blood-orange lips; women with half-open lips showing off the whiteness of their teeth; dark girls with shapely backs; one girl who walked through a puddle with her saree lifted above her ankles, and another who walked with swinging hips, like in *Rathi Samrajyam*; some with their heads bowed, scared even to look up; others who stared you down; women who walked with a smile inside them; those whose eyes spoke to you; others who gave you sidelong glances. You wandered among them, taking in their smells. You were still a schoolboy, so you did not attract undue attention. If anyone did notice you, they misconstrued your lustful look as one of casual curiosity and passed by without commenting.

That year, the festival at Karikkat Bhagawathy was an orgiastic experience for you. The festival grounds were suffused with femininity. There were stalls selling kohl, bindis, glass bangles and hair extensions. You roamed everywhere, squeezing through the crowd, brushing against women and inhaling their fragrance.

On nights when sleep eluded you, you tossed and turned in a torrid, dreamy state until you fell into an exhausted sleep in the early hours of the day.

Finally, the torment ended. Kamadeva left with his quiver of arrows one day, and you were suddenly free of the wild passions and desires that had consumed you. But the memory of those days of intense arousal lingered. Even now, past your seventieth year, you can recall it all with startling clarity.

11

YOUR SIBLINGS

Ramakrishnan, Shivaraman and Vasudevan may be your blood brothers, but you also thought of everyone else as your siblings. Even Pankajakshi, whom you once desired to see naked, was a sister to you. When you met her some two dozen years later and addressed her as 'chechi', you could see the twinkle in her eye.

What about Paru?

After all these days, you think of her too as your sister. You are aware of tongues wagging, speculating about you— on the wrong side of seventy—and her—not yet twenty-five. But you truly see her as a little sister.

How does she see you though? As an eccentric old man? A grandfather? An elderly uncle? She tends to speak to you with alarming, if indulgent, familiarity as 'eda Unni'shna' or 'eda chekka'. You don't know who you are to her. You may trust most people blindly, but not her. She's a chameleon. She tries to charm and seduce you only to discover your secrets. Her sole objective is to keep Konnath Pappan happy and consolidate her position at *Aagolam*. Everything else is a charade, lies. For you, she is exactly that—a liar!

Back when Kamadeva shot his arrows remorselessly at your heart, you had begun to look at your 'sisters' differently. You thought they dressed revealingly and smiled seductively at you; they filled your entire being with lust until you ravished them in your fevered imagination. Later, when you looked back on those moments, you felt a deep sense of loathing for yourself.

When a smug Kamadeva finally backed off with the arrows still rattling in his quiver, you started to win back your sisters one after the other. You wrapped clothes around their nakedness. You wiped the sweat off their foreheads, necks, the valley between their breasts. With solicitous, brotherly love, you planted kisses on their foreheads. You felt great joy and solace in redeeming your sisters, and you prayed that Kamadeva would never come into your life again.

What about after your marriage? Would you keep Kamadeva out of bounds even then?

The truth is, you weren't really concerned about marriage. You asked yourself this question: must one only marry a woman? Can't one be married to writing? After all, there was no guarantee that a woman would present you with a child; Sathiyechi continued to be childless. But writing could never be sterile or barren. Writing delivers— booklets and book cubs, if nothing else.

While you were working at Kalyani Talkies, two weddings took place in your family: Kausalya's and Shivaraman's. Kausalya's was not unexpected, but the news of Shivaraman's wedding came as a shock to most people.

Kausalya had by then received a few marriage proposals. A tailor, a watch repairer, a mason—she had seen the concrete worker before and noted his steely arms and broad chest. 'Would be fun to be crushed in those arms . . .' she thought in spite of herself. The next proposal was from Karanan, a house painter. Your father humiliated him and sent him away saying, 'You are not good enough for my daughter.'

'Let me tell you, if it goes on like this, she'll remain unmarried,' Lakshmikuttyamma said.

'She's our only daughter. I'll marry her to a government officer. No one else needs to come salivating.'

Many trooped in and trooped out. Finally, one man was found acceptable by all—Jayasheelan, a postal clerk from a good family. Your father took the proposal forward without so much as having a word with Kausalya. When you realised this, you spoke to her.

'Do you like him?'

'What's there to not like?'

'That's all I wanted to hear. I'm relieved.'

Jayasheelan was a good-looking young man, educated and sensible. He walked with a stoop, almost like a hunchback, that was his only fault. It's those who lack self-confidence that usually walk in this fashion, but very soon you came to realise that he was far from under-confident. Once, when a policeman tried to browbeat him at the post office, without even lifting his head, Jayasheelan said, 'Oye, this is not your police station, it's a post office. Scram or I'll call the police.' You liked this man who was prepared to summon the police to discipline a policeman!

Another day, you saw Jayasheelan taking part in a political rally. As he swept past like a hurricane with his head almost hidden in his chest, his clenched fist rose higher than anyone else's. The slogans from his solitary throat reverberated as if a hundred voices were shouting together. Watching him, you thought he was a good match for Kausalya.

Meanwhile, Vendor Goyindan had decided that his only daughter's wedding should be a celebration for the whole village. He began making all the arrangements early. The house was renovated six months before the wedding. A goldsmith spent sleepless nights fashioning ornaments for the bride. Sitting cross-legged on the floor, he used his bamboo blowpipe to kindle the fire and melt the gold. Sarees were bought all the way from Kozhikode, and Kanjeevaram and Banaras silk sarees formed rainbows in the house.

One week before the wedding, a shamiana was erected in the front yard, its arches decorated with palm leaves. Kausalya's silk blouses were sent to the town for stitching, causing Shivaraman to protest. Already, he was without much work. The villagers refused to give him anything to stitch; they only trusted him with hemming the edge of a mundu. Very occasionally, an elderly man would hand him fabric from the mill to make a loincloth or two. Vendor Goyindan's son had to be satisfied with such work while dreaming of stitching silk skirts and velvet blouses. But this was the unkindest cut of all, not getting to create his own sister's trousseau.

'Nothing good will ever come to you!' he cursed his parent and siblings.

'Why would you get someone else to stitch her wedding clothes when I'm right here? She's my sister, isn't she? You forgot even that,' he railed at your mother.

'Why're you screaming at me? If you have anything to say, say it to your father.'

Shivaraman did not have the courage to stand up to his father. He knew he would not be able to utter a word in his presence.

Everyone in the village had been invited for the wedding—the blind, the lame, the mute, no one was left out.

'Why are you inviting so many people?' Velukutty asked, astonished. 'Isn't that a lot of money to spend?'

'Kausalya is my only daughter. If the gods would come at my invitation, I would ask them too.'

Your father wrote to Vasudevan in Bombay: your sister is getting married. You have no other sister. You should come. I will celebrate her wedding with pomp. I don't need your help. Let that not stop you from coming.

There was no reply. Every day, your father went to the post office and queried, 'Any letter from Bombay?'

'No, but why have you walked all this way, Vendor, in this hot sun? If there's a letter or a telegram, we'll bring it to you. What else are we here for?'

Some days later, he sent a telegram. That, too, got no response.

'I don't have a son called Vasudevan any longer. If he so much as steps inside this house, I'll break both his legs,' he declared, trembling with rage.

Many years had passed since Vasudevan's move to Bombay. He had not come even once to visit you. Everyone believed he would come for Kausalya's wedding at least, but he didn't.

After that, they stopped waiting for his return. Vendor Goyindan felt as though he had performed the last rites for his son while he was still alive, but what else could he do?

After the wedding feast featuring eleven dishes and two payasams, all the guests dispersed. When it was time to leave, Kausalya's eyes welled up.

'Don't cry, Kausalya. You're not really going away, are you, it's just across the river,' your mother consoled her. The breadth of a river. As long as there's a boat to ferry one across, that's no distance. Your amma will take the boat to come to you, your mother reassured your sister.

Kausalya left, trusting that assurance. And you hurriedly moved into the room that was hers. You could stop sharing with Shivaraman now. You would have a room all to yourself like you had always wanted.

Around you, the village was changing. New shops opened, all of them doing good business. The only thing lacking was an umbrella store. To buy an umbrella, one had to travel to the town.

'Tailoring is not for you. Go and bury your machine somewhere. Start an umbrella store. The monsoons are coming, there'll be good sales,' Vendor Goyindan told Shivaraman.

'That's not a good business to get into. It's not going to earn me lakhs, is it? And what will I do after the rains, when there's no demand for umbrellas? Twiddle my thumbs? Sit on my hands?'

'Even Karikkat Bhagawathy can't save you!' Vendor Goyindan stomped off without another word, angered by such unreasonableness.

A moplah from Keenicherry, the nearest village to yours, started an umbrella store that same year. It expanded quickly. People found the colourful Colombo umbrellas attractive. Until then, they had only seen the regular black ones. The moplah sold multi-coloured umbrellas with flowers and polka dots on them. Even those who had no need for umbrellas bought them.

When the monsoon got over, the moplah started selling footwear. The umbrella store pivoted to being a footwear store.

'Learn from him how to trade.'

'I'm not a trader.'

'Then what are you?'

'I'm a tailor.'

'Phthoo,' Vendor Goyindan hawked and spat on the ground.

Not long afterwards, this brother of yours surprised everyone. The man who used to sit in front of the sewing machine swatting flies the whole day got married without telling anyone. But that was not what stopped people in their tracks. The girl he married was beautiful. So stunning, in fact, that you could not believe your eyes.

'What made Vatsala marry this man? Does he have a steady job? Is he earning enough?'

You've always known that life throws up dark imponderables from time to time. The usually scrupulous Vendor Goyindan had gone out of his way to help Erattu Velukutty in a few dubious land deals. In that last exam you wrote, although you knew the answers, you copied from your friend. Now, Shivaraman's marriage reinforced your belief in the unpredictability of life.

Shivaraman registered his marriage at Keenicherry without anyone else getting to know. At the registrar's office, he did not care that the window frames and bars were dusty, the windowsills grimy with caked mud. A pipal tree stood outside the building, its leaves covered in dust. Inside, files and bundles of papers were stacked neatly on shelves and on top of cabinets.

After paying the registrar his dues and his witnesses a few rupees as baksheesh, your brother came home. He was wearing a starched white mundu and shirt. You wondered who had done the washing and pressing for him. The bride was wearing a silk saree and blouse. Who had bought these for her? Tradition demanded that the groom buy the bridal dress and the gold chain she would wear around her neck. The chain she had on must weigh three or three-and-a-half sovereigns. Where had your brother found the money for it?

'What business do you have here?' Vendor Goyindan blew in like a typhoon, folding his mundu and tucking it in, ready to do battle. 'Get out! This is not your home and you are not my son. Get out of my sight.'

One glimpse of your apoplectic father was enough to scare you. But neither your brother nor his new wife showed any fear.

'Where else am I supposed to go? This is my house.'

Shivaraman had never spoken to anyone, let alone his father, with his voice raised. You wondered where this new-found audacity came from. Did getting married to a girl do that to him? 'If that's the case, I'll get married too,' you told yourself. You badly wanted a bit of nerve.

Shoving aside your father, your brother strode into the house. He went directly to his room.

'Where's the chopper?' Vendor asked Lakshmikuttyamma. 'I'll hack him to pieces. I'll chop him up and feed the dogs.'

'Lay one finger on me and you'll know what this tailor is made of.' Shivaraman went into his room and bolted the door behind him.

How does a lowly earthworm rise up and spread its hood like that?

Vendor Goyindan rushed forward and unleashed a kick at the door. It stayed firm. Vendor staggered as if the door had kicked him back. Lakshmikuttyamma grabbed his arm and told him tearfully, 'Enough! He is our son, isn't he? He had a crush on her and now he's married her. Come away, we'll talk things over in good time.'

Your mother led your father into their bedroom and bolted the door behind her.

You turned to your sister-in-law. 'Who stitched this silk blouse for you, Edathi? Did my brother do it himself?'

'Nah, I got it stitched in town,' Vatsala said. 'You work in the cinema talkies, don't you? I love watching movies. You'll take me to see every one of them, won't you?'

12

YOU AND HITLER

Your youth flew by as if on wings. If you cock your ears, you can still hear the flapping, the loud chittering as though from a flock of sparrows flying by. It was the end of the sixties and the beginning of the seventies. A time when all that you had considered dear receded from you. You suddenly turned into an introvert and a loner.

'Those who are in the habit of thinking become recluses,' you told yourself. The only thing that kept you alive was the desire to write. But not on the subjects that most mainstream writers worked with. For some time now, you had been aware of the blood of two communities that had spilt on the path you were on. You wished to write about that.

'What? There's such a problem in our midst? Impossible!' Balan looked at you, surprised. The breeze from the ceiling fan flattened the springy, disobedient hair on his head. 'Why do you have to write about imaginary things?'

You broke your silence then. 'Everyone likes writing about what's in front of their eyes. I intend to write about stuff that's kept hidden from us. That's what will bring readers to me. You and I may not be able to see these readers, but they're there, hidden from view.'

There was a smile in the corner of Balan's eyes. He agreed with you.

'I want to live with writing as my partner,' you said once. You were twenty-five years old.

Balan had been your best friend since your school days. He was a better student than you, and escaped the cane. However, each time it lashed your buttocks, he writhed in pain. Even in his seventieth year, he could not bear the sight of anyone in pain. He had specialised in oncology, and his life's mission was to alleviate the pain of cancer patients. 'Why do terminal patients have to live in agony?' he said to you. 'It's much better to inject them with poison and end their pain.'

He had started a campaign once, for legislation that would legalise mercy killing. Since then, he had remained at the forefront of the battle for euthanasia, travelling all over the country to drum up support.

You met often, your friendship growing stronger over time. In your troubled old age, it was he who showed you a way out.

During the years when you were employed at the theatre, Balan came often to meet you. He had just finished medical college then.

Although there was now a nameboard that identified you as the manager, you continued to do the same work—issuing tickets to women through the ticket window on the left and to men through the window on the right.

He sat gazing at you as you went about your work, occasionally smoking a Player's. Seated under the metal sheet roofing, he would soon start to perspire.

When the bell rang to signal the start of the evening show, you closed the ticket counter and sat down to chat with him.

'Such boring work! Is this what someone like you should be doing?'

'I don't find it boring, Bala. Every job has its own dignity.'

'So, you plan to spend your whole life tearing off tickets and selling song books?'

You took the burning cigarette from between Balan's fingers and took a puff. You were in the habit of smoking when absorbed in thought. Something that had not missed Balan's notice.

'I don't plan to work for long. I want to write, you know that.'

'Why aren't you writing then?'

'I have to cleanse my body and mind first. Only then can I write.'

'You mean they're not clean now, your body and mind?'

'No. Smell my clothes and you'll know.'

Balan stretched his neck like a crane, flared his nostrils, sniffed.

'Your shirt reeks of stale sweat. That's because you sit and work in this shed without any ventilation. Go home and take a bath. Use enough soap and this smell will vanish.'

'Bala, this isn't the pong of sweat. It's the stink of Hitler's and Mussolini's uniforms.'

'Where did you get their uniforms from? You're mad.'

You didn't like that one bit. Yours was a long friendship, but sometimes Balan failed to understand you. Sometimes you spoke in a language that did not make sense to him. You had the mind of a writer. Balan, a doctor, could only understand that which was logical.

You wanted to explain to him that communalism and racism lay in wait every moment, trying to sneak into your heart. You would not yield, but they lurked on your skin, waiting for an opportunity to afflict you. That's what caused the stink. When it was beyond sufferance, you would tear off your shirt and fling it away. Some days, even your mundu had to be tossed off. One such time, Kausalya saw you lying naked in the darkness and you had to buy her silence with two rupees.

*

Now that you had your own room on the ground floor, you felt there was no need to wait any longer. You were ready to write.

Let's go over the geography of your house once more.

It was a thatched house, rather small, with verandas on three sides. The floor was plastered with cow dung. Outside, on the left side of the compound, green coconuts were piled high. Beyond that patch lay a coconut pound. When there was no more room in the pound, coconuts would be spread out on the veranda. During the monsoon, the smell of damp husk lingered in the air.

In the barn at the rear of the house, cows stood ruminating: you had three cows and a bull. Okra, beans, spinach and aubergine grew in the compound, and on the right side were stacked piles of hay.

From the veranda, one entered a central room, a long and narrow one. In a corner stood an old but sturdy table and a chair. Both gave off the distinctly unpleasant smell of bedbugs. The chair creaked when someone sat on it. You remembered seeing a kerosene lamp on the table all through your childhood. It was called the No. 6 lamp. Every day, Lakshmikuttyamma would clean its smoke-stained glass with a piece of cloth.

At night, the yellow-copper light from the lamp would paint the walls. On the table, stacks of paper were neatly arranged. Occasionally, Vendor Goyindan could be seen seated at the table, going through a stack, referring to papers and making notes. He ate his meals there too.

The ground floor had two rooms. With their tiny windows and low ceilings, they let in very little light even during the day. One of these rooms was used by Vendor Goyindan. This was where his wooden trunk containing cash, deeds and documents and the Waterbury's Compound bottle with the key of the trunk were stored. Your mother and Kausalya slept in the second room. Some days, late in the night, your mother would go missing and Kausalya would start to sniffle. One night, scared of the darkness, she went up to her father's room and heard her mother's whispery voice. Her father and mother seemed to be sharing some secret. She called to her mother in a low tone.

'Molu, go and lie down, Amma will come in a minute,' her mother said.

The next morning, your father seemed to find fault with everything that Kausalya did and scolded her continuously, even boxing her ear once.

You shared your room with Vasudevan, as Shivaraman did with Ramakrishnan. When Vasudevan left for Bombay, you tried to take over the room, but Shivaraman beat you to it. When you went to the room that night with a book in your hand, you realised that Shivaraman had locked the door from inside. You had to take refuge in Ramakrishnan's room. When Ramakrishnan married Sathi, you had to vacate it and move in with Shivaraman. Then, when Shivaraman married Vatsala and, ignoring your father's protests, brought her into the house, you were left with no place to sleep.

'You can sleep in my room, Kausalya is not there,' Lakshmikuttyamma said.

'Aiyyo, in your room?'

'Why can't you sleep in my room?'

'Amma, why don't you sleep in Achchan's room? I need a room to myself.'

'Are you also planning to bring a girl home like Shivaraman did? I'll kill you!'

Your mother picked up her tired old quilted mattress and blanket and moved into your father's room. She spread a mat on the floor, unfolded the mattress on it and lay down, covering herself with the blanket.

And so, with the departure of Kausalya, you finally got your own room. After a long, long wait.

When you moved in, you found the room redolent with the smell of coconut oil. The turned rollers on the bed's headboard were stained with oil from your mother's and sister's hair. A small wooden almirah was set in the wall. When you opened it, you were assailed by the piercing smell of lemongrass oil that your mother used whenever she had a cold. You set about cleaning the room immediately.

At the ticket counter of Kalyani Talkies, you had stashed away a couple of books and magazines to leaf through whenever the tedium of the job overwhelmed you. These were the first things you took to your room. When you went to the town to meet the film distributor, you brought back a thick notebook and a bottle of blue ink. You already had a fountain pen firmly clipped to your shirt pocket. All you needed now was a table and a chair. You had the carpenter Kunjan make these for you.

Everything had come together—you had your own room, table and chair, pen, ink and paper. All you had to do was sit down and write.

'I'm not going to do anything today. I'll lie on this bed looking at the world through the window and think for a while,' you said to yourself. You were always in step with your thoughts. Your brain worked more than your body, and without rest, as though you did not know there was a border between thoughts and dreams. Sometimes they felt the same.

Between dreams and thoughts, where is the space for writing? Do thoughts follow writing or does writing follow thoughts?

You liked to believe that thinking is both exercise and meditation.

*

Would you continue as the manager of Kalyani Talkies? Or did you plan to give it up? It was you who asked the question, and you who had to reply. But you were unable to.

You sat thinking and smoking a cigarette in the empty, kennel-like room with the ticket counter. When the monsoon arrived, windy and cold, fewer people showed up. Rather than shivering in the theatre, they preferred to stay home. Some days, not even ten people turned up for the late show. Most lay snoring in their beds, snug under their blankets.

'Even if there are only ten, it doesn't matter. Don't stop the show.' Velukutty was categorical.

Lightning. Thunder. The rain tore through the holes in the dark sky. You had thought that no one would turn up and you could switch off the generator, lock up and go home early. You would gobble down some food, lock yourself in your room, then sit down and write. That was the plan.

You had been playing hide-and-seek with writing. Sometimes it would be at arm's length. Sometimes it was beyond divination. Today, at this moment, the words were right in front of you. Today, you would write.

The movie of the day was *Shyamalachechi*, starring Sathyan and Ambika. When you were readying to lock up the theatre, two drunks turned up to watch the movie.

'There's no late-night show today.'

You spoke deferentially, hiding the irritation that you felt. Velukutty's instructions were clear: cinema goers should be spoken to with the kind of reverence you would show your own parents. You complied as best as possible.

Was it not enough that they were drunk? Did they need to see the late-night show as well?

'Why not?'

'There's no audience.'

'Why, aren't the two of us enough of an audience for you? Start the silima, man!'

'Why don't you go now and come back tomorrow? There's no one to operate the projector. Kunjiramettan has already left.'

The projectionist had indeed gone home. You thought back to the time when Kunjiramettan had been laid up with a chest congestion and fever. For those two days, you had taken on the role of projectionist. This had made you go up in Velukutty's estimation, but you were filled with dread—would your boss dismiss Kunjiramettan and foist that job too on you? Erattu Velukutty had a devious mind.

The drunks started to get testy. You lost patience and went to switch off the generator. The men lurched forward with the intention of beating you up, but they couldn't see anything in the dark. The first punch landed not on you but on the other drunk. He hit back. While they abused and hit each other under the impression that they were giving you the treatment, you hightailed it to Velukutty's house. You handed over the day's collection and hurried away without giving him an opportunity to ask questions.

You walked briskly, shining your flashlight. You wanted to get home and start writing. It was like the urge to pee. When the bladder is full, the lower belly starts to ache. When the urge is to write, the chest aches. You could feel yourself filling up with scenarios, the words gushing forth.

The house stood drenched in darkness. You had been procrastinating for months; today would see it end. You thanked Lord Varuna for making it rain tonight. Velukutty had cursed the rains. One man's happiness is another man's sorrow, you reflected.

Everyone was asleep. Through a door that was ajar, you could see the light from inside. Your mother was waiting for you, half asleep. Not wanting to disturb her, you opened the door gently. The hinges bellowed like buffaloes. Your mother woke up and rubbed her eyes.

'Why don't you sleep, Amma? Why do you wait up for me?'

'If I sleep, who will serve you dinner?'

'I can eat on my own.'

'Men shouldn't be cooking or serving food. That's women's work.'

You couldn't argue with your mother. Without saying anything more, you took off your shirt, hung it on the clothesline, swapped your wet mundu for a dry one and sat down to dinner. Your attention was not on the rice and buttermilk curry your mother had made for you. Your mind was busy with thoughts of writing. You could not tarry a moment longer. If you did, the words would vanish. Without finishing the food on your plate, you shook the rice from your fingers, scrambled up and used the water from the *kindi* to wash your hands and to gargle, then rushed to your room and shut the door behind you.

The pen in your right hand, a burning cigarette in your left hand. Beyond the window, lightning flashed without the accompanying sound of thunder. Everything had come together. Now to start writing. One . . . two . . . three . . . Start!

Alas, Karikkat Bhagawathy, the moving finger could not write. Although the nib was placed on the paper, not a word came out of it. You shook the pen vigorously. Ink drops plopped onto the paper and the floor. You put the pen to paper again, but not a single word could be formed. Disappointed, you stood up and paced the room a few times.

That did not help, so you paced some more. In that manic phase of walking in the weak yellow light of the 40W bulb, you pulled off your clothes like Victor Hugo and became lost to yourself. You had read somewhere that Victor Hugo sat down to write only after shedding his clothes.

Finally, the words emerged and embraced you. You ran to the chair and picked up the pen. You wrote whatever came to mind, not thinking about what you were writing. Afterwards, you crumpled up the papers and threw them out into the darkness that waited with its mouth open. You watched as the night chewed up everything and ingested it with great relish.

13

YOU AND YOUR DRINKING HABIT

Your dear friend Balan took up a government job. His first posting was at the government hospital in a faraway town. To reach there, one had to cross the railway tracks and take a muddy, smelly path through the swamp. You wished Balan had found a better place, not this old, rundown hospital with its rusted and broken gate.

Until he moved there, Balan lived and worked in the town closest to the village. He lived in a large house—his own tharavad in the middle of a large piece of land in which coconut trees, areca palms and mango trees grew close to one another. Sparrows and warblers perched on their branches and pepper vines grew on Indian coral trees.

After graduation, Balan had started a private practice in town, the board outside his room proclaiming Dr Charoth Balan, M.B.B.S. In the beginning, most of the patients he saw suffered from mild infections or diarrhoea. When word spread that his treatments were effective, others began approaching him for consultations. He cured consumption, provided relief to patients of rheumatoid arthritis and asthma. His practice flourished and he grew to be well liked. It was at this juncture that he got the government job.

'Unni'shna, I'm leaving. I've got into government service.'

'Why do you need another job? Don't you have a roaring practice here?'

'I must study further. A government job is better for that. I can take study leave.'

Balan had bought a Premier Padmini car and drove to and from town. To the hospital, he wore a mundu with a black border.

Meanwhile, you continued to be the manager of Kalyani Talkies.

When Balan turned up at the theatre, he would sit at the ticket counter and chat with you.

'I feel bad when I see you in this shed. You shouldn't be working in a place like this. You're more intelligent than I am, yet . . .'

You were a good student during your school days, although you had neither focus nor ambition. Balan had both. Perhaps that was why he had become a doctor while you remained a talkies manager.

'Come with me to the town,' Balan said to you. 'I'll find you a decent job there.'

You missed some of what Balan had said in the din from the theatre. A love song was playing. You had instructed Kunjiramettan to keep the volume low, but he never listened. If the volume was low, the audience would start catcalling to show their displeasure. 'I can't bear the loud sound. I'll go mad if I have to,' you would say each time.

'You skinflint, increase the bloody volume. We've paid good money to see the movie. We're not freeloaders. Turn it up, you money-grubbing louse!'

Kunjiramettan kept the volume high to avoid becoming the subject of such abuse. Especially when it came to songs. Only then could the audience feel the thrill.

'What do you say?' Balan persisted.

'I'm all right for the time being. When I'm tired of it, I'll tell you.'

'As you please.'

Balan sounded disappointed. The town had a few establishments owned and run by Gujaratis, some of whom he was acquainted with. He could have got you a clerk's job with ease. You could have stayed with him in his big rented house. He had a maid who cooked and cleaned for him. You could have had a comfortable life there. A clerk's job had a certain dignity too. You would have had plenty of books to read, and the time to read them. You could have watched new movies. However, none of this appealed to you.

You knew, of course, that you would someday bid adieu to Kalyani Talkies. You wanted to make a living out of writing, without having to do a regular job. You had done your calculations. Soon, you would be rid of the deafening duets, the shrill whistles and catcalls, the abuse.

'Eda, I've got some whisky in my car. Shall we have a drink?'

'Sure, let's.'

It was exactly what you wanted. A mouthful of whisky.

Balan fetched a bag from his car, out of which came two glass tumblers, half a bottle of Scotch whisky, a bottle of boiled and cooled water and a small ice box packed with ice cubes. Also, a bag of spicy mixture to follow each gulp of the drink. The glasses carried the branding of some pharmaceutical company.

An hour had passed since the evening show began. The late-night show was still two hours away. Till then you had all the time in the world. You could do anything—think, daydream, land on the moon, even sleep. There were days when you did sleep, slumped on the chair, only to be startled awake by the catcalls and whistles from the hall. If the film snapped in between the show, there would be booing and hooting, which ceased only when Kunjiramettan unwound the reels to find the snapped ends, scratched each one with a rusty, broken blade to allow for better adhesion, then glued them together before starting the projector again.

When the heroine walked in wearing a low-slung, diaphanous saree through which her navel peeped, you would know instantly from the sharp intake of breath and the collective sigh from the audience. Someone would caterwaul and shout, 'Edi, wear it even lower.' Others would respond with a sudden burst of howls and cheers.

Balan and you clinked glasses and took a sip each. As the whisky went down smoothly, you felt energised. Although it was dark outside, inside you was cool sunshine.

The racket from the theatre increased. The heroine had entered the pond with two handmaidens for her bath.

Balan was the first one to drain his glass. He dropped some of the spicy mixture into his mouth, then took a couple of generous sips. He was a disciplined drinker.

You always started conservatively, with a small sip, then gulped down what was left in the glass. Although your taste buds craved the sharp saltiness of the mixture, you did not yield. You only wanted to drink. When your glass was empty, you started to smoke a cigarette.

'I became a doctor, had a successful practice. And now I am in government service. You've always wanted to be a writer. Why haven't you become one yet?'

'The words have to come. They are bottled up inside. A few have emerged after much effort and cajoling. I know there are more inside, but they're stuck for now.'

'What's the point of carrying them around inside you? You have to write it all down and get it published. How else will people come to know of you, how will you become a writer? Bloody fool!'

You sat there drinking whisky and chatting till the evening show was over. There was a large crowd for the late-night show too. Bathing scenes and displays of flesh were always a big draw. Balan watched with amusement as you dispensed tickets to those who had queued up outside. He was used to accepting money after examining patients with a stethoscope and writing out prescriptions. The money you accepted was not yours; the money he took became his own. In the mornings, he would do free consultations at his house before leaving for the hospital.

'I'll go now.' Balan picked up his car keys and stood up. It had started to drizzle. A cool breeze touched them before heading east in the direction of the river. It must be raining heavily somewhere close by. With his car's headlights piercing the darkness, Balan drove away.

Pleasantly drunk as you were, you could feel the happiness spreading through you. You smiled to yourself. You were fond of alcohol, but you would not drink toddy or arrack or the local, low-priced brandy or whisky. If you drank, it had to be the good stuff. But where would you find the money to buy high-quality whisky? Usually, you made do with Hercules XXX rum. Even Old Monk was a luxury.

Drinking in the company of Balan soon became a habit. You discovered that a little brandy or rum loosened your tongue and made conversation easier. After two large pegs, you became positively garrulous. On one such occasion, you said, 'You keep asking why I'm not writing. The truth is, I've started to write a little. I know I should do more. But when I'm ready, the words will emerge by themselves. Till then, be patient.'

You took another sip of your drink. 'The words are screaming inside me. They gnaw my innards like a pack of rats. Right now, there's a big block inside me that's stopping everything. It's stopping my writing too. You want to know what the hindrance is? It's those people who reside within me, like aliens. And they're not just in my body, they're in every person's body. Didn't Hitler die many years ago? You asked me that once. But Hitler and others like him cannot die. I've prised them out of my heart, but they continue to live on in my skin. I have to exorcise them from my body and keep them away by ring-fencing myself. Only then will I be able to write. Bala, being a writer is not an easy thing. It's the trickiest vocation in the world. Whenever I start on something, people try to stop me . . .'

'Unni'shna, who are these people?'

'Do I have to tell you that? Don't you know?'

'Tell me, who are they?'

'From the past, of course. These are people who do their damnedest to stop writers from writing anything. Hitler,

Mussolini, Franco. Even our Stalin can be counted among them.'

'They have risen from their graves to impede your writing? You're stark raving mad!'

'They don't die. Ever. Even if they die, they go about trying to haunt writers. Their ghosts hover around all the time. This is not new, you know. Even Mark Twain was haunted by ghosts.'

'Let's forget Twain for the time being. He was a racist.'

'He was not haunted by the ghosts for being a racist. It's because of the language he used. His book was banned for containing vulgar words not fit for decent society. Do you know, even if a writer is an apologist for Hitler, Hitler's ghost will come and haunt him? His kind will not let writers survive.'

'Hitler and Mussolini have nothing better to do than come after Vendor Goyindan's son? This is all your imagination. You are trying to justify your inability to write, making excuses for not writing.'

'My dear friend, you know and understand medicine, but you know nothing else. Hitler and Mussolini and others like them are not human beings. They are phenomena. They live among us as various incarnations. Writers can see and recognise them easily, others not so easily. You are unable to see them because you're not a writer.'

'Let such phenomena take care of themselves then. Let's have a couple of pegs and go to sleep.'

'True. Let me throw the pen into the bin and down a few large pegs. Much more sensible!'

A bottle filled with alcohol is superior to a pen filled with ink. Enter bottle, exit pen. You laughed.

That night you sat with Balan and, instead of having two large pegs, you had four.

Once, when Balan had to go on work to Madras, he insisted that you join him. You would have liked to take the train for your maiden journey and wander through Moore Market. But you had no money for the fare and other expenses. More importantly, your boss Velukutty would not grant you leave. He believed that if you were absent, the show would stop at Kalyani Talkies. You sat at the box office and issued tickets, sold the song books, started the generator and ran the projector. In short, you did all the work. Kunjiramettan took advantage of this. He knew that even in his absence, the show would go on because you were there.

In the morning, on the way to the theatre, you went to Velukutty's house.

'What brings you here, Unni'shna?'

Velukutty was preparing to go for his bath, his body shining with the Dhanvatharam oil he used. He was adamant about bathing in the pond every day.

'I need to go to Madras.'

'Go then, who's stopping you?'

'I need a week's leave.'

'Impossible.'

'Aiyyo!'

'If you go away, the silima won't run.'

'I'm not going to be here forever. One day I'll leave.'

'Are you threatening me?'

Velukutty rolled his eyes. Rohini arrived just then, dressed in a short skirt, though she was a little too old for skirts. She wanted to order something from Madras in case you were going—an electric iron. She had never seen one, but she had heard about it. Until she got one, she would have to continue using her box iron filled with coconut-shell embers.

'Achcha, let Unni'shnettan go to Madras.'

'Phhaa, go inside!' he snapped at her.

She was not the type to leave.

'Kunjiramettan is there to start the generator and run the projector,' you said. 'Anyone can issue the tickets and sell the song books. And surely you can check the accounts, boss? I'll be back in a week's time.'

'I can check the accounts. I've studied up to eighth class,' Rohini chimed in.

'Scram, girl! What business do you have here, where men are talking?' Velukutty threw her an angry look, then sought to quell her with a death stare.

'Come on, boss. What if I fall sick? You won't give me leave even then?'

'Fall sick first, and then we'll see.'

You left, disappointed. There was dew on the wild plants growing on either side of the path. The pointed tips of leaves glinted like needles in the sunlight. You cursed your boss. 'Velukutty, I'll burn down your Kalyani Talkies. You'll understand then who this Unni'shnan is,' you muttered as you walked behind your shadow, which marched ahead.

Your shadow reached the theatre first, with you right behind. You were there to check the accounts before the film distributor's representative arrived. But you were not in the mood to work. You lit a Charminar and became lost in thought.

In your head, you were already on the train to Madras. The next morning, after getting off the train, you booked yourself into a lodge, had a bath and ate a breakfast of idli, sambar and coconut chutney. Then you left to see the city. You wandered through the famous Moore Market that everyone talked about. Many kinds of fabric and readymade garments were available there at low prices.

You wanted to buy something for everyone back home. Unfortunately, as usual, you had no money. Your pockets were empty. You did not feel bad about it, though. Poverty never bothered you. You were resigned to hardship. You knew that if by some miracle you were to become a rich man overnight, you would take no pleasure in it.

14

YOUR MARRIAGE

All through the years that you worked at the theatre, Balan remained deeply concerned about your future. Thanks to his intervention, a large-hearted and equally large-bellied Gujarati in Kozhikode arranged a writer's job for you. But you kept him waiting.

'What should I tell the Gujarati?'

'Nothing.'

'They won't wait for long. Don't you want to be a writer? This job is exactly that. You join as a writer in the company and then become a "writer" writer.'

You said nothing, just looked beyond Balan's head at the treetops that had been washed clean by the rain. You were sitting on the red-cushioned cane chair in the patio of Balan's house. The aroma from the kitchen, of dal being tempered, made you salivate. At Balan's house, tasty food and a wide variety of alcohol were guaranteed. You were always happy to visit him. By the time you left, you would have tanked up on alcohol and food. His bar was a veritable library of alcohol, and now it seemed he had started to build a library for books as well. Every time you visited him, you saw more and more new books. Was he spending all his salary on books and liquor?

Sometimes you were possessed by the urge to write, and when that happened, you would write oblivious of your surroundings. Even while people waited impatiently for tickets and hollered at you, you kept writing without a care.

'You bugger, what are you doing?'

Velukutty happened to be passing by, and hearing the ruckus, hurried to the theatre to investigate. The sight of you with your head bowed, writing furiously, enraged him. You rubbed your eyes and looked up as if you had woken from a deep sleep. It took you some time to become aware of your surroundings.

'Boss, my apologies. I dozed off.'

'You write in your sleep? What the hell are you scribbling? Am I paying you sixty-five rupees of the finest every month for this? Give out the tickets, you sonofabitch!'

Velukutty snatched your book and threw it out. You flew out of the shed after the book as if you too had been flung out. You picked it up and held it close to your chest as you might an infant. Then you went back inside and started to issue tickets to the foul-mouthed cinema lovers shouting profanities at you. After watching the scene for a minute, Velukutty hawked and spat to express his disdain before walking away.

After that, you did not feel like writing any more. You wished Balan would turn up with his bottle-in-a-bag, but he did not. When the movie started, you sat around listlessly, trying to pay attention to the dialogue and the songs. But your mind strayed each time you started to count the cash and work on the accounts. You kept losing count and having to start all over again. Finally, you gave up and leaned back in the chair, preparing to doze.

Once the late-night show was over, you switched off the generator and walked through the darkness to Velukutty's house. You handed over the day's collection and the accounts and noticed that Velukutty was looking at you in a peculiar way.

'I abused you a lot today. I called you a bugger and a sonofabitch. But whatever I say, you don't seem to improve. Son, why are you like this?'

His words sent you into a tizzy. The man had never spoken to you in this manner before. The same mouth that had called you a bugger a hundred times was now calling you son. There was a gentle smile and an amiable look on his face. You decided there was foul play afoot. Anyone in your position would have thought the same. No one could do such a somersault in the space of one night.

Determined not to get caught in whatever snare he had set for you, you reciprocated with a charming smile of your own and took leave of him.

'Be careful. Pit vipers may be out at this time of the night.'

You acted as if you had not heard. Was there a more venomous pit viper than Velukutty in these parts?

*

Vendor Goyindan was sad that you could not land a more suitable and better paid job. The thought stayed with him like the sting of snuff as it went up his nostrils. He had not sent you to college spending a potful of money for you to end up as a cinema hall manager. He blamed himself for finding you the job in the first place. It wasn't fit for a graduate.

'Eda, are you planning to spend all your life cooped up in that silima theatre?' he asked, fanning himself with a towel.

It was a sunny day, though there was also a fine drizzle. His body tended to absorb heat more than others' and he sweated even on cool, rainy days.

'Achcha, you were the one who found me the job,' you retorted.

You were planning to get into bed after lunch and read a book, perhaps even take a nap. The weather—bright sunshine and rain at the same time—had most fortuitously set the stage for this. Today there was no matinee show. For the last three days, they had been showing *Thayin Karunai*, a Tamil movie released in 1965. It had few takers and the hall was practically empty. The late-night show had already been cancelled, so had the matinee. Only if you got the print of a new release would the shows resume. So you had some unexpected time on your hands. Apart from reading and a possible siesta, you had a few things to mull over too.

'When I saw you loafing around, unable to find a job, I had to suck up to Velukutty and fix you up there. Are you blaming me for that, you ungrateful wretch? How old are you now?'

You remained silent. You already knew where your father was headed with his imprecations. The question of marriage follows the question about age.

'Eda, do you know, at your age I was already a father of two kids.'

Vendor Goyindan had married Lakshmikuttyamma at the age of twenty-two. Within three years she had given birth to future grocer Ramakrishnan and tailor Shivaraman. Vasudevan followed.

'Eda, I can't step out of this house. The whole village is asking—why is a twenty-five-year-old still single, doesn't he want a girl?'

'Let them say what they want. I'm not marrying just yet.' You spoke firmly and picked up the book lying on the bed. Reading yourself to sleep after lunch—wasn't that one of the great pleasures of life?

You found it hard, however, to concentrate on the book; stray thoughts filled your mind with disquiet. If you were to make a list of priorities, writing would be on top, while marriage would be somewhere at the bottom. And yet, you were still to write anything remotely satisfying. Once, you had stayed up all night, scribbling, like a child trying his hand on a slate and writing his first words. You filled the pages with nonsense, then crumpled them into a ball and tossed them out of the window.

'Did anyone shit paper here last evening?' asked Cheeru, who was sweeping the yard with a towel wound around her head to keep away the early morning chill.

'Yes, Cheeru, those are the paper scraps I excreted yesterday,' you said to yourself.

Gradually, your marriage grew into more than a private concern for Vendor Goyindan and Lakshmikuttyamma. It became a public issue that perturbed the denizens of your village. They started to turn up with unsolicited proposals.

One of these was an alliance with Velukutty's daughter, Rohini.

Velukutty himself arrived at your house one day, without warning. He closed his umbrella, placed it on the veranda, hawked and spat, then climbed up the steps and did a quick survey of everything.

'Velukutty, is that you? Come, come . . .' your father welcomed him. Pushing the chair on the veranda towards him, he said, 'Sit down, please sit down.'

'There's no time to sit and chat,' Velukutty said, after he had seated himself. 'I'll come straight to the point. I heard you are looking for a girl for your son, is that right?'

'Yes, that's right. He's past twenty-five already, Velukutty.'

'When there's a girl in my house, why do you have to seek elsewhere?'

This was unexpected. No self-respecting father would turn up at a boy's place offering his daughter's hand in marriage. What could have prompted Velukutty to abase himself like this? Rohini was just approaching marriageable age. What was the hurry?

Erattu Velukutty was one of the wealthiest men of the village. He had acquired large tracts of land within a short time. However, his family lacked pedigree; they could by no means be considered 'old money'. And Velukutty's mother, it was said, couldn't be sure who had fathered him.

The sight of a silent Vendor made Velukutty narrow his eyes. The muscles of his neck tightened.

'Goyinda, why are you silent?'

'Let me think it over, Velukutty.'

'What's there to think about? You know me well, and your son is the manager of my silima talkies.'

'Give me two days. Marriage is not child's play, is it? One must think it over.'

'All right. You think about it as much as you please. Let me know after two days. We'll decide everything else after that.'

Velukutty stood up and picked up his umbrella. There was a drizzle; the sun had gone behind the clouds.

'Have a glass of tea at least . . .'

'No, Lechmikutty. I don't drink coffee, tea and all that.'

'What about 'orlicks?'

'No,' he repeated, walking down the steps. From the manner of his departure, Vendor Goyindan knew he was unhappy. There was a veiled threat in his words.

'Velukutty doesn't look too pleased. Will he kick our Unni'shnan out of his job at the theatre?' Your mother was anxious.

Vendor Goyindan did not reply. He went back into the house, pulling the towel from his shoulder and cracking it twice like a whip.

Velukutty walked down the wet gravel path and disappeared from Lakshmikuttyamma's view. Only his shadow lingered.

So, would you end up marrying the buxom, fair-complexioned Rohini?

15

YOU AND BELLY LAUGHTER

Balan's marriage to Kamalakshi took place without any warning, even before he had finished his postgraduation. You were peeved because he gave you no indication of it. You had been friends with him since school. You told each other everything. You even drank together. Yet, Balan hid the news of his wedding from you. He told you only after he had got married.

To you, it felt as though Balan had become suddenly invisible; he had faded into the darkness and you were left searching for him. How could you not be peeved?

When the lights dimmed and the movie started, you swept the coins from the day's ticket sales into the table drawer and emerged from the kennel-like shed. You beckoned to Balan, who was waiting in his car. In order to escape any unwanted attention, he sat with the tinted glasses rolled up. The sight of a doctor waiting in a car in front of a theatre—the Red Cross sticker on the windscreen was a dead giveaway—was enough to pique curiosity.

Balan followed you in with his bag. This time, he had a full bottle of brandy in it. After placing it on the table, he closed the tin door of the shed. He had just placed on the table two glasses that he had washed and shined himself, and was about to open the bottle, when he was interrupted by frantic thumping on the window.

'Two tickets for the benches. Make it fast, dick-face. The movie's started.'

'Take the money first. Only then hand over the ticket. Otherwise, they'll dash into the theatre without paying, and you'll never be able to identify them.' Velukutty's words came to your mind as you took the money and tore off two pink tickets.

'Why're you scowling?' Balan asked.

'You didn't breathe a word to me. Ours is a friendship that goes back more than twenty years. Yet . . .'

'Eda, it was a decision made on the spur of the moment. I booked a trunk call and informed my parents. If you had a phone, I would have informed you too.'

'Do you need a phone for that? Don't you have a car? You could have driven down and told me.'

'I'm sorry. I was under some stress.'

Balan poured the brandy and topped it with soda from the marble soda bottle. You clinked glasses.

'To your health and your wife's.'

You clinked glasses again, with more force than was necessary. Luckily, they did not shatter.

Balan and his wife were both doctors, while you were an ordinary cinema theatre employee who knew nothing about medicine or health. Yet, here you were, wishing two doctors good health.

'You must come home soon. Kamalakshi has to leave in a few days.'

'Where to?'

'Aligarh. She works in the medical college there.'

'Why does she work so far away? Don't we have hospitals and patients here?'

'She studied there—at Aligarh Muslim University. Do you know, she is a Nampoothiri. Pure stock, one hundred per cent Nampoothiri. And yet, she went to a Muslim university and took her degree there.'

'How long have you known each other?'

'A mere two weeks. She's also an oncologist. We got married so we can treat cancer patients together, alleviate the pain of others.'

'She studied in Aligarh, does that mean she eats beef?'

'If needed, she'll eat you too.'

'My God! Can you find me a girl like her?'

'I heard some news too. That you are to marry Velukutty's daughter. And that he's going to give you a cinema theatre as dowry.'

'Get lost!'

You emptied the glass and banged it down on the table. You transferred all your anger onto that glass, and it guffawed at you. It was one of the two glasses that Balan carried in his bag along with the bottle. The bottle kept changing, whisky to rum to vodka to gin, the glasses remained the same.

As the brandy hit you, you became loquacious.

'What you heard is correct. Velukutty boss came home to meet my father. I thought something had gone wrong at the theatre and he had come to tell me about it. You know there are problems all the time. The panchayat officials keep harassing us. They say they need fifty free tickets for every movie. Velukutty offered five, but they said no way. So I offered twenty, and we reached a compromise.

'But that's not the story. Velukutty had come to meet my father, not me. He came to talk about me, umbrella in hand and holding up one end of his mundu—it's vulgar, the way he does it. And it's not just the way he holds the mundu, Bala. Everything about him is obscene. No one likes him. But he's filthy rich, so everyone hides their dislike and pretends to be respectful. He came to say that I should marry Rohini. That was his demand. My father said he would think it over. I said I'm not going to . . .'

'So what I heard is true!'

'Cent per cent.'

'Why are you rejecting her, though? You'll get a theatre as dowry.'

'Who needs that man's theatre, one that stinks like a urinal?'

You had forgotten that you were sitting and drinking in the same pee-pot theatre.

Balan left at 9 p.m., the car's headlights lighting up his path through the drizzle. You too wanted to glide through the darkness—not in a car, but on wings. The mist thickened around you; your head became foggy. There was still the late-night show to come, so you couldn't leave any time soon. You decided to settle down with your thoughts instead.

You were keen to meet Kamalakshi. What was she like, what did she have that made Balan marry her in such haste and secrecy? Was it her looks? Her proficiency at work? Her attitude to the world, perhaps?

As if he had read your mind, Balan arranged for the two of you to meet not long after.

Although he had invited you to his house a few times, you had not been able to find the time to go over. With his asthma playing up, Kunjiramettan had stopped coming to work. So you had to perform double duty, leaving you with no time or interest to do other things. Your boss saw this and announced, 'I'll fire that bugger Kunjiraman with a kick on his backside. I don't want him in my theatre anymore!'

Knowing your tough schedule, Balan brought Kamalakshi to the theatre. The evening show had started, and you were in the office counting cash when you heard the car door slam. Through a gap in the tin door, you saw Balan and Kamalakshi walking towards you.

'If you don't come to meet Kamalakshi, Kamalakshi will come to meet you.' Balan's words made his wife smile. She had springy hair and a small mouth with plump lips; her skin was even lighter than Kausalya's.

Balan placed his bag on the table.

'Kamalakshi leaves tomorrow. How can she go without meeting you? So, I brought her here.'

He opened the bag and took out three glasses.

'He only has time to talk about you. Even on our first night, he was talking about you. Right, Bala?'

'True. And then she said—Bala, why couldn't you have married Unni'shnan?'

They laughed together. Her laughter sounded like marbles rolling around in a crystal glass.

Balan poured rum into the glasses and topped it with Coca-Cola. They clinked glasses. Cheers!

'Balan will be coming to Aligarh for Bakrid. You should come too, Unni'shna!'

'He doesn't have time to come to our place to meet us, and you are talking about going to Aligarh!'

Balan refilled their glasses.

'Kamalakshi, I'll come to Aligarh. I love to see new places.'

'Oh yeah, he's a big-time traveller. Like our Ibn Batuta.'

Balan rocked with laughter, spilling his drink.

'Listen, Kamalakshi, the longest journey he's made till now is from his house to Ve . . . Ve . . . Velayudhan's teashop near the ferry landing. Unni'shna, you must have been an immovable rock in your previous life. Wherever you land up, you grow roots there. You don't stir.

'How many times have I told him to chuck this job and move to Kozhikode? The Gujarati is waiting still, with a writer's position. But he won't even get out of this shed.'

'What he says is true, Unni'shna. Don't spoil your life by sticking to this dead-end job.'

'I know all that. I'll leave this job soon. I'm fed up too.'

'Insha Allah,' the antarjanam said.

*

A few days after Velukutty turned up with his proposal, you and Rohini happened to meet. You had gone to Velukutty's house to discuss replacing the projector, which had been breaking down far too often. You had to be back at the theatre at least half an hour before the matinee, so you were in a hurry. While you were discussing the possibility of leasing another projector, Rohini came into your field of vision. She wore a short skirt with tiny polka dots; her hair was tied back in two plaits. Around her neck was a string of black beads.

'Achcha, I want to talk to this man.'

Her words surprised both Velukutty and you. Velukutty had been hearing her voice from the time she was a toddler. When she was an infant, he had heard her happy gurgling, her wails of indignant protest, her childish prattle. When she grew up, he had listened to her hearty laughter, her grievances and grumbles. But he had never heard this tone before.

You were irritated at being referred to as 'this man'. You had been to their house several times in the past, but she had never so much as acknowledged your presence. If she was around when you climbed the steps, she would give you a sidelong glance and hurry inside as if there was a fire to be put out in the kitchen. But she stood in front of you now, her head held high and her gaze steady. You were the one who flinched.

Velukutty stood there looking flabbergasted.

'Did you really say that?' Rohini asked you.

'Say what?'

'That you don't want to marry me?'

You chose to remain silent. You didn't know how to reply.

'Why are you silent? Has the cat got your tongue?'

'I did say it.'

'What is it that I lack? Do I not have everything that a woman should? Come, take a good look. Then tell me, what do I lack?'

She moved closer and struck a pose, her head thrown back, chest thrust out and arms akimbo, looking like a drawn bow. You could not have found fault as far as her appearance was concerned. Young though she was, womanhood seemed to have filled her out far more than was warranted.

'You lack nothing.'

'Then why did you reject me?'

'Because I don't need you.'

She shot you a look that scorched you all over.

'From tomorrow onwards, don't come to work. If you don't need Velukutty's daughter, then you don't need Velukutty's theatre either. Do you understand?'

'EDIIIIII . . .!'

Velukutty, who had stood stunned and mute until now, bellowed with rage, making the world around them tremble. Rohini acted as if she had not heard him. When Velukutty approached her with his leg raised to kick her, she swerved out of his line of attack with the agility of a doe.

You turned and went down to the yard, then stood for a moment, folding and tucking in your mundu. The road was empty. You took out a Scissors cigarette from your pocket and lit it, then started walking home.

Absorbed in your thoughts, you passed your house without noticing and had to double back. You felt a certain sympathy for Rohini, but you could not help laughing aloud. Ha . . . ha . . . ha . . . The look on Velukutty's face!

16

YOU AND YOUR LIFE AS A WRITER

You would not allow your life to be borne away by the tide—like a hay stalk carried to the river in the rainy season through gutters, streams and rivulets, knocked around by every impediment along the way. While still an adolescent, you had decided that you would take the rudder of your life into your own hands. The decision to send your father alone to the eye hospital in Vadakara while you went to the library had its origin in the more fundamental decision to remain in control of your destiny.

All this time, you were drawing the map of your life. If anyone else tried to set the course for you, you would step in and correct it immediately. When you saw that the marriage line on the map was pointing towards Rohini, you erased it altogether. When the time felt right, you would draw the line yourself. Until then, that part of the map would stay blank.

When you decided that you would give up your job at the theatre, it was a well-thought-out decision. Your monthly income of Rs 65 would cease. But you would redeem precious time that would otherwise have been lost to you. Which was more valuable? Rs 65, or the time you would reel back in?

Velukutty did not give you permission to leave. He had no love for you, felt no particular concern or sympathy, but he was aware that without you, the theatre would suffer. You knew how to start the generator, operate the projector and keep the movie running; you were capable of writing synopses for the new releases; the proceeds from the ticket sales were accounted for to the last paise, no short-changing at all. Whenever summoned, rain or shine, you would report to Velukutty at his house. Where was he going to find your replacement?

'My daughter is a windbag. Don't let her words drive you away.'

'My mind is made up. I have to leave.' The firmness in your voice surprised even you.

'Have you found another job, Unni'shna?'

'No.'

'How are you going to live then? You should have enough money for your tea and cigarettes, at least?'

'That's not an issue, Velukutty sir.'

'Think it over once more, then let me know.'

'It's a decision I've taken after a lot of thought.'

'So what? Think it over once more.'

The two of you were standing in front of the ticket booth. Catcalls and cheering could be heard from the theatre. There was the sound of clashing swords amidst the drumming of horses' hooves. Unseen objects tumbled and crashed.

Earlier that day, Rohini's words had struck Velukutty's hairy ears when he emerged from the puja room after his morning prayer. 'If Unni'shnan wants to leave, let him go. I'll find you ten men more capable than he is.'

He said to you, 'Okay, if that's the way you want it, so be it.'

As Velukutty started to walk away, dragging his tyre-sole sandals, shrill whistles erupted from the hall. He felt as if someone had slapped him on the face.

Once Velukutty disappeared from sight, you woke up from your reverie. You had no clear idea where you were headed. All you knew was that the road ahead would take you towards writing. Your life as a writer was about to begin, and you would enter it like a cool breeze through an open window. There were no more impediments to block your path.

The next morning, you handed over the keys and account ledgers to Velukutty. As he took them, Velukutty's fat fingers trembled.

'Unni'shna, wait!'

'Keep this.' Velukutty thrust a few folded five-rupee notes into your hand. You started to protest, then saw his expression and quietly pocketed the money before walking away. It would come in handy for tea and cigarettes.

'Sonofabitch!' You thought you heard someone comment from behind.

When Balan arrived in his Premier Padmini, a burning cigarette between his lips, you broke the news to him without any explanations.

'Good, it's a wise decision! But how're you going to live? You should have enough money for at least the basic necessities. Who'll give you that?' Balan was impeccably dressed as usual in a starched, spotless white shirt and mundu. Only his hair was dishevelled, having caught the wind.

'I'll do some odd jobs. Two rupees a day is more than sufficient for my needs.'

'Who'll give you that on a daily basis?'

'I'll take tuitions for children. If need be, even for grown-ups. Velukutty told me just the other day that he wants to learn English.'

'So, you've resigned your job as manager of his cinema theatre to teach him English?' Balan laughed, showing his even, white teeth, and you joined him. For the first time, you realised that you had a sense of humour and that your words could make others laugh.

Although the news of your quitting caused your father some anxiety, he made no comment, keeping his thoughts to himself.

One day, Balan arrived at your house. You sat together in your dark room and chatted for a long time. You had bought a bookshelf when you first started working. On the narrow bed placed against the wall was a new mattress and a set of pillows you had bought; the old, moth-eaten ones had been discarded. The table built by Kunjan carpenter was also ready and waiting for you.

'Bala, get your bag from the car.'

'Let's not . . .'

'I need to celebrate my freedom. I need a couple of drinks. What do you have in your bag today?'

'No, Unni'shna. Let's not drink in your house.'

'We must!'

You argued, but Balan did not succumb. He respected your father and mother too much to drink in their house.

Eventually, you went with him to his house, where a bar awaited. Bottles of Old Monk, Honey Bee Premium brandy, McDowell's No.1 and so many others. The library of liquor made you envious.

You drank more than your usual quota that night. At some point, you began to feel as though you were walking through a tunnel made of quartz. Crystal-clear water flowed from springs that lay over the quartz walls and turned into a stream as you walked onward. You dunked your head in it, laughing. Nude women were swimming around you. When you tried to grab them, they swam away, giggling, drifting away like water lilies separated from their stalks. Only one woman tarried, blocking your way.

'Why did you say you don't want me? Am I not a woman? What do I lack? Take a look!' She placed her hands beneath her breasts and thrust them towards your face. 'You bastard, do you need to see any more?' She started to spread her legs, the water climbing to her knees, but you pushed her down and fled towards the mouth of the cave, treading water all the way. But Velukutty was waiting at the exit with a net. He threw it at you, spreading it wide, and you went down. The quartz started to split and water cascaded down. Caught in the net, you started to sink to the bottom . . .

Did the dream mean anything at all? 'Life has meaning; therefore, dreams must also have meanings,' you told yourself.

Although time hung heavy on your hands, you were unable to produce anything worthwhile. So you decided to learn how other writers churned out books so easily. But you didn't know any writers. You hadn't even met any. Around that time, you heard about the writing routine of Ernest Hemingway. Every morning, before the sun rose, he sat at his writing table. First, he read through the previous day's work and only then did he start to write. No one came to disturb him on those cold, silent mornings, and he continued to write until noon. As soon as he stopped writing, he felt an emptiness inside him. He called it a pleasurable emptiness. You decided to try this out. You wanted to know what pleasurable emptiness felt like.

You tidied up your writing desk, filled ink in your fountain pen and placed it neatly next to your notebook. After a dinner of rice and mussels cooked with coconut and mustard that your mother served up, you paced the moonlit yard for a long time.

You had read somewhere that walking stimulates creativity. Tolstoy was said to have paced up and down his drawing room deep in thought until the carpet became threadbare along its centre. In your house, there was no drawing room and no carpet. You had never even seen a carpet.

You had heard that the best carpets were made in Persia. Why had that land not produced renowned writers like Tolstoy? You paced the yard past midnight, imagining that the moonlight falling on the ground smeared with cow dung was your carpet and planning what you would write the next morning.

'From tomorrow, I'll wake up early and start writing,' you vowed.

When your legs started to tire, you went in and lay down on your bed. That was all you remembered. You opened your eyes to your mother's voice.

'How can you sleep like this? Go, brush your teeth and come and have tea. I can't keep warming it up.'

As you sat up yawning, you imagined the sound of mocking laughter. It came from your writing table. The fountain pen you had filled the previous night seemed to join in the laughter.

You were agitated the whole day. Balan's bar kept popping up in your mind. If only you had such a bar at home. 'I'm not an alcoholic, but sometimes alcohol calms me down. That's why I drink,' you told yourself.

You had a bath, changed your clothes and walked to the ferry landing. Velukutty was in Ve . . . Ve . . . Velayudhan's teashop, having tea. He had pulled his mundu high above his knees, exposing his thighs. His wife must not be at home to make him tea. But he did have a slut at home, his daughter! Couldn't she have made him a cup of tea?

'Maa . . . maa . . . Manager, whe . . . whe . . . where are you headed in this bla . . . bla . . . blazing sunshine?' Ve . . . Ve . . . Velayudhan enquired. Velukutty looked at you and smiled a sour-as-kokum smile.

You pretended not to have heard and stood gazing at the approaching boat. You were in no mood for conversation. At that moment, even if Velukutty had questioned your parentage, you would not have reacted. You had to get to town as soon as possible.

You could hear Ve . . . Ve . . . Velayudhan asking if you wanted tea, but you turned away and fixed your eyes on the river. You could barely conceal the tide of self-loathing that rose within you.

Velukutty let down his mundu and approached you. He smelt of some cheap soap. Did he use washing soap to bathe?

'Edo, I have some news for you. My daughter is getting married.'

You kept staring at a crane that was swooping down over the water in search of food. He probably thought he could shock you with the news, but your face remained expressionless.

'Why are you silent?'

'What should I say?'

'You haven't asked who the boy is.'

'I don't want to know!'

'Phthoo . . .' Velukutty hawked and spat and walked away.

You had no interest whatsoever in knowing who Rohini was to wed. You jumped into the ferry, impressed at your own agility. The boat filled up quickly. The majority of the passengers were headed to the town.

The boat made slow progress, like a pregnant woman close to term. The tide was coming in, and punting against it was not easy. You cursed the sea impatiently, 'Thou shalt turn into a desert!'

When the boat made the landing on the opposite bank, you were the first to leap out. You folded up your mundu and walked quickly through the slush. You took out a cigarette from your pocket, lit it and started to smoke as you walked.

The town became visible as soon you reached the riverbank. This was where the villagers came when they had to buy an umbrella before the monsoon or allopathic medicines when sick.

Shops were visible in between the houses on either side of the tarred road. You lit another cigarette and cursed and abused everyone who came to mind. Your legs started to move faster. The boundary between walking and running blurred. Anyone watching would have found it difficult to decide whether you were walking or jogging.

A car came alongside, almost brushing against you, and stopped.

Lowering the glass, Balan asked, 'Unni'shna, where are you off to in this heat?' He could see that you were in distress, racing as though pursued by a swarm of hornets.

'To the liquor store, where else?'

'Why are you going there?'

'To buy milk,' you said, mocking your friend.

He opened the car door and stretched his head out. His unruly hair looked like a hornet's hive.

'Get in.'

'I'd rather walk. You do what you have to do.'

The store was not very far away. Maybe a ten-minute walk from here. You just had to turn left at the cashew-nut factory and it would be right there.

Balan stepped out of the car and blocked your path.

'You don't have to go to the liquor store. Come with me. I'll give you whatever you want.'

'I'm not coming anywhere.'

Balan frowned. 'Then don't come. Wait here.'

He turned and took out a half-empty bottle of Old Monk from his bag. Exactly what you had been thinking of. You grabbed the bottle from Balan's hands.

'Get in, I'll drop you home.'

'No!'

Crossing the bridge would mean driving about five miles. The ferry ride was shorter and quicker.

You walked back, cradling the bottle as you might a baby. You accosted all the acquaintances you ran into on the way and exchanged pleasantries with them. You laughed and even shook hands with some of them.

*

After many days had crawled by in this fashion, out of nowhere, inspiration struck. In spite of yourself, you picked up the pen and started to write:

Kunjachchu Master was born in Cheriyath village in the first year of the twentieth century. To be precise, in 1901. He was the eldest son of the farmer Poraprath Chathukutty and Kunjichirutha. Although Kunjichirutha had given birth to nine children, only four survived. One fell victim to smallpox. Another succumbed to cholera. The third was gored to death by a cow when he was eight years old. And two died of the plague.

Of the four children, only Kunjachchu Master studied, until the seventh class. The others did not attend school at all. Their village had only two or three people who could read and write, and they were all from the upper castes.

From a young age, Kunjachchu was a non-conformist who broke all the rules. He was able to join the school only because he was determined to. He was sent away thrice, having gone without a slate or pencil and clad only in a mundu held up by a string made of plantain fibre. He did not suffer the same fate a fourth time because Sree Narayana Guru had arrived by then, and schools started to sprout along the route he took. Many children like Kunjachchu were able to receive a rudimentary education at these schools.

Kunjachchu got high on breaking rules. He started his transgressions with Ambu the astrologer. This happened long before Mahatma Gandhi exhorted people to break the law by making salt.

Ambu the astrologer was walking along the ridge between the fields in his tyre-sandals, holding a palm-leaf parasol. They both stood on the ridge looking at each other. The astrologer tied up his tuft of hair, which had come loose, and ordered, 'Get out of my way.'

'There's enough and more space for you to pass by.'

Although Kunjachchu moved to the side and gave him more room, Ambu was furious. Poraprath Chathukutty's brood should be stepping down into the muddy field and giving him the whole breadth of the ridge. He could not stomach the impudence. But when he tried to kick Kunjachchu, the boy feinted like a kalari expert and evaded him. Ambu swore and cursed and threatened him, but nothing would make the boy budge. Finally, Ambu admitted defeat, brought down the raised hood of his vanity, and edged past Kunjachchu. As he left, he shot back a curse. 'Your end will be at the hands of moplahs.'

Hearing this, Kunjachchu could not help smiling.

But not many days were left to the Moplah Rebellion. Many were to die, stabbed, speared and hacked. Was that the astrologer's prediction then, that Kunjachchu would become a victim of the Malabar Rebellion?

You stopped writing and flexed your back, then lit a cigarette and read what you had written. 'Good.' You nodded your head, passing judgement on your own writing.

Kunjachchu became the adjunct of your first novel. You found the word 'protagonist' distasteful. There is no need for any story to have a protagonist, male or female, you thought. Every character is an adjunct. There can be no minor characters or a support cast. Everyone is an adjunct in a story.

You started to make steady, if slow, progress. Today, after filling the fountain pen nearly to bursting, this is what you wrote:

Kunjachchu Master was miserable as he watched the two communities start to regard each other with distrust, resorting to violence whenever the opportunity arose. Dark clouds descended, presaging a great tragedy, and from these dense clouds emanated a burning heat that spread far and wide. Watching hatred engulf his people, he could feel his body and his innards burn up. The scorching sensation was unbearable.

Kafka's Gregor Samsa had found himself turned into a monstrous insect as he sought to escape his miserable life. Kunjachchu Master, who had not even heard of Kafka, had no such powers. He divested himself of all his clothes and dived into the village pond as if fleeing from death. It was the easiest way to be rid of the blistering heat. On that blazing afternoon, the pond was deserted, most people having finished their bath and washed their clothes earlier in the day. The water was cool, and jackfruit leaves and algal bloom greened the surface. Kunjachchu Master swam beside tadpoles and striped murrels in the depths of the pond until, gradually, his body and mind started to cool down.

'What is this? Are you bathing in the nude?'

Ambu the astrologer, an umbrella tucked in his armpit and towel in hand, could not believe his eyes. The umbrella with the curved handle went with him everywhere. A relative from Colombo had gifted it to him, and he used it not only for protection from sun and rain, but also to hit the stray dogs that sniffed and tailed him.

The sight of Kunjachchu Master in the buff doing somersaults in the water enraged Ambu, who was old enough to be his father. His hands itched to thrash Kunjachchu black and blue with his umbrella, like he beat the dogs. He refrained only because Kunjachchu Master, though of a low caste, was a teacher who had studied till the seventh class. Ambu found himself troubled by the thought of the children taught by such a person.

'Eda, Kunjachchu, enough of your fun and games. Get out of the water.'

'Let me cool my burning insides in this water. What is it to you, astrologer?'

Kunjachchu Master dived and came up with water spouting from his mouth like a fountain, provoking Ambu even more.

'Eda, the whole village bathes in this pond. If you want to bathe naked, come in the middle of the night and bathe to your heart's content. No one will see you and no one will say anything. Now come out of the water and wrap a thorthu or something around your waist.'

This was the man who, with his cowrie-shell divination, had predicted that an unpropitious planet alignment and an inauspicious star would prevent Kunjirama Poduval's youngest daughter, Revati, from ever getting married. The girl had killed herself by jumping in front of a train.

As he swam around vigorously in the pond, Kunjachchu Master subjected Ambu to a gimlet stare that flashed over the water like a death ray and smashed into Ambu's chest.

'Don't meddle with me, Kunjachchu!'

Ambu shouted the warning while tying up his tuft of hair that had come undone, even as the frown on his sandalwood-paste-anointed forehead deepened and wriggled like an earthworm.

'Go and mind your own business. I'll come out of the water only after my mind and body have cooled down.'

At that moment, Ambu's eyes fell upon Sarojini, who was coming up the narrow lane to the pond. On her shoulder she carried a bundle of clothes for washing. The old man felt as if he had been kicked in the solar plexus.

Sarojini had dropped out of school while still in the first standard. She was Ambu's illegitimate daughter, born to Manikyam, the wife of master carpenter Gopalan. The twenty-five-year-old beauty was employed in the cashew-nut factory.

'Aiyyo, Sarojini, stop right there, don't go towards the pond.'

The astrologer ran towards her, dropping his umbrella and towel. Sarojini stopped, wondering how this man, who was old enough to be her father, was able to run so fast and why he was so panicked. She did not know, of course, that it was her own father who was blocking her way. Even the cuckolded Gopalan did not know this truth.

'Don't block my way, old man,' she said. Slapping away the hand raised to restrain her, she sashayed towards the pond, a bottle of coconut oil and a bar of perfumed soap in her hand. Ambu followed her, protesting. Sarojini wondered what had happened to the old man, who normally acted as if he did not see her whenever their paths crossed. As she walked ahead, slapping away his hand again, Kunjachchu Master breached the surface like a whale.

Sarojini pushed the old man aside and approached the steps of the pond.

You put down the pen, stretched, then fastened your lungi that had come loose. You lit a cigarette and started to pace the moonlit yard. You felt as though your brain was being bathed in moonlight and caressed by the cool breeze. Like a small child, your mind danced with happiness.

You realised that the tip of your pen's nib yielded not only ink but pleasure too. This was a revelation to you, that pen and paper could produce such happiness. After smoking two more cigarettes one after the other, you returned to your room, flicked the bed sheet clean and stretched out on the bed. The night breeze entered through the window and stroked your forehead like your own mother might. Somewhat reluctantly, the moonlight too entered the room and sat beside the bed to give you company. Recognising that all of this emanated from your writing, you paid homage to the god of writing and slowly slipped into sleep.

The next day, when you read your creation to Balan in his house, a smile bloomed on his rum-touched lips. You had made a new acquaintance tonight—Jamaican white rum. As you read, the dull red rays of the setting sun stole in through the curtain-less windows and lit up the bottle.

Your poison was Hercules XXX, standard army issue. Occasionally, Old Monk, which you considered a luxury. It was your friendship with Balan that made it possible for you to get to know exotic rums such as this one.

From Balan's expression you inferred that he liked what you had written. You were astonished, therefore, when he said, 'Dear Unni'shna, what rubbish have you made up? We live in Kerala, not in France, da. How do such ideas even get into your head?'

'What's wrong with what I've written?'

'There's nothing right about it.'

'Meaning . . .?'

'If teachers who teach small children start bathing naked in the village pond, the villagers are not going to let it happen.'

'Bala, you must believe it. He jumped into the pond to cool the heat within him. I want to do that too, often. I too burn up inside.'

'There are no flames inside you. It's just your imagination.'

'So, my writing is not believable?'

Your voice reflected your deep disappointment.

'Okay, I believe what you say. But why are you sitting around holding that glass and not drinking? Has rum become unpalatable just because you've written a few lines? At this rate, by the time you finish writing a novel, you'll stop having rice too? Unbelievable!'

'So, you don't approve of what I've written?' you asked again.

'Poda, who says I don't approve of it? But your readers must accept it too, right? I did tell you, we're not in France. Such writing won't work here. You'll be buried alive.'

You slammed your half-filled glass down on the table. Balan laughed; the rum had started to hit him. He had already refilled his glass four times.

'Don't get upset. Your writing is top class. Have a couple of double pegs and go home and write. What you said is true. We drink rum and bathe in the nude in the pond for our own sake. We can't spoil our lives for the sake of Ambu the astrologer, who knocked up master carpenter Gopalan's wife. Drink up, da.'

You sat there, drinking rum and chatting till the bronze red light turned into a grey darkness. Balan had a cook named Malini; she had left after preparing rice, prawn chutney and mackerel curry for your dinner. The two of you warmed up the food and ate, then you left for home.

You knew by now that Balan had started to accept the truth of your writing. You found the thought comforting. You went home, gliding over the plush carpet that the Jamaican rum had spread in front of you. You felt like you had grown wings where your legs had been. With a decent amount of rum inside you, you could walk on your wings and fly with your legs.

You hurried home, yearning to hold the pen again. When you reached, the house lay enveloped in darkness, except for a sliver of light that came through a gap in the door.

17

YOU AND KUNJACHCHU MASTER

One night, you were overwhelmed by the urge to write. You ate dinner, downed a glass of water, then washed your hands and headed for your room like a passenger aiming to board a train that he could hear thundering into the station. As the sound came closer, you picked up your pen, ready and filled with ink, and started to scribble in your slanted, only occasionally upright, handwriting.

You picked up the story from where Sarojini, the daughter of the master carpenter and his two-timing wife, was seen sashaying towards the pond. But first, you scanned through what was already written to fix the words in your memory. Should you flesh out the character of Sarojini a little more? She knew nothing of her own illicit birth or that Ambu the astrologer was her biological father. Should you give more space to this existential crisis? After some more reflection, you decided that such an elaboration was uncalled for.

You wrote:

Sarojini approached the steps leading down to the pond. Kunjachchu Master was doing somersaults in the middle, splashing water in all directions. He could feel the heat inside him dissipate through his nostrils and every other orifice as steam. The relief made him blind and deaf to his surroundings. For a moment, he forgot that he taught young, impressionable children.

Ambu the astrologer, who was right behind Sarojini, tripped on a stone and fell on his face, his nose smashing into the ground. When his efforts to rise failed, he raised his head and looked piteously at her. Anyone seeing him then would have mistaken him for a crocodile.

'Molae, Sarojini. Don't go into the pond . . .' he croaked, sounding like a frog had got caught in his throat. 'Don't go, molae . . .'

He could not imagine his daughter seeing Kunjachchu Master naked. His head seemed to be spinning faster than Lord Vishnu's Sudarshana chakra.

The way the old astrologer was behaving, Sarojini was convinced that something interesting was going on in the pond. Curious, she hastened towards its edge. But all she could see were two feet sticking out of the water. The next moment, there was a churn in the middle and ripples spread out across the surface as the feet disappeared and, in their place, Kunjachchu Master's head appeared. Water dripped from his hair as if wrung out of his head.

As he sucked in air and opened his eyes, Kunjachchu Master saw through the curtain of water the image of Sarojini hurrying towards him. He regained his senses immediately. She was an old student of the school where he taught. He put on his most solemn look.

'Sarojini, please hand me that thorthu,' he said.

'Are you done with your bath?'

'Umm . . . yes,' he said loudly so his voice would carry to her. How was she to know that he was not having a bath? He was just trying to cool the fiery heat inside him by thrashing about in the water. Only Kunjachchu Master knew how deeply he felt the impact of communal conflict in the town, the palpable build-up to violence.

'Did you stop because I've come?'

'I told you to hand me the towel, not ask questions!'

'I knew it. You don't like me, do you?'

'Stop playing the fool and toss that towel to me.'

'No way! Do you think this is your school where you can order me around? This is the village pond. If you want your thorthu, come and get it. I'm not giving it to you,' she said bluntly.

She wondered why he did not want to come out of the water and get the towel himself. And then it hit her. He was bathing in the nude! When he had done that somersault in the water, she had fancied she saw a glimpse of his muscled waist. Now she realised she wasn't wrong.

'I know.'

'Edi, what do you know?'

'Why you are not getting out of the water. Stay there. I'll scream and get the whole village down here. Let everyone see the spectacle.'

'I'll come out and take the thorthu.'

'I'd love to see that! Come, come out . . . who's stopping you?' she challenged.

Kunjachchu Master trod water, still submerged below his neck. Water dripped from his hair into his eyes like tears.

'Why aren't you coming out? I'll tell the whole village. Shameless fellow!'

'Get lost!' he bellowed. Losing patience, he began to swim towards the bank. Just in time, Ambu the astrologer scrambled up from the ground and limped forward to pick up the thorthu. He threw it towards Kunjachchu Master. Sarojini wanted to kick the old man in his belly, but her leg would not obey her. Perhaps somewhere in her body lurked the knowledge of who he was to her. She used her eyes instead to land a kick on him, and went down the steps to the pond. The moss-covered steps were slippery, as if covered with slimy snails.

Kunjachchu Master, who had only leapt into the water to be rid of the unbearable flames of hatred that had enveloped his town, paid a steep price for his impetuosity. Sarojini carried the tale of his experiment with bathing in the nude to everyone in the village. Although those who knew him well did not believe her, a few others did. They started to look at him as though he were a strange animal. Men advised their wives and sisters to give him a wide berth.

'He should have at least remembered that he is a teacher.'

'I won't send my child to a school where that shameless fellow teaches.'

'He should be thrown out of the school. Only then will I send my Lakshmanan and Ananthan there.'

The villagers said many such things and took many such vows. Someone eventually carried the news to Kunjachchu Master's father, Poraprath Chathukutty. He was milking his goat at the time, beside his hut. From its full udders, milk squirted into the pot with a hiss. Occasionally, the goat turned its head and looked at him. 'Leave some milk in there for my kids,' it appeared to be telling him.

'Why is it such a big deal? Are people supposed to bathe in their suit and hats?' the farmer demanded.

Not everyone was as ingenuous. The other three teachers in Kunjachchu Master's school were from the higher castes. They thought this was an ideal opportunity to get him out. They started to mount pressure on the caretaker of the school, Kandan Nair. Over the next few days, many parents withdrew their wards.

'Enough of your teaching, Kunjachchu. They are not going to change even if you want them to. Take a shovel and come with me. We'll till the land,' said Poraprath Chathukutty. He was short and stout, with limbs that resembled mahogany trunks. He wore only a loincloth inside the house. When he went out, he wrapped around his waist a discoloured towel that was frayed from repeated washing and had holes in it.

Eventually, it dawned on Kunjachchu Master that he had been foolish. Deep inside, though, he believed he had done the rational thing. When the lava welled up and scalded him, what else could he do? After much thought, he decided to approach Kandan Nair and plead his case. He had no desire whatsoever to lose his job. He believed it was one that bestowed the highest dignity on a person.

'Ah-ha, come, come. I knew you would turn up eventually.'

'I have to seek your pardon. I've done something I never should have.'

'It's too late for you to realise your folly. Even the school superintendent can't save you now.'

The school superintendent was an Englishman named Gunther. All the schools in the area reported to him. He had paid a visit to Kunjachchu Master's school once, riding his *bicycle, dressed in a shirt and trousers and wearing a hat, all the way from Kozhikode.*

'In the name of Kunkichchi Bhadrakali, please don't dismiss me.'

'It's too late, my man. A signed complaint from the villagers is already with Gunther sayyiv.'

'Aiyyo! Who has signed it?'

'All the parents and guardians. And Ambu the astrologer. If you are not chucked out, they say no one will send their children to school. You might as well leave now. Don't waste your time trying to press your case.'

'Please listen to what I have to say.'

'I don't want to.'

'I jumped into that water because there was no other way. My insides were on fire. I jumped in to douse the fire.'

Kandan Nair, clad as usual in knee-length pants, stared at Kunjachchu Master uncomprehendingly.

'I am tense. I can't sleep at night. My heart tells me that we are heading towards a terrible tragedy. The two communities are sharpening their daggers and swords under the cover of darkness . . .'

'Why do you need to lose sleep over that?'

'How can someone with a conscience find sleep at such a time?'

'Get out of here. You and your conscience! As if no one else has one.'

Kunjachchu Master was despondent. No one seemed to understand him.

The elementary school with four standards had thirty-one students. They had to pay a fee of two annas in the first standard, three annas in the second, five annas in the third and half a rupee or eight annas in the fourth. Most of the low-caste children who attended the school could not afford to pay any fees. Kunjachchu Master was paying for four such children—Nanikutty, who was in the first standard, Chirutha and Kelappan in the third standard and Mathu in the fourth standard. Every month, Kandan Nair would deduct one-and-a-quarter rupees from Kunjachchu Master's salary of seven-and-a-quarter rupees.

When it became clear that he would lose his job, Kunjachchu Master began to fret about the future of these children. Who would pay their fees now? Kandan Nair would probably expel them. He was always trying to find ways of cleansing the school by expelling low-caste students. Kunjachchu Master had just presented him with the perfect opportunity.

'I have a request. I'll find the money somehow to pay the children's fees. Don't send them away; they're intelligent children. Let them study and make a good life for themselves.'

'First take care of yourself, then worry about those children. What's the use of studying anyway? They're not going to end up as magistrates. Get out of here. I don't have the time to listen to your grovelling.'

After two weeks, a peon from Gunther's office handed over the dismissal order signed by the sayyiv himself. The peon drank tender coconut water, popped an elaborately made paan containing cured catechu and tobacco into his mouth, then climbed back into the bullock cart and left for Kozhikode.

After his dismissal, Kunjachchu Master seemed to be in a constant state of rage. Although he was a young man, permanent frown lines appeared on his forehead. Those lines of worry soon started to pulsate and convulse, as though taking on a life of their own.

Once, an acquaintance who was walking by with a hoe on his shoulder ran into Kunjachchu and asked politely, 'Where's Master headed to?'

'Go and call your bloody father a master. Not me!' Kunjachchu exploded.

With nothing to do, Kunjachchu walked around, stoning any crows or dogs he came across. His rage unquenched, he started to stone bullock carts that passed by the huts. He stoned an elephant that was walking by with palmyra fronds in its trunk, on its way to the temple festival of Konkachi Bhadrakali.

When his rage finally subsided, he slept the whole day, curled up on the mat in his hut.

He tried to get work in a tile factory, then a plywood factory. No one was ready to employ him. News of his digambara-style bath in the pond had reached everyone's ears. Who would want to employ such a wanton man?

Kunjachchu realised that he couldn't stay on in the village. He would have to cross over to Colombo in a sailing ship. A journey without the possibility of return...

*

The news that Kunjachchu Master was joining a school in Tirurangadi sent shockwaves among his detractors, including Ambu the astrologer and Sarojini, who had been going about slandering him. The Malabar Rebellion was drawing closer; the sound of its footsteps could be heard from a distance. Sporadic attacks had taken place here and there.

'He's going to the place of the rebels.'

'It's the money. They say he has been offered a big monthly salary. Bhadrakali! I never knew he was so greedy for money.'

'Is money more important than one's life?'

Some of the villagers came to him and demanded that he stay back and not move to the land of the moplahs. Some pleaded with him, others threatened him. But Kunjachchu Master stood firm: despite all their protests and pleas, he would move to Tirurangadi.

'We can only counsel him, the rest is up to him. He's educated and is supposed to know what is good and what is not.'

'What do you mean "educated"? He's going to the land of the moplahs!'

One day, Ambu the astrologer appeared in front of Poraprath Chathukutty's hut, leaning on his umbrella from Colombo, his tuft of hair untied and a folded thorthu on his shoulder. He had never visited a low-caste's house before. He believed that the rules of caste and pollution were God-given and he should not be the one breaking them.

'Where's your boy?'

When he saw Ambu the astrologer in his yard, Poraprath Chathukutty stood rooted to the spot.

'What do you want?' Kunjachchu Master came out of the house, fastening the mundu around his waist and coughing. The astrologer countered the cough with a fart.

'Dear Kunjachchu, don't go to the land of the moplahs.'

'What if I go?'

'I'm ready to fall at your feet. Just don't go!' Ambu the astrologer pleaded with folded hands.

'Who are you to tell me not to go? Weren't you the one who got me thrown out of the school? And yet you are not satisfied! What more do you want? You want me to starve to death too?'

The astrologer stood there lost for words.

'I don't want to see your face. Please leave.'

'Kunjachchu, your egotism will make you breach all limits.'

The astrologer tarried for a little while and then left.

Kunjachchu was paid a salary of seven-and-a-quarter rupees at his village school. In Tirurangadi he would only make six-and-a-half rupees. Here, he had his own hut and his mother cooked for him. In Tirurangadi he would have to pay rent. If he were to cook for himself, he would have to buy rice and groceries. But money could not be the main consideration. He hated his people for branding him as a dissolute man just because he had jumped into the pond with no clothes on. And he needed a job to survive. He did not want to depend on his father, whose life was already a daily struggle with the land.

The villagers were still gossiping about him when Kunjachchu Master set out with a small metal trunk in his hand. Before leaving, he took off the gold ear studs set with red stones that he had worn since childhood and handed them to his mother.

'Why are you doing this?'

'I may not return.'

You'll die at the hands of moplahs. Ambu the astrologer had made the prediction, and now Kunjachchu Master was headed to a place where moplahs were the majority. He was not superstitious, but he knew he was going to a troubled place.

18

YOU AND YOUR SECULARISM

You wrote only one novel. But the memory of those days, when you wrote all day, remained in your mind like the clear waters of a lake. You travelled back often to relive that time.

Writing a novel was like catching a tiger by its tail. You held on to the tail and got dragged to wherever it went. If you let go, the tiger would turn on you and tear you to pieces. So, tail in hand, you stumbled behind as it prowled and dashed around. When it got into the water to drink, you followed. When it clambered up a tree, you were right behind, clutching its tail. When it leaped on its prey, you tumbled after it. When it mated, you did too. When it slept, so did you.

You started the day with these lines, the tail still in your hand:

Tirurangadi, Malappuram, Kondotty, these were all hotspots of strife and violence. Even at midnight, the police could be seen patrolling the fields and lanes and alleys. Fear and hatred smouldered in people's eyes. This was the Tirurangadi that Kunjachchu Master arrived in, clad in a coarse mundu and shirt, and carrying his metal trunk.

The road was deserted. A herd of goats passed him by and crossed the dirt road. There was no shepherd in sight.

'Who are you? Where are you going?'

Two young men seated on the retaining wall of a culvert stood up and approached Kunjachchu Master, eyeing him with suspicion. They were members of the Khilafat movement. Since his mundu was fastened on the right side of the waist, they knew he was not a Muslim. That only made them more suspicious. Any non-Muslim outsider would have to be questioned. Sometimes, even Muslims were interrogated.

'Where are you coming from?'

'From the north. Cheriyath.'

'Why have you come?'

'I'm the new teacher at the school here. Kunjachchu Master.'

'Oh, you're the new master? Alright, you may go.'

When he started to walk past them, one of the men called out, 'Teach the children and behave yourself. Don't poke your head into things that don't concern you. Or your head could go missing. Don't say we didn't warn you.'

He found a thatched hut to rent, east of the civil court, beside a stream where cattle were bathed. It had two rooms, a low ceiling and tiny windows, and was dark inside. It belonged to the butcher Sulayman, who had a shop in the market. With his bulky arms and legs, broad chest and slightly bloodshot eyes, he looked exactly as Kunjachchu Master would have expected a butcher to look.

'What will you take as rent?'

'I don't need rent, Master. Why should I charge you rent when you are teaching our kids to read and write? You can move in whenever you want.'

'No, let's not do that, Sulayman. I get a salary from the school.'

He moved in only after he received an assurance from Sulayman that he would accept a small sum as rent.

He set aside one room for reading and sleeping, the second for cooking and eating. A stove was already in place. He bought some pots and pans and a coconut grater from the market. He had not cooked even a bowl of kanji for himself all these years. But he started enthusiastically and found happiness in it.

'Why are you cooking for yourself? My Aishu will cook for you. Her mutton biryani will transport you to heaven. She's a magician in the kitchen.'

Kunjachchu Master declined the offer with graceful formality. Aishu arrived with firewood for the stove and a coconut to grind for the curry.

Bird's eye chillies and curry leaves grew on his plot of land. The branches of the moringa and mango trees were bowed down with drumsticks and ripe mangoes. Nothing was lacking in this place.

Kunjachchu Master's life in Tirurangadi fell into a routine: teaching at the school, cooking, eating, reading and sleeping. In the evenings, he went for long walks. He was particularly fond of strolling in the area around the Tirurangadi mosque.

One day, the mufti of the mosque, in his turban and long white garment that came to his knees, called out to him.

'Ah, there you are, Master. Come, let's have a cup of tea together.'

Even though he wasn't in the mood for tea, Kunjachchu Master accepted the invitation and went with the mufti into a tiny teashop. It was the only shop on that stretch of the road. They had a cup of strong tea each while the mufti narrated the history of his predecessors at the Tirurangadi mosque. The first mufti was Habib-ibn-Malik, the son of the mufti of Chaliyam. The qabar in front of the mosque was that of Odakkal Ali Hassan Musaliyar, who was originally from Ponnani. It had become a hallowed spot.

On some days, Kunjachchu Master woke up at 4 a.m., had a bath and went to the temple to pray. He never missed going on the solstice. The temple was an hour's walk from his hut. He enjoyed the walk, going through the darkness to reach a place of light.

One day, as he was walking to the temple, Kunjachchu heard the jingling of cowbells behind him. A bullock cart came and stopped beside him—or was it the shadow of a cart?

He could see only a part of the driver's face in the light from the lantern in the cart. The driver was as black as a buffalo. Beyond the shapes faintly painted by the light around the bullock cart, waves of darkness lapped as far as the eye could see. As though the darkness itself was transforming into wind.

'Where are you going in the dark?'

Only then did Kunjachchu Master realise that there was a second person in the cart. It was Mammadkunju, a wealthy man who was known to be the owner of half a dozen bullock carts.

'I'm going to the temple.'

'I'll take you there. I'm going that way anyway.'

Kunjachchu Master hesitated, then climbed into the cart and sat facing Mammadkunju. In the dim light, they could barely make out each other's faces. There was a lush beard on Mammadkunju's broad face, but no moustache. A bluish-green hue lingered above his upper lip.

'One of my sons is studying in your school.'

'How many children do you have, Mammadkunjikka?'

'Ayy, not so many! Only eleven. Or maybe twelve.'

They continued to chat as the cart made steady progress along the path. When the light from the lantern dimmed, Mammadkunju raised the wick. A rooster crowed from somewhere close by; towards the east, the sky turned pale. Kunjachchu Master could feel the chill on the sides of his ears.

He got down at the turn-off for the temple. The lane was too narrow for the bullock cart; he would have to walk the rest of the way. The sun was yet to rise, but people were coming and going, some with torches in their hands. The faint light of dawn was drowned by the orange light from these torches that were made from dried coconut fronds.

Mammadkunju took out a British rupee from his capacious pocket.

'This is for your god. Please drop it in the box for offerings.'

Holding the silver coin in the palm of his hand, Kunjachchu Master stood watching as the cart disappeared towards the east. The temple bells could be heard in the distance.

It was a short walk to the temple. Kunjachchu Master stood in front of the sanctum sanctorum and prayed with folded hands. He dropped the silver coin that Mammadkunju had given him into the hundi and added an anna. When he returned after his prayers, with sandal paste on his forehead, he felt peaceful and calm.

The violence that had been smouldering till then broke out in full force and became a conflagration. Daggers, choppers, *swords and axes emerged in the night, in search of human bodies. Kunjachchu Master watched the water in the stream turn red and thick with blood. When cows and buffaloes bent to drink the water, their mouths turned red. His mind in turmoil, he stayed inside, looking out through the window, his hands clasped around its sooty bars.*

With the pen in your hand, you sprawled across the table like an old man, your writing at an end. The hand holding the pen started to tremble slightly. You could see the Malabar Rebellion that took place half a century ago playing out again in front of you; you could smell the blood. You felt one with Kunjachchu Master as he sat helplessly in the dark hut that belonged to Sulayman.

You took out the bottle of Hercules XXX rum that was hidden behind a stack of books in your almirah and poured the quarter that was left in it directly into your mouth. It shot down your gullet like fire water, burning all the way. Your vision dimmed; with both hands you groped for a cigarette on the table. Even in the light of the 40W bulb, you couldn't see the packet that lay in front of you. The military issue rum had intoxicated your eyes too.

*

'Aiyyo, Unni'shna, why did you drink the rum neat? It will corrode your intestines!'

You drank that rum many years ago. But Paru makes it sound as though it had happened just this instant. She is seated on the floor near you. She holds on to your legs and raises her head to look up at you. Your hair has turned completely white in the past few days. Your throat works as you swallow your own saliva constantly, painfully. Your days are numbered; you can count them on your fingers. But you continue to read out pages from the book of your life.

'Paru, bring me some water.'

She hurries to the kitchen and fetches a glass of cool water from the clay pot kept there.

'Open your mouth.'

She pours the water into your open mouth. You drink it greedily. You can feel the burning sensation in your belly calm a little.

'And then . . .?'

'And then what . . .?'

'You didn't write anything more that day?'

'No, I didn't. I needed more rum. I poured water into the empty bottle, sloshed it around and drank that.'

'Aiyyo! You're the limit! I feel sad, Unni'shna.'

'Paru, don't get all sentimental. I don't like it.'

'I am not the one who is sentimental. You are looking back and getting all worked up about things that happened long ago. Isn't that right?'

'But I'm not sad about anything.'

'You mean you're happy?'

You resent the constant barrage of questions she throws at you.

'You stopped at the point when the Malabar Rebellion started in Tirurangadi. How did you write the rest? When did you write it?'

'That's not for you to know. You already know a lot about me. Enough, no more.'

'Aiyyo, why shouldn't I know more?'

'Too much information is not good.'

'Who else will you tell, if not me?'

You remain silent. On her nose glints a gold stud that looks like a firefly. There are times when you are overcome with desire for her, though she is young enough to be your granddaughter. The nose stud is what ignites the lust. You avoid looking at her then; you look elsewhere and hunch over, reminding yourself that you are an old man.

Even in your youth, you never had an active sex life. You had installed your writing in the place of sexuality. Your intellect, energy and imagination were devoted entirely to your writing.

'Please go and sit somewhere else for a while instead of pestering me.'

'All right, I'll leave. But first tell me how you did it. Did you write the next part of the novel after pouring water into the rum bottle and drinking it down?'

Although it is not easy to bring back those memories, they do eventually come back to you. That sultry night when you put down on paper Kunjachchu Master's life in Tirurangadi. A night so hot and humid that even the trees sweated.

You wrote:

Kunjachchu Master had been smoked out of his native place by Ambu the astrologer and Kandan Nair. Later, they regretted what they had done. When the Rebellion broke out, Kunjachchu Master was not even twenty years old. The astrologer's conscience told him that if Kunjachchu Master were to die at such a young age, God would never forgive him.

The old man felt a fondness and sympathy for Kunjachchu Master that he had never experienced before.

One night, with a thorthu thrown over his head for cover, he went up to the grove where the family deity presided. As he approached the grove at midnight, the fragrance of champaka flowers wafted towards him. At that hour, no one who valued his life would go anywhere near the place. Only the gods and dead souls were out and about.

Ambu the astrologer stood in front of his family deity, Konkachi Bhadrakali, with folded hands.

'Devi, I have a request. Nothing should happen to Kunjachchu. I cursed him unintentionally. He's a fine young man. He's educated and sensible. When he fooled around in the village pond, I couldn't control myself. I'm an old fogey, Konkachi . . . When March comes around, I'll make a vellattam offering. I'll also perform annadaanam. Please keep Kunjachchu safe. Have mercy upon me.'

Where was Kunjachchu when the Malabar Rebellion broke out? What was he doing?

Tirurangadi was in flames. Countless people from both communities lost their lives. Many British police officers also died. The British hanged Ali Musaliyar—with whom Kunjachchu Master had tea when he first arrived—in the Coimbatore Jail. When Variyankunnath Kunjahammad Haji was placed in front of a firing squad, he asked not to be blindfolded. In his Ayurveda hospital, P.S. Warrier provided shelter to Muslim families when their men were taken away by the police. So many incidents, so many such tales . . .

The people around Poraprath Chathukutty, meanwhile, remained blissfully ignorant of all that was happening. Not even a scrap of a newspaper reached them, and they had not heard from Kunjachchu Master either.

'Looks like he's lost,' said Kandan Nair.

'Kunjachchu? Where will he go? He'll come back here,' said Poraprath Chathukutty.

A rumour spread among the villagers. The rebels suspected Kunjachchu Master of being Colonel Humphrey's spy, so they had killed him and impaled his head on an upright spear, then paraded it around. When he heard this, Poraprath Chathukutty laughed. 'They can't even touch a hair on my son's body. And you are talking about cutting off his head! What rubbish!'

At long last, while being carried in a palanquin to the neighbouring village, Ambu the astrologer saw a sight that pleased him even more than his first glimpse of Sarojini's mother, Manikyam. Kunjachchu Master was striding along with his left hand holding up the hem of his mundu. In his right hand was a steel trunk. As the palanquin passed him, although unaware of who was inside, he moved to the side, bowed and offered a greeting with folded hands.

Poraprath Chathukutty was right. Neither the British nor the rebels were able to touch Kunjachchu Master. Because he was never alone. Truth and integrity were always by his side.

19

YOU AND YOUR NOVEL

The first edition of *Digambaran* sold out in two months and became the subject of conversation whenever and wherever people met. Critics held forth on the book enthusiastically. They emphasised that, with his maiden novel, Unnikrishnan, a previously unknown writer, was making history; citing multiple sources, they established that this was a secular novel that spoke to the times they lived in. Since all you wanted to do was to write, such appreciation thrilled and inspired you. How could you not feel chuffed when you thought of how far you had come from those days when you scribbled on pieces of paper at Velukutty's theatre? How could you not feel elated and enthused?

One day, your photo appeared in the newspaper. Until then, you had seen your face only in a mirror. You had never been to a studio to have a photograph taken. Kausalya had been very keen to take a photo with you by her side. 'Edi, when you get married, you can have your pictures taken at the studio. I'm not going anywhere,' you would say.

This was around the time of the fourth assembly elections. A coalition government headed by C. Achutha Menon had been sworn in. The newspapers were full of it. Your photo appeared across two columns, in between the political news and alongside a photo of Pookoya Thangal, the Muslim League candidate who had won from the Kunnamangalam constituency.

When she saw the photo, Kausalya detached her baby daughter from her breast, dressed her in a frock, quickly changed into a saree and took a bus to the junction near your house. She was in a hurry to show your photo to your parents.

'Ammae . . . ammae . . . look at this!' Kausalya tripped on her saree and nearly fell as she rushed into the house. When Vendor Goyindan and Lakshmikuttyamma came out onto the veranda, she held up the sheet with your photo as if she were showing them a winning lottery ticket. Her daughter sniffled and pawed Kausalya's chest with her tiny hands, her lips seeking the source of milk. She bit Kausalya's breasts with her toothless gums, but Kausalya was too excited to register the pain.

'Where's Jayasheelan?'

'He's not back yet. I came as soon as I saw Unni'shnettan's photo. Here, look.'

'Unni'shnan's photo? When did he become so famous?'

Vendor Goyindan could not believe that his son was an equal of Pookoya Thangal. He looked at the photo again and again to make sure it was his son. Yes, there you were, your shiny black hair oiled and neatly combed back except for a few stray curls; a finely shaped nose; a thick black moustache that filled the space between the tip of your nose and your upper lip; and a short neck. Your photo was on one of the inside right pages, opposite the obituaries. If it had slipped a little bit to the left, it might have ended up amongst them. You couldn't remember who had taken the photo, where or when. Journalists were like phantoms. No one knew when they would appear or where they would disappear to.

'Ettan has become a big man,' Kausalya said, her face shining with pride.

'Oh, it's not such a big thing, is it? When Uncle Choyan died, his photo also appeared in the newspaper. And he was only a coconut-tree climber.' Your mother's words rang true. Uncle Choyan had died at a ripe old age, and his photo had appeared in the obituary column. Your mother seemed to think that for someone's photo to appear in the newspaper, all they had to do was stretch out and die.

Vendor Goyindan remained silent. He did not betray the happiness that was bubbling up inside him like toddy fermenting in a pot.

The next day, when you fastened your mundu around your waist, lit the first cigarette of the day and opened the door to step out, your eyes fell upon a floral wreath kept on the veranda. Stuck into the wreath of cheap marigold flowers and leaves was a piece of white paper on which was stencilled in large letters: RIP. The blood drained from your face. All the happiness inside you flew out and away like dry leaves in a high wind.

'Eda, what's written on that paper?' your father asked, coming up behind you and looking anxiously from your face to the wreath on the floor.

'Oh, nothing, Achcha. It's wishing my soul eternal peace.'

'What?' Your father looked at the wreath with distaste. He was aware that such things were placed on dead bodies. As if to expel the wrath inside him, he hawked and spat into the yard.

'Who put it here?'

'Who knows?' You spread your hands in a gesture of ignorance.

How had his son earned such enemies when he was incapable of hurting even a fly? With his reading confined to title deeds and testimonials, Velukutty had not read his son's novel. He had picked it up once, flipped through it and dropped it back on the table. Could the book be the reason for this wreath being placed here anonymously? Vendor Goyindan was annoyed.

As your father stood watching, you picked up the wreath and threw it towards the billy goat tethered in the yard. The goat turned its head away, although it was usually ready to nibble at anything it came across. You picked it up again and threw it into the swamp some distance away, at the bottom of a hillock. It floated on the muddied water, refusing to sink. You were enraged. Instead of throwing it into the swamp, you should have poured kerosene on it and set it alight. But that splendid idea had not occurred to you.

You went to the well and drew water. It was only after pouring twenty buckets of cold water over your head that your fury abated to some extent.

'Don't try to scare me with a snake made of a palm leaf,' you muttered.

'Achcha, they are cowards. If they had something to say, they could have come and said it to me. They don't have the balls to do that.' Vendor Goyindan nodded in agreement, but his anxiety did not lessen.

'Unni'shna, what have you written in the book?'

'It's a novel, Achcha.'

'What's a novel?'

'A novel is a story of people who are in pain,' you said, punning on the word 'novvu', meaning pain.

'So why are these people angry with you?'

'They don't like people who speak the truth.'

'Who are they?'

They are not Muslims. Of that, you are sure.

Although Vendor Goyindan did not understand everything you said, he firmly believed that you had done no wrong. 'Unni'shnan is *my* son,' he said to himself in order to reinforce this belief.

The next day, you received an anonymous postcard written in an untidy hand.

> *You sonofabitch, what wicked things have you written in your book? By teaching children to read and write, teachers mould the next generation. You have insulted the entire community of teachers by writing about someone who swims naked in the village pond in broad daylight. If you dare to write anything of this kind again, we will break your spine. Fucking whoreson.*

The letter did not name the 'we'. It could not be a teacher, or teachers, you knew.

'The teachers of this land are sensible, they stand for truth and justice,' you told yourself. 'They would never write an anonymous letter like this.'

A few days later, another postcard arrived. It contained only a few words.

Even if you are a Thiyya, you are a Hindu. Do not forget that.

During these critical days of your life, Balan was not around. He had gone to Delhi to attend a medical conference, following which he went to Aligarh to visit Kamalakshi. He had mutton biryani and rasmalai with her, slept with her, then returned to Delhi and spent four or five days there. He was trying to drum up support from like-minded people in his fraternity for euthanasia.

'Eda, why are you so despondent about this? The wreath is a sign that your novel has found its mark. But if you feel so strongly about it, we can lodge a police complaint,' he said.

'No. Let them come and place more wreaths, I don't care.'

It seemed you had regained your self-confidence.

Balan told you about his efforts towards legalising euthanasia. He had tried to discuss the matter with doctors in Delhi, with legal luminaries, volunteer organisations and palliative care–centre managers. But he just couldn't take the discussions to the next level, where they could become a springboard for meaningful action. A few of the people he spoke to looked at him as if he had blown in from another planet. Some were shocked. Some remained unmoved and noncommittal. Some railed at him and insulted him. 'You sound like a vampire,' one man shouted.

'Unni'shna, I won't step back. One day, everyone will know that I was right all along. Mercy killing will become legal in this country. It may take a decade, maybe two or three. But it will happen, you watch!'

'Bala, I am with you all the way. I think death would be a deliverance for terminally ill patients who have no way back. Everyone will realise this, if not today, then very soon.'

Balan continued to talk about euthanasia, and you about your novel. You offered each other a little shade where you could seek a modicum of inner peace. Balan was ready to wait as many years as it would take to realise his goal, but you did not have the luxury of time. Writing was your lifeblood. If it was blocked, your veins would bulge and burst, and you would fall dead, vomiting blood. For you, every second counted.

Unknown to you, your second novel was taking shape in your womb. From the time you became pregnant with it, like Lakshmikuttyamma during her pregnancies, you started to retch and vomit. Morning sickness had you in its iron grip. It was then that Pilakkunnan, the publisher of *Digambaran*, arrived with his oversized shirt-pocket stuffed with papers and currency notes. He used his umbrella as a walking stick and, as he mounted the steps, placed his index and middle fingers on his lips and spat out a stream of red precisely, like a jet.

'Edo, Unni'shna, your novel is charging forward like a wounded wild boar. I'm bringing out the third edition. Here, take the spoils.'

Pilakkunnan handed over a pile of currency notes. The note on top had a fresh dash of paan-stained spittle. You placed the money between the window bars without counting them.

'Count it! I've never paid a writer so much money, ever!'
You had no interest in counting the money.
'Now do it without losing any more time.'
'Do what?'
'Write your next novel, what else?'
'Aiyyo!'
'There's no aiyyo! Start to write! How many bottles of rum do you need? How many packets of cigarettes? Don't hesitate, just tell me. I'll have them sent over immediately.'

Pilakkunnan stood like a tiger in front of you, exhorting you to catch his tail. You would not fall for it. If you took the tail in your hands, you would find yourself endlessly running behind it. You would have to climb trees, pounce on prey. You had barely managed to get rid of one tiger. And here stood another, right in front of you. When the tiger yawned, its foetid breath filled the space between you.

The novel was inside your head, but nascent still. It lay as an embryo in your womb.

'Edo, why are you silent?'

'I need more time. I have a story in mind. But it needs to be developed, fleshed out. I can start writing only after that happens.'

'I am sure it's grown enough. Yank it out of you. If required, do a Caesarian and pull it out.'

You remained silent, unable to respond.

'How many days do you need to write it?'

'It's a sensitive subject. The Thalassery communal riots. I have to make sure I don't rub anyone the wrong way.'

'Nonsense! Then don't write at all. You're fit to be Velukutty's manager, nothing more! Don't rub anyone the wrong way, I believe!'

You were prevaricating. You had the entire novel ready in your head. It would be set during the Thalassery riots and its adjunct would be Kunjachchu Master. When the Malabar Rebellion happened, he was about twenty years old. By the time the Thalassery riots took place, he would have touched seventy. You had decided that Kunjachchu Master, whose life spanned two eras and two riots, would be the primary adjunct of your new novel too.

'What will the title be?'

'I haven't thought about it.'

'Well, don't stress about it. I'll give you the name. *Digambaran Two*.'

'No. I'll think of a better name.'

'All right, if that's how you want it. I'm leaving now. I'll come again after a week. By that time, you should have started writing the novel. Eda, writers should not be good only at writing. They should have some business sense too. You know that proverb about fishing in muddy waters? Your novel has already muddied the waters. Get in there now and gather up the fish!'

*

On a hot April night, when even the stars were sweating in the sky, when Shivaraman's and Ramakrishnan's bedroom doors were closed and your father and mother were fast asleep, you sat down at your writing table. Your upper body was bare, like Victor Hugo's. There was a bottle of rum and a glass in the wall cabinet, but you did not touch them. You were going to write with all your senses about you. The new novel had started growing within you as rough scraps and little shards and strands. It spun around in circles, squares and oblongs, gradually starting to take shape. Everyone in your family was asleep. You were waiting now for the gods to go into repose.

In the new novel, Kunjachchu Master was seventy and still a bachelor. He had decided to live in the midst of history rather than in the confines of a household. Ambu the astrologer and Kandan Nair the school caretaker had no place in this new novel, which was set in 1971, during the Thalassery riots. His parents, Poraprath Chathukutty and Kunjichirutha, had also ceded space, as had Mammadkunju. They were not even in your thoughts. This new work would be all about Kunjachchu Master and a few other adjuncts around him, some of them spitting venom and some, like deities, on the side of righteousness and truth.

When danger approaches, an alarm goes off somewhere, even if nobody notices it. You planned to begin the novel with this sense of danger. Pulling up your mundu above your knees and scratching the tip of your left ear, then your right ear, then the tips of both simultaneously, you started to write.

The large bronze bell in the bell tower of Arakkal palace had been installed by the Arakkal family four hundred years ago. Every day, the bell would be rung five times, signalling the time of prayer, from Salat al-fajr or Subahi till Salat al-'isha. The tolling of the bell would carry even to those who could not hear the muezzin's call to prayer.

One day, the bell rang at an odd time, its sound travelling many miles beyond the palace. It is said that sometimes, when a great tragedy is about to take place, the sound of bells from places of worship can be heard hundreds and thousands of miles away.

Old Kunjachchu Master closed the ledger he had been writing in and stepped out of the rice wholesaler's shop near the Mattambram mosque where he was employed as a bookkeeper. He could see people running down the road. In their hands were truncheons, meat cleavers and choppers.

'Old man, go and hide inside. Those are our men.'

The rice merchant, Kalanthan Haji, a fez covering his head, pulled Kunjachchu Master into the store and pushed him into the dark godown in the rear where bags of rice were stored. Bandicoots scampered among the bulging rice sacks. When one bared its fangs and leapt up towards his chest, he slapped it away.

In the semi-darkness, Kunjachchu Master strained to hear the sounds coming from outside. Cautiously, he opened the rear door of the godown and peered out. Kunjachchu Master was not a coward who would hide in a godown in the company of bandicoots while history was writing itself. Folding up his mundu, and with his arms swinging, Kunjachchu Master strode out, and into history.

20

YOUR VACATION

You had the feeling that a sailing ship laden with sorrows had reached the shore of your life.

Unaware of your feelings, Pilakkunnan would turn up regularly to check on the progress. He was in a hurry. He did not believe in procrastination; what had to be done must be done forthwith. When he saw that you had not got very far with the novel, he went into a tizzy. 'Useless fellow! Lazy, that's what you are.'

You did not speak about the sorrows and disappointments that agitated you. You did not tell Pilakkunnan the reason you could not write. He would never understand, however many times you told him. You remained silent, as if you had swallowed your tongue. You had nothing to say to him.

Whenever he visited you, you would be rendered incapable of writing a word. He left you with a feeling of disquiet even if you had started the day calmly. Yet, he kept up his visits. Once, he arrived carrying buffalo meat.

'Boil it with salt and turmeric and preserve it. Whenever you feel like eating it, take a portion, add ground chillies and make a curry with it. Or else, add spices and roast it. It will go well with the rum you drink. Once they are both inside you, you'll be able to write without any further goading.'

For some reason, you were afraid to write. When you picked up the pen, your hand would start to tremble. You had visions of your corpse lying with floral wreaths stacked on it.

One night, you prepared yourself and picked up the pen, ready to write about Kunjachchu Master, who had just emerged from the rice godown of Kalanthan Haji behind Mattambram mosque. That was when you heard the barking. It came from the darkness beyond your window. It sounded like a creature that could tear a person to pieces. No one kept a dog in your neighbourhood, so it must be a stray. You wondered what could have triggered the barking. A dog is a loyal and affectionate animal. You knew that it could not have a grudge against you. It must have barked as a friendly warning, maybe to remind you that some great danger lay in wait for you.

Ignoring the warning, you tried to climb back into your writing and set sail on a new journey. You heard the barking again, louder this time. The boat was marooned. You put the pen down and bent over the desk like your back hurt. Your forehead touched the table on which the paper and pen lay as you prostrated yourself before your writing.

You invoked Karikkat Bhagawathy and went to the window. When you looked out, you saw nothing but darkness. You shone a torch and strained to see as far as you could, but there was nothing. 'It must be my imagination,' you told yourself.

You took off your shirt, switched off the light and lay prone on the bed, trying to sleep. But sleep stayed away as if it had a quarrel with you. You tried lying on your side, then on your back, but there was no trace of sleep to be found anywhere. You tossed and turned, went out and peed beneath a coconut tree whose crown glowed in the moonlight, then poured yourself a glass of cool water from the clay pot and chain-smoked till dawn. And then your eyes closed and you slept.

You woke up late, when the warmth of the sun made sleeping uncomfortable. You went looking for footprints in the yard near your window. Could it be that the barking you had heard was only the fabrication of a tired mind?

'Ammae, did you hear any sounds in the night?'

'I heard your father's farts, nothing else.'

'So you didn't hear . . .'

'What's wrong with you? Brush your teeth and come and have tea.'

Yes, it must have been your imagination. It had happened before, on nights when it was warm both outside and inside and you were particularly tired. Once you had thought that Sathiyechi had given birth to a child and Ramakrishnettan, suspecting you to be the father, had beaten you up and driven you out of the house.

You waited for night to fall so you could start writing again. You lit a cigarette and planted yourself in front of the table. You shook the pen to make sure there was enough ink in it. A few drops fell on the cow-dung floor, and some on your mundu.

You wrote:

Leaving the godown behind him, Kunjachchu Master found himself in front of a small house. The majority of the ancient-looking moss-covered tiles on its roof were broken. There was no road here worth the name. He went past that house and reached another that had a goat tethered in its front yard. Red-tinted coconuts hung from dwarf coconut palms. He stopped there, unable to decide which direction to follow to reach the road.

He was aware that wandering alone in such a deserted area was fraught with risk. The doors of the house creaked open and through the gap an old Muslim man wearing a checked lungi emerged. He could tell from the way Kunjachchu Master wore his mundu that he was a Hindu. Stealing glances in all directions, the man said softly, 'Son, you'd better leave here immediately. This whole place is full of our people.'

Kunjachchu Master believed that no one would hurt him. Like Lord Buddha, who walked on both sides of the river at the same time, he lived his life as a Hindu and a Muslim. He did not believe in religion or caste. So why would anyone want to kill him?

You had reached this point in the story when a pack of dogs rushed towards your house and stood barking under your window. You were shocked to hear them howling. Yama, or Kaalan, as he was known here, must be very close. You had heard that when someone was close to death, dogs would howl as they watched the arrival of Yama on his vehicle, the buffalo. Even if humans were oblivious of his proximity, dogs could smell his presence. Was Yama coming in search of you? But why? What wrong had you done to be subjected to capital punishment?

The pen in your hand hit the wall and fell to the ground, as if someone had snatched it from you and flung it away. You rose from the chair, ran to pick it up and inspected it. The nib was broken. Gathering your courage, you went out and shone a torch into the darkness. Was it truly only your imagination?

As you walking back to your room, the hand holding the torch trembled.

You poured water into the glass that sat beside the clay pot and drank it in one gulp. But your throat was still parched; you felt dehydrated. You picked up the broken pen and caressed it like you would a baby. *Digambaran* had been written with it.

The next day, you took the ferry to town and tried to get the nib changed. The pen repairer's name was Paithal. He took the pen, examined it and, scratching the grey stubble on his chin, declared, 'This can't be repaired. Buy a new one, that's better. I have a few Hero pens, they're in great demand. What do you say? Shall I give you one? It writes as if it has loose motion. There's no pen in this world that can best a Hero.'

You bought a new pen, took the ferry and returned home. You vowed to yourself that, notwithstanding the number of dogs that howled, you would write tonight. You felt as though Karikkat Bhagawathy had appeared before you, to warn you that if you did not write soon, you would never be able to write again.

It was impossible to write during the day; the sun stripped everything bare. You needed darkness and stealth.

Until the day was burned out and the night rose from the shroud of darkness, you stayed out and went for long walks. When the dusk was delivered in its blood-red mattress, you thirsted for a taste of rum, but you had promised yourself that you would not write a single word when drunk. All the writing you did would be while you were fully conscious and sentient. Liquor was embargoed.

After a dinner of kanji with jackfruit on the side, you smoked a cigarette, seated on the poorly lit veranda, and attempted to arrange your thoughts. But when the words, instead of evoking images and word-paintings, began to take the shape of dogs, you became annoyed and went into your room. You shut the door and latched it, then sat down at the table as mottled wood owls started to smash themselves against the wooden bars of the window. The barking of dogs accompanied their loud, shivering, heart-shredding calls.

You wanted to call out to your mother, but you had become mute. The end was near, you had no doubt about it. Why else were the owls and dogs calling so piteously?

*

'It's just your imagination.'

'No, I heard it with my own ears. The howling of the dogs, and the owls.'

'Did anyone else hear them?'

'No.'

'Unni'shna, those dogs and owls are not outside the house. They are inside your mind. You need to drive them out. Let me help you with that.'

'No one can help me.'

'Yes, they can.'

'The owls are calling right outside my window. Do you think I can't hear them?'

Balan gripped your hand firmly.

'What you need is sleep. If you get a good night's sleep, everything will go back to normal.'

'How can I sleep when my mind is disturbed?'

'Keep the outside light on when you sit down to write at night. That way, if the owls appear outside your window, you'll be able to see them.'

'Should I light up the skies too? Isn't that where the owls fly down from? Go away, da. You don't understand my problem.'

Balan thought about it for some time, then cleared his throat and said, 'I'd like to tell you something, Unni'shna, but don't get upset. I have a friend, a psychiatrist, in Kozhikode. Let's go and meet him.'

'Are you turning me into a mad man?'

You gave Balan an angry look, the kind of look the fiery theyyams prancing on fire pits throw at their devotees. You were a gentle person. Your laughter, the way you looked at people—everything about you was gentle. But you had been transformed into someone else.

Balan seemed to understand what you were going through. He spoke softly, like a father to his son. 'I'll give you a small pill. Once you take it, your mind will become calmer. You'll get some sleep too. Shall I?'

'Give it to me then. And if you have some poison, give me that too.'

Balan was filled with sympathy for his childhood playmate, anxious to help you out of your depressed state.

There were bags under your eyes. Your forehead looked as if it had been scored with the sharpened spine of a palm leaf. There were dark patches on your cheeks. In the past, you never left the house in anything but a starched shirt and mundu. Now your shirt was buttoned haphazardly. The edge of your mundu was streaked with mud.

'Isn't this our Vendor Goyindan's son, Unni'shnan? What has happened to the young man?' Weaving like a drunk, you turned around and looked balefully at the two villagers who had spoken.

Another day, Velukutty appeared in front of you as you were walking along, unshaven and dishevelled. After examining you from head to toe, he said, 'I didn't even recognise you, Unni'shna. What has happened to you?'

'Nothing's happened to me; you mind your own business.'

You had no interest in having a conversation with Velukutty. But when you tried to walk past him, he caught hold of your shirt sleeve.

'I won't let you go away like that. You were once my employee. I need to know what's wrong. Do you need money? Tell me, I'll give it to you.'

You stood there as if someone had sewn your lips together.

'So, that's what is—you need money. Eda, Unni'shna, I begged you not to quit. I told you I'll hike your pay by ten or twenty rupees. You spurned my offer. Now look at you, loitering about without any income.'

Velukutty took a five-rupee note from his pocket.

'Keep this. As long as this Velukutty is alive, you won't have to live like a vagabond. Whenever you're in need of money, come to me; I'll help. And one more thing . . .

Rohini has nothing against you anymore. She asks about you all the time.'

You acted as if you had not heard him.

'You were not destined to have her as your wife. What's the use now of talking about it? Everything happens as Karikkat Bhagawathy wills it.' Velukutty sighed deeply.

You were already walking away. He hurried after you and tried to press the money into your palm. You slapped his hand away and walked faster.

Balan drove up in his car just then and stopped next to you.

'Where are you headed, Unni'shna?'

'Nowhere.'

'Get in, I'll drop you home.'

You got into the car and sat beside Balan. He smelled fresh, as if he had just had a bath. He spoke to you without taking his eyes off the road. 'Da, you need to have a strong mind. Only then can you become a writer. You have a childlike heart. Writing is not for you.'

'Do you mean that a writer should be stone-hearted?'

'Come and stay with me for a few days. When I return from the hospital in the evening, we can drink rum and discuss Camus and Castro. And after dinner, you can write. I'll keep watch. No mottled wood owl will come anywhere near you. Do you know something, Unni'shna? I own a gun now. I'll use it to shoot down anyone or anything that bothers you.'

Balan did own a gun. Burglars had tried to break into his house recently. He had bought it only to frighten them away. They wouldn't know that he had not bought any bullets.

Despite Balan's insistence, you refused to stay at his place. He was certain that the fear that had infected you like a virus could be cured through counselling. But you were not ready for it. So, he decided to give you a small dose of benzodiazepine to calm your nerves and help you sleep. He had brought the medicine with him.

'You should take it. It's just 0.5 mg. A tiny dose, no harm will come of it.'

You took the pill and threw it out of the window.

'I don't know what to do with you,' Balan said helplessly.

*

You could not live without writing. But you were unable to write. What was the way out?

You loved life as much as the sea loves the shore. Your grouse was that life did not reciprocate even an iota of that love. The thought of suicide had never occurred to you. How could someone with a lust for life end his own life? Instead, you began to seriously consider the option of taking a vacation from life and going somewhere else.

You would return to this life only when you felt certain that you could continue to live without writing. Day and night, you went about engrossed in such thoughts. Eventually, one night, while dark clouds were extinguishing the stars one by one, you decided to head out. It was the most painful decision you had ever made.

You knew that Balan and Kamalakshi had gone to Palakkad to spend time with a cancer patient who was in agony. That morning, after your oil bath, your hair combed back neatly, wearing a double mundu and white shirt, and with empty hands, you stepped out of your life and disappeared.

21

YOU AND THE POLICE

When you left home without saying goodbye, your family was thrown into turmoil. They couldn't sleep, they couldn't eat or drink. Your mother was optimistic, but your father had no hope that you would return.

'Why are you starving yourself like this? Unni'shnan will come back. Where can he go?' Lakshmikuttyamma would console Vendor Goyindan.

'One took the train to Bombay and never returned. Now my Unni'shnan also has disappeared. I can't go on suffering like this. Why is God being so unkind to me?'

In the case of Vasudevan, Vendor Goyindan knew that he had gone to Bombay. But where had Unnikrishnan gone? Where could one go searching for someone who had taken a leave of absence from his own life?

'Karikkat Bhagawathy, why have you given me such unbearable pain . . .?'

Although he wanted to cry, he was unable to. Vendor Goyindan was now a grandfather, and old men have no right to cry. As one ages, one's liberties become curtailed, especially the liberty to cry. Infancy is far better. When sadness melts one's insides, one can at least flail one's arms and legs and, with clenched fists and arched back, bawl open-mouthed. If there was a train that could travel from old age to infancy, Vendor Goyindan would be the first to purchase a ticket and get on board.

No one saw you leave that day. Ramakrishnan's and Shivaraman's doors were shut. Vendor Goyindan was awake but still in bed with his eyes closed. Lakshmikuttyamma was snoring, unaware that it was dawn already.

When she woke up, your mother pulled her thick grey hair into a knot at the back of her head and made her way to the thatched toilet. Then she entered the kitchen and placed the long-handled aluminium pan on the stove to heat water for tea.

You would sit on the veranda with your morning tea, unwashed, not having bothered to brush your teeth. Vendor Goyindan, on the other hand, would not even drink water without brushing. Ramakrishnan and Shivaraman had no such habits. If there was tea, they would drink it. If not, they were okay with not having any. Of all of Vendor Goyindan's children, you were the only one who was stubborn.

You were not in your room when Lakshmikuttyamma came with your tea in a bell-metal tumbler. The bed had been slept in; the sheet was wrinkled.

'Your tea is here. If you feel like having it, come and get it.' She spoke loudly, but you were too far away to hear. Your mother did not know this. And anyway, for a mother, however far her son has gone from her, he is always beside her.

She waited for you, but you did not return home that night. The next day, Ramakrishnan and Shivaraman were among those who sat with their eyes peeled, waiting for your return. Sathi and Vatsala gave them company. In the days that followed, all the villagers waited for you. They said, 'Unni'shnan is not a child to run away. He will be back, Vendor.' Nobody knew that you had left your family and your village with no plan to return soon.

'He must have gone to that doctor friend of his.'

There was only one place you went to regularly: Balan's house. Your parents were aware that their son visited his friend often to have a drink or more, even if they never let on that they knew.

On the third day, when by high noon you had not turned up, your mother's hopes suddenly wilted. Her mind filled with the image of Karikkat Bhagawathy. Whenever she was struck by sorrow or anxiety, Lakshmikuttyamma turned to the goddess for consolation. When she was happy, she did not need any of the gods. 'Go and live in some wilderness,' she would chide them. There were people who believed that the gods dwelled in the firmament, much farther and higher than anyone could reach. Your mother, however, believed they lived in dark, dense forests. She chose to worship at temples because she did not know the paths that led to the jungles and because ferocious animals roamed in them.

'Where has my Unni'shnan gone, oh God? Why can't you go and look for him?' she railed at her husband, who sat on the veranda like a wet hen.

'Where do I go and search for him, Lakshmikutty?'

'Call Balan doctor and ask him. He has a telephone.'

'I don't have his number.'

'Why do you need a number to call anyone? Can't you just call?'

There was no telephone in your neighbourhood. Your father and mother had never seen a telephone. Eventually, Vendor Goyindan went to Velukutty's house. Velukutty had bowed to Rohini's insistent pleas and grovelled before the local MLA to get a telephone connection.

'Don't worry, Vendor. I'll find out where your son is and bring him to you, well and truly trussed up,' Velukutty declaimed as if you were a wanted criminal. When he placed a sympathetic hand on your father's shoulders, his fingers wiggled like a crab's legs.

'May I call Balan doctor? Perhaps he'll know where Unni'shnan has disappeared to. They are good friends.'

'That drunkard doctor has spoiled Unni'shnan. Do you know, that Nampoothiri woman, his wife, also drinks like a fish?'

Vendor Goyindan thought this was abominable. He closed his ears with invisible hands.

'Come in, Vendor, and call the doctor.'

The telephone stood next to a picture of Parassinikadavu Muthappan, covered with a red silk cloth like a corpse.

'Do you know the doctor's number?' Vendor asked.

'Have you come to call him without his number? Do I need to do that too for you?'

'You must help me.'

'Maybe Rohini will know. Let me ask her.'

There was no telephone number that Rohini did not know. She had the numbers of Karikkat Bhagawathy and Konkachi Bhadrakali too, should anyone care to ask.

They tried his number over and over again, but Balan could not be reached. How was Vendor to know that he had finished his palliative care duties in Palakkad and taken the train to Aligarh with the antarjanam?

Disappointed, Vendor decided to return home.

Velukutty followed him outside. 'Vendor, can I ask you something? Was there a tiff between you and your son?'

'What kind of tiff, Velukutty? Don't start any rumours. I'm distraught as it is.'

'Then why did Unni'shnan leave?'

'Velukutty, please keep quiet!'

'So now, I'm the bad guy? I asked because I want to help you find Unni'shnan. But here you are, jumping all over me! This is Kali Yuga. One mustn't help anyone. Go away then, it's your problem.'

Noisily scraping his tyre-soled sandals against the floor, Velukutty went back into his house. Secretly, he was happy that you had disappeared. He had nothing against you, but he did have a grudge against your father. He believed that your father was the reason you had rejected Rohini. Velukutty had been dead keen for you to marry his daughter.

As the days passed, everyone in the village helped look for you, including your brother Shivaraman, who was always sniffling like a puppy around his wife Vatsala, and Ramakrishnan, who seemed cursed to remain childless. Only Velukutty, the villain of Karikkat, went around saying things like, 'Vendor, let those who want to leave, leave! You still have two sons. Why do you grieve so much?'

Then, one day, the phone call came. From a long distance. The undulating ring of the telephone was reminiscent of a snakehead murrel swimming through the water, twisting and turning. It was Velukutty's telephone that was ringing non-stop.

'Velukutty boss, this is Dr Balan.'

'Oh! But no one here is ill,' Velukutty wise-cracked.

'I need your help. I need to talk to Unni'shnan's father urgently. Please fetch him; I'll call again after half an hour.'

Balan cut the call. Long-distance trunk calls ate up a lot of money.

Velukutty went to fetch Vendor Goyindan, who sat down next to the silk-covered phone with a bowed head. The phone rang twice. Each time he picked it up, the line was disconnected. The third time, he heard Balan's voice at the other end.

'Doctor, Unni'shnan is missing.' Vendor spoke plaintively before Balan could say anything. Balan was calling from Aligarh. When he realised this, Vendor asked anxiously, 'Doctor, is he there with you? Has he come there?'

He was certain that if you had to go somewhere, it would be to Balan's. He knew you had no other friend.

'I'm calling you to find out about Unni'shnan. He hasn't come here. Don't you have any news of him?'

When he heard this, your father gasped for breath, as if he were climbing a hill. His knees buckled under him.

'Have you informed the police?'

'Aiyyo, the police? No.'

'You should inform them immediately. There's nothing else we can do. Let them search for him. That's their job.'

'I don't understand what's happening.'

'Don't worry. I'll be there soon.'

'How soon?'

'Very soon.'

Your father did not have to go to the police station. The police came to him.

Three policemen from Moozhikkara arrived in Karikkat in a rickety jeep that rattled all over. A cloud of dust hung in its path. The villagers chased the vehicle, braving the dust, until it came to a stop in front of Vendor Goyindan's house. They couldn't contain their curiosity. First, Unnikrishnan had gone missing. And now the police had arrived.

Ramakrishnan had left for his grocery store and Shivaraman and Vatsala for their tailoring shop. With a wad of tobacco stuffed between his molars, Vendor was seated on the veranda, nursing painful thoughts.

The policemen leaped out of the jeep into the yard.

'Aiyyo, you're here! I was thinking of coming to you. We have no information about Unni'shnan. What should I do now?'

Of the three policemen, two were barrel-chested and stocky, and looked like brothers. The third was lean and lanky.

'Then why didn't you come to us?'

'I thought I would come with Balan doctor after he returns.'

'Who's this doctor?'

'Unni'shnan's friend.'

'You don't have to come with or without anyone. We'll find your son, wherever he's hiding.'

'Why should my son hide?'

'Edo, Vendor, that's what we also want to know. Where's he hiding?'

Your father felt his head going numb. His mouth was dry.

'Tell us, where is he hiding?'

The tall policeman went up to Vendor Goyindan and shoved his lathi into his belly. Vendor's innards convulsed. He keeled forward and nearly fell.

'I don't understand.'

'Don't you read the newspaper?'

'No.'

'Don't you listen to the news on Akashvani?'

'We don't have a radio.'

'Alright, then we'll tell you what's happening in this land.'

Exactly a year after the shooting and killing of their young leader Arikkad Varghese, a group of Naxalites had come out of hiding and attacked a police jeep. One policeman was killed and two grievously injured. Similar attacks took place in south Wayanad. Varghese died on 18 February; you had disappeared on 16 February.

'Vendor, don't act as if you know nothing. Your son has gone to Nilambur forest. We need him alive, so that we can shoot him dead like we shot that Varghese. Get into the jeep, you sonofabitch!'

The tall policeman pushed your father into the jeep. Although thin, his arms were like steel. Your mother came running, wailing loudly, 'Aiyyo, please don't take away Unni'shnan's father.'

'Don't worry, sister. We have some questions for Vendor. After we're through with him, we'll drop him back here.'

What the police wanted to know was how long you had been involved with the Naxal movement. And who you were connected with. Also, whether you had ever visited Andhra Pradesh.

The police jeep turned into Paathimukku and went past Shivaraman's tailoring shop. There were two sewing machines in the shop now. Vatsala was seated at one. Flush against the wall was a table on which lay a big pile of clothes waiting to be cut and stitched. In his store nearby, Koman Chettiar sat behind earthen pots and pans stacked all the way up to the ceiling. Sodden from the rains, the walls of the shop looked ready to collapse at the slightest provocation.

Speeding past Chettiar's shop, the jeep headed towards Ramakrishnan's grocery store with its thatched roof. The walls showed signs of seepage here too. Leaving behind Choyi vaidyar's shop, the vehicle turned onto the main road to Moozhikkara. Vendor Goyindan sat hunched on the floor, as though the roof was leaking.

A week later, the policemen brought your father back in the same rickety vehicle and kicked him out as if he was a football. Most of his bones were fractured. His face was covered with bruises and blood clots.

After that, the villagers stopped looking for you. Perhaps you really were hiding in Nilambur forest.

'I've been saved by Karikkat Bhagawathy,' Velukutty told himself. He could not believe that you had joined a group that went about decapitating landowners and businessmen. He was a landowner and businessman too. How could he not be afraid? He ran his hand over his head to make sure it was still in place.

You, of course, were not in Nilambur forest; you were nowhere. Forget being with people who chopped off heads, you were with nobody. You were on a leave of absence from life itself.

Gradually, the villagers, and even your parents, forgot about you. In the fertile soil of Karikkat, where you were born, not even a stalk of grass served as a memento of you. You were erased from everyone's memories.

BOOK TWO

22

YOUR REBIRTH

As the rays of the setting sun reflected off the glass façade of the mall-cum-multiplex, passengers disembarked from a bus that had made its way there from the south. Among them was an old man with a cloth bag hanging from his shoulder. His face was calm like an ocean that had run out of waves. On his grey head, a few black, curly hairs survived as reminders of a youth long gone. He wore a clean mundu with a black border and a white linen shirt. On his feet were a pair of shiny leather sandals. A cigarette packet was tucked into his shirt pocket, but no pen.

This was you—Unnikrishnan. An old man whose best years were well behind him.

In your absence, Karikkat had changed almost unrecognisably.

The ferry landing and the boat had disappeared. Ve . . . Ve . . . Velayudhan's teashop was missing too. The dirt road between the river and the land where the teashop stood was wider now, and tarred. A new bridge had come up, adjacent to the spot where the teashop once stood. That must be why the ferry and the boatman had been pushed into oblivion. Only the river remained, yet to be banished from its place.

When the conductor had asked where you would get off, you said, 'Paathimukku.' He asked you where that was, and you replied, 'In Karikkat.' But the conductor didn't know a junction by that name. A man who looked even older than you had been listening to your conversation. He asked, 'Do you want to go to Nayanar junction?' You gave a slight nod that could have been interpreted either way. When the bus stopped at Nayanar junction, the conductor ribbed you gently, 'Get down here, karanavar. Here's your Paathimukku.'

You extracted a cigarette from its packet, lit it and, sucking in a mouthful of smoke, looked around you. You were setting foot on the soil of Karikkat after a very long time. A stormy sea seemed to rage inside you. The old Paathimukku was indeed the new Nayanar junction. You noticed the red flags fluttering from the top of trees and lampposts. On the other side of the road was a massive building that housed a mall, a hypermarket and a multiplex. Cars and motorbikes were parked haphazardly on both sides of the road.

Paathimukku was once the centre of the village. Ramakrishnan's grocery store was here. So was Shivaraman's tailoring shop. When you left more than thirty years ago, it was flourishing. He was no longer just stitching hems and old men's loincloths. With help from Vatsala, he had started to make shirts and women's blouses. Both husband and wife were very busy. There were days when they returned home late at night. But their tailoring shop too had disappeared.

You remembered that, as a child, you would take the narrow trail through the banana plantation, past the temple grounds, to Choyi vaidyar's herb store. Whenever you developed scabies or had diarrhoea, your father would take you to see the vaidyar. The herb store too had disappeared.

Your mother used to buy her earthen pots and pans from Koman Chettiar, knocking with her knuckles on each pot to make sure it was not cracked. If she didn't have enough money, Koman Chettiar would say, 'Lachmikuttyamma, you can take as many as you want. Pay me when you have the money.' Your mother would buy some pans and narrow-necked pots and walk past the small kiosk of Kunkar, who sold paan and cigarettes, on her way home. Neither the pottery store nor the paan kiosk were around anymore. Paathimukku had been almost entirely effaced. In its place stood Nayanar junction.

You walked towards your house along unfamiliar roads, not the old path that was usually under water. Once, you would have taken a shortcut through Kelu Asan's property. A long time ago, in the days when you were busy uncovering hidden things, you had spotted an earthen pot hanging from a rafter on the veranda of his house. When you brought it down and undid the cloth that covered its mouth, Kunjiraman, Kelu Aasan's eldest son, had come rushing towards you, causing you to drop the pot and break it. A few pieces of bone lay amid the ashes that fell out of the pot. Was Kelu Asan's soul still wandering somewhere? A smile formed on your lips.

You walked along for a while more, then stopped, bewildered. The banana plantation and the path through it were missing. There were only tarred roads and buildings as far as the eye could see. Internet cafés, women's garment and jewellery shops and electronic stores. Your house lay due east from Paathimukku. With tall buildings blocking the view in every direction at Nayanar junction, you couldn't tell east from west. After walking along a road on which autorickshaws plied up and down, you decided to ask someone for directions to your own house.

'One moment,' you said, accosting a young man. He looked at you as though annoyed that you had a question for him.

'Where is Vendor Goyindan's house?' you asked the young man. He wore a pair of distressed jeans with holes at the knees. Probably pretending to be poor.

'Vendor Goyindan? Who could that be?'

'Unni'shnan's father.'

'Which Unni'shnan?'

'The manager at the cinema talkies . . .'

'Talkies?'

'Yeah, Velukutty boss's Kalyani Talkies.'

'There's no cinema talkies here. We have a multiplex. Go and ask someone else, old man. I'm kind of busy.'

He left, clearly in a hurry. Everyone in Karikkat looked busy. No one had the time, the inclination or the patience for small talk.

You looked around, unsure. There wasn't one familiar face in sight. How could there be? You had returned home after so many years. All the boys you knew had turned into young men and the young men had become old. You spent a few minutes smoking a cigarette and reflecting on your next course of action. Then, suddenly inspired, you walked ahead and turned right.

You were thrilled when Kelu Asan's house came into view. The thatched roof of the old building had been replaced with tiles. You took the shortcut through the yard and were hailed by an old man who walked out onto the veranda leaning on a walking stick.

'Who are you?'

You immediately recognised him as Kunjiraman, Kelu Asan's son. Time had deconstructed the young man and reconstructed him to look exactly like his old father.

'I'm just passing by.'

'Can't you take the road? Do you have to trespass?'

Kunjiraman widened his purblind eyes and fixed them on you suspiciously.

'Doesn't this path lead to Vendor's house?' You had taken this route at least a thousand times.

'Why have you come now to meet Vendor?'

You kept quiet.

'How are you related to Vendor?'

'I lived here for some time.'

'When was that? I haven't seen you around.'

'It was many years ago.'

The old man thought for a while before asking, 'Where are you coming from?'

'Far away.'

'Meaning?'

'From beyond thirty-five years.'

You looked around and realised that there was no exit at the end of the shortcut. A house blocked the way. There was a car shed in front, but no car. No one seemed to be around either.

Kunjiraman surveyed you from head to toe.

'Why are you silent? Why have you come to meet Vendor? I don't think I like your shifty eyes.'

You realised there was little to be gained from tarrying here. There must be another way to your house.

Before you left, you asked, 'Kunjirama, did Kelu Asan's soul get moksha? Or is he still wandering?'

The bewildered old man stared at your departing form. Memories started to form like dark clouds in his cataract-dimmed eyes. Rising to his feet shakily, he said, 'Who are you, really?'

You walked away as if you had not heard him. You chose another road and asked for directions from people you passed, but no one could help you. Finally, a man with a head as grey as yours looked closely at you and said, 'Vendor's house? Come with me.'

You followed the genial man, dodging the growling autorickshaws that zipped by. The road had undergone a transformation, but it was becoming familiar the longer you walked. You didn't need anyone's help from here on.

'Over there, that's Vendor's house.'

It was a mansion. The gate was locked. A dog barked from inside the compound. A nameboard on the gate announced, 'Dr Rayaloth Balakrishnan Nambiar, BSc., M.B.B.S., D.C.H.' You gazed at it like a man walking in his sleep.

Yours was a small, thatched house. The floor was plastered with cow dung and there were verandas on three sides. In the barn to the south of the house, cows stood ruminating. Okra, beans, spinach and aubergine grew in the compound, and on one side were stacked piles of hay.

That house where you lived from infancy to youth had ceased to exist.

What had happened to your house? What happened to your brother's grocery store, and to Shivaraman's tailoring shop? You wanted to know everything. To see everything. But you did not want to be recognised. You wished to live the rest of your life unknown, and in peace.

All these years later, you still loved life as deeply and passionately as ever. Your love had not diminished one bit with the passage of time. You were also clear about how you wished to spend the rest of your days. You had drawn a map of your future life, and there were no great explosions or rebellions in it, as in the past. You just wanted to bask in the light of the sun in Karkitakam. To live within an illuminating blaze of light flashing with brilliant little sparks before leaving the world forever. Would your wish be fulfilled?

An invisible dirt road lay under the tarred one you were walking on. In your mind's eye, you saw the imprint of your footsteps on it. You reached the riverbank, where once there was a ferry landing and boats. You longed to drink a cup of tea from Ve . . . Ve . . . Velayudhan's teashop. But all that your eyes sought was gone. The sun was getting warmer, and you could only see cool-drink and fruit-juice shops. All the kiosks had disappeared. Had Kottoor Krishnan's bakery also met the same fate? The memory of his hot onion vadas lingered in your mind. You had forgotten nothing.

You walked over the bridge to the other side of the river. It was the first time you were crossing the river on foot. On a rainy day, long ago, when you rode the boat with your umbrella open, the wind had blown it out of your hands. You watched it skim the surface of the muddy water and disappear from view. You father had bought that umbrella for Kausalya. You were in the ninth standard then. Where was Raman Kutty Master, who had found nirvana in caning your buttocks? Was he even alive?

A right turn after the cashew-nut factory brought you to the liquor shop. Your supply of rum used to come from here. You preferred Old Monk, but usually had to be content with Hercules XXX.

The cashew-nut factory was a memory now. The liquor shop was no longer there. Paathimukku, the ferry landing, the boat, your house, everything was gone. What was left then? Where were your parents, your siblings, your childhood mate, Balan? Where were Velukutty and his daughter Rohini, who had hankered after you? What of the cinema talkies where you sold tickets and song books?

You had forgotten nothing except the writer in you. You did not know the author of *Digambaran*. You did not even know that a man like that was once alive.

But Paru knows everything.

23

YOUR NEW DOMICILE AND HOUSE

When you and Balan met that day, the light was seeping through little jagged breaks in the dark monsoon clouds. You stood gazing at each other, unable to speak. Balan's mind was in turmoil; yours was serene. His hair had turned white like yours, as if lime wash had splashed across his head. He had put on weight; his cheeks and chest had become fleshy. The extra fat seemed to have shrunk his short neck even further. He was wearing a white shirt with black buttons over his mundu. A gold-capped fountain pen was clipped to his pocket. Tucked into his waist was a packet of cigarettes—State Express 555—and a lighter.

His breath carried the scorching smell of whisky and cigarettes. The silence grew heavier. Balan seemed to be gasping for breath. You had never seen him so overwrought. He had been with you every step of the way—through the highs and lows of childhood and youth. You were inseparable, so much so that people would say, 'These two will end up getting married.' And yet . . .

'I can't believe my eyes.' Balan's eyes brimmed with tears. 'You could have said one word to me before running away!'

'I couldn't. My mind was on fire.'

'We never hid anything from each other. We told each other everything. Yet, when it came to this, you didn't trust me.'

'Please forgive me, Bala.'

Balan took your hand in his and led you to the sofa. A wedding photo was displayed on the wall—it was Balan's daughter, Devangana. The house itself was large and surrounded by high walls. A shiny black sedan stood in the porch.

'All you had to do was consult a psychiatrist. But you weren't ready to do that. And look, you've wasted the best years of your life.'

'Let's talk about something else. Isn't your antarjanam here?'

'Kamalakshi has gone to meet her mother. She's nearly hundred years old.'

'Whose photo is that on the wall, your son's or your daughter's?'

'That's my daughter. We have only one child, you know. And I have some news for you. My Kamalakshi has earned a place in history. To the best of my knowledge, she's the first woman in India to develop alcoholic cirrhosis. She's under treatment now.'

'She can treat herself, can't she? She's a doctor, after all.'

'Eda, we are both oncologists.'

You nodded your head. You wanted to be quiet and listen to him.

Balan wanted to hear what you had to say. He shot off two questions that you had been anticipating.

'Where were you all these days, Unni'shna? What were you doing?'

'I was nowhere.'

'Use a language that people can understand. I'm fed up with your Vedanta gibberish.'

'I was fed up too. Which is why I went away.'

'At least tell me what you've been doing all these years.'

You said nothing. Balan took out a cigarette and started to smoke. When he offered you the packet, you shook your head. You had not stopped smoking, but you were in control of it, and of your mind. You were the schoolmaster standing with a cane in his hand. You were also the student with an upturned palm ready to receive the caning. In fact, you had become a school all on your own—teaching, learning and punishment all in one place.

'All right, Unni'shna. If you don't want to say anything, I won't ask, okay?'

You nodded.

'Is there something you want to know? Did you hear about your father's death?'

'No.'

Your father would have been over a hundred years old by now. So the news of his death did not surprise you.

'Everyone dies when they grow old. Yet, your father's death . . .'

The two years before you left had been stormy. But you had no idea what had happened in your absence. You were too far away.

'The police took your father away.'

'Why?'

When Balan told you about that day and all that followed, you could not believe your ears.

After the police dropped him back to his house, Vendor became bedridden. Choyi vaidyar gave him full-body massages and prescribed various Ayurvedic concoctions and decoctions as well as herbal oils for his bath, but nothing worked.

'He died with your name on his lips.'

Vendor died suffering because of you. Yet, you were on his mind as he lay dying, and until his last breath. You were the cause of your father losing the last link to life before he was fully done.

How did you feel when you heard this? Did you feel guilty? Did you feel regret? Did you silently seek your father's forgiveness? Or did you justify your actions as causing harm only unintentionally? All you said to Balan was, 'I have no control over anybody else's life, or death.'

You wanted to smoke a cigarette. Balan's eyes were fixed on your face as you leaned back on the sofa with a Charminar between your fingers. He seemed to be finding it hard to believe it was you. His face shone with the pleasure of getting back, at least in his old age, the friend he had lost in his youth. Memories from the past—dark, radiant, colourful, faded, fractured—flashed through his mind. Time turned into a mirror, and the images reflected in it of the both of you moved him deeply.

He said softly, 'Unni'shna, you committed a grave mistake. There were people here who loved you. You pushed them all into an abyss of sorrow. If you didn't like living amidst us, you could have left. But couldn't you have done that after giving us at least a hint? You just told me you have been "nowhere". Is that even possible? And what does returning now prove? That you were somewhere. That you could have dropped me a letter sometime. It would have been a great relief to know that you were alive. Your father wouldn't have died so early. And in the end, you have turned up, haven't you? But only after the death of your father and mother, who kept waiting for you. Whatever you may say, you're responsible for their death. You can't escape that.'

'Is my mother dead too? When?'

'Why do you want to know that? You never loved your parents, did you?'

Lakshmikuttyamma did not live very long after Vendor's demise. Having lived as his shadow for so long, she missed having someone to be a shadow to. There was a time when your home was like a crow's nest, noisy and raucous all the time. After your disappearance and Vendor's death, it fell silent, as if it was midnight all the time. Sathi would help Lakshmikuttyamma with her chores and spend the rest of the day sleeping. Vatsala and Shivaraman left in the morning for their tailoring shop. One by one, the cows disappeared from the barn; there was no one to look after them. Little by little, spinach, okra and snake gourd stopped growing on the land. Wild vines, nettles and weeds took over instead. Ramakrishnan and Sathi had no interest in anything. Then, Vatsala gave birth to a stillborn child.

'I don't have the good fortune to be a grandmother. I must be a great sinner,' your mother lamented.

One day, she sprained her back after a fall in the bathroom and became bedridden. 'Now you must be happy, you wench,' she said to Karikkat Bhagawathy. 'Gouge out both my eyes too. Then I can stop seeing things as well.'

Vasudevan never returned from Bombay. Sathi never became a mother. Vatsala had a stillborn baby. You went missing. Your mother used to say that a crow had flown off with you. As she lay curled up under her blanket one rainy night, she dreamed that a crow flew away with you in its beak into a sky filled with dark clouds.

'You and your blasted dreams! What will you dream of next? A dog running away with me in its mouth?' Vendor had asked.

A dog had taken away the writer in you. That was a truth no one knew.

'I still can't believe it, Unni'shna.'

Everyone you ran into told you this. You were being rescued from a collective amnesia. Some of the old-timers who had forgotten you started to remember again. Most of them found it hard to believe you were back.

They did not know that you had only two options: either return to life or kill yourself. You could never kill yourself. You loved life too much for that. So, after thirty-five years, you chose to return to life.

'I'll leave now.'

'Where are you going?' Balan asked anxiously. Perhaps he was worried that you would disappear again. 'Don't go anywhere. Stay with me. Let's celebrate your return. I have an unopened bottle of Black Label somewhere.'

He rose to his feet, opened the refrigerator and peered inside.

'Da, there's some roast beef here. Kamalakshi made it the other day. We can really celebrate tonight.'

'No, Bala. I need to go.'

'Okay, if you must.'

Balan had realised by now that you were the sort to leave, not stay.

Folding up the sleeves of your shirt that had slipped below your elbows, Balan asked, 'Where are you staying?'

'In a lodge.'

The lodge, Nani Palace, was opposite a furniture shop on the road to the bus terminal. Your room number was 6. It was on the first floor, which had a row of six rooms and only one bathroom. The underwear and lungis that were left to dry on the half wall of the building could be seen from the road.

Your room had a table and an almirah; the other rooms did not have an almirah. You had nothing to store in it, though. You had returned empty-handed from your leave of absence, like a newborn.

'When I have this big house, why do you need to stay in a lodge? You should come and live here.'

'No. For the time being, I'll stay there,' you said politely.

'Stop being so stubborn, Unni'shna. That's what has brought you to this.' Balan sounded irritable, displeased.

You placed a hand on his shoulder and said softly, 'Don't be upset with me, Bala. All these days, I've lived alone. I don't think I can live with anyone now.'

'Am I a stranger to you?'

You smiled at Balan without saying anything and walked down the steps, across the brick-paved driveway and through the gate. Across from the house was a banana plantation. The wet greenness of the plantain leaves cooled your eyes. Although tarred, the road was potholed here. There wasn't much traffic, or dust.

A ten-minute walk brought you to the main road. You look a limited-stop bus that went via Karikkat. Although you longed to sit down with Balan and pour yourself a peg of Black Label, you did not yield to the temptation. You had complete control over yourself now.

*

When Paru entered the footwear shop, the eyes of the obese shopkeeper with a gold chain around his neck went straight to her feet, visible beneath the churidar she wore. Her sandals were worn out, and her shoulder bag bulged from the stuff she had packed into it. The only bit of gold on her body was her tiny nose stud.

'Da, Ajeesh, see what this girl needs,' he said from behind the counter.

A youngster who had been dusting the footwear on the shelves approached her.

'I don't need sandals. I've come for something else.'

'What do you need then?'

'I've come to find out something.'

'So, you're a CID?'

'I'm a journalist. Please help me. Have you heard of someone called Unnikrishnan?'

'Which Unnikrishnan?'

'He lives close by. He's old. He always wears a clean, starched mundu and shirt.'

'Does he use footwear? What is his occupation?'

'I don't know, but I need whatever I can get on Unnikrishnan. If you know anything, please tell me. It would be a great help.'

'What is his caste?'

'I don't know.'

'Whatever I ask you, you don't know. You're a shoplifter, I know it. You have a crooked look about you.'

She threw him a disgusted look.

'Go away!' he said. 'We've just opened the shop. Don't spread your inauspiciousness here and jinx our business.'

Deciding that there was nothing to be gained from staying there any longer, Paru shifted her heavy bag from one shoulder to the other and started to walk, keeping to the side of the road. When she came to a house next to a textile store, she stopped and went inside. An old man relaxing in an armchair, his legs up on its arms, was waiting for her.

'Come, come, come,' he said.

She climbed up the steps to the veranda, sat down beside him and offered him a smile.

24

YOUR DEATH AND CHILDREN'S RHYMES

You were unable to stay very long at the Nani Palace lodge.

The toilet caused you the biggest headache. You could tolerate most things, but not those dingy walls and the oily, grimy floor. It was important to you to keep both body and mind clean—you would rather go hungry than live in unsanitary conditions.

When you moved to Kundachira, you had a girl coming in to sweep every day. But after she was done, you would sweep the place all over again, dissatisfied with her work. The thing that had bothered you the most at Nani Palace was the sight—as soon as you entered the place—of underwear and lungis spread out to dry on the half wall.

One day, you lost your patience and screamed at one of the lodgers, 'Edo, do you really need to display all these in front of my room? Take them away or I'll throw them out on the street.' The man laughed vacuously, not quite understanding. Provoked, you used a stick to flick the underwear down to the ground below.

After this incident, you took a small house on rent. Why did you choose this unfamiliar area to live in? Was it because there were no houses available for rent in Karikkat? But no, that was the land of memories as far as you were concerned, of Kalyani Talkies and Paathimukku. Memories that dogged you as laughter and tears.

These days, you disliked recalling events from the past. You knew about the passing of your parents. Once you were able to discover what had happened to your siblings, you could obliterate Karikkat itself from your memories and get on with life.

Kundachira was neither a town nor a city, it was somewhere in the middle. It had a bus terminal with a few shops around it, including two mobile recharge kiosks and a TV and food-mixer repair shop. A teashop stood at the corner where the road from the bus terminal met the main road. Passersby stopped to eat bondas and drink piping-hot tea seated on a bench outside the shop. Whenever you passed the shop, Ve . . . Ve . . . Velayudhan would swim into your memory. You had no idea if he was still alive.

By now, all your relatives and acquaintances would have become old. In your mind's eye, the majority were grey-haired and wrinkled, with saggy jowls and bags under their eyes, and creaky knees.

You had first looked for a house in the area between Kundachira and Moozhikkara.

'What's your occupation?'

'Nothing in particular.'

'How will you pay the rent?'

'Why do you need to know that? I'll pay you the rent promptly on the first of every month. I'll pay an advance too. Isn't that enough?'

'Let me think about it. Come back after a couple of days.'

It was a clean, if small, house. The front veranda did not have a grille. You disliked grilles, they gave a house the appearance of a jail. You decided to take the place and pay whatever the owner asked for as rent. But then, you heard a voice behind you.

'Who will give their house to someone like you, without a job or any visible means? You don't have to come here again asking about this house.'

You were disappointed.

After many such rejections, you eventually found a house. It had a patio and a front yard. After moving in, you planted fruit trees and flowering plants all around the house.

In the mornings, after drinking a glass of cold water and donning a cap to protect your head against the dew, you would walk up and down the yard, expelling the stale air in your lungs and breathing in fresh air. You subscribed to an English and a Malayalam daily. After your walk, you picked up the newspapers and sat on the patio, scanning the headlines. After that, you made yourself a glass of black tea, added a few drops of lime juice to it and returned to the patio to read the papers from front to back. By 8 a.m. or so, you would be done.

After that, changing into a fresh mundu and shirt, you would walk to the kiosk around the corner for milk and cigarettes. You smoked ten cigarettes a day. Sometimes you finished your quota before lunch. When that happened, whatever the temptation, you refused to touch another cigarette.

Even while having vodka or brandy with Balan in his liquor library, you drank in moderation. Your discipline amazed Balan.

'Da, Unni'shna, how did you become like this?'

Once, Balan was the disciplined one. Now, despite being doctors, neither Balan nor Kamalakshi seemed to have any self-restraint. When it came to alcohol, they were like unbridled horses, galloping away in all directions.

After returning with the milk and cigarettes, you changed into a single thorthu and applied gingelly oil all over your body. You would then use the toilet, brush your teeth and shave. After your bath, you would make idlis for breakfast with batter that had been prepared the previous evening. Using a mini food-mixer, you ground some coconut chutney with bird's eye chilli.

After breakfast, you would change and go out once again, your oiled face shining in the sun. You walked all the way to the fish market, about a kilometre away. All the fishmongers there knew you. They would give you fresh fish that had not been preserved in ice or ammonia. 'Why is Unni'shnan so late today? I had some fresh blood snapper which Khadar boss snapped up a little while ago,' one of the fishmongers might say to another.

'What's your name?'

One day, an old man appeared before you as you were leaving the fish market. Below his mundu, his legs were covered with grey hair. You did not like the question. It was only to loveable little children that such a question could be posed, as one fondly took their chin in one's hand. Why was it being asked by this old man of another just passing by?

'I've seen you somewhere. You look very familiar. That's why I asked.'

Although he was older than you, he looked much younger. He was tall and stooped a little as he stood in front of you, raising his eyes but not his head.

'My name . . .'

'I didn't ask your name.' You were irritated.

'My name is Jayasheelan.'

'What, Jayasheelan?'

As if he had not heard the question, he continued, 'Who are you?'

'Me? I'm a nobody.' You spoke without even the pretence of amiability.

Something came to you then. While speaking with his head bowed, he had raised his fist twice as if shouting slogans. A bulb lit up in your brain.

'Are you Jayasheelan, who used to work in the post office? Kausalya's . . .?'

'Umm . . .'

You stood there, staring at each other.

'Everyone thought you were dead.'

No, you had only gone to sleep. Thirty-five years of sleep. Although death and sleep rub against each other, they are not the same, you wanted to say. They are distinctly different.

It seemed inappropriate to continue the conversation standing in front of the fish market, so you led Jayasheelan to a teashop on the other side of the road. You sat down on either end of a bench. Flies were landing in and taking off from puddles of tea that had spilled on the table. The smell of sizzling banana fritters was all-pervasive. You ordered tea and blew into it before drinking.

You wanted to ask about Kausalya. How many children did they have? What were they doing? Where were they staying? If possible, you wanted to meet Kausalya.

*

'Isn't this Kausalya's house?' Paru asked, approaching the yard with her head covered with a dupatta.

Although the front door lay open, no one seemed to be around. Through the open door, a photograph of a woman, framed and mounted, was visible in the reddish glow of a zero-watt bulb under it. As she stood there, hesitating, she noticed the switch to the left of the door. The symbol of a bell on it banished any doubt. She pressed it thrice. A man appeared, tying and untying the lungi he wore. He looked like he was eating something. She must have interrupted his breakfast.

'Sorry, is this Kausalya's house?'

His stoop became more pronounced and his face grew dark. He wiped his mouth with the back of his hand and looked closely at Paru.

'What do you want?'

He noticed that although her eyes seemed tired, she had an attractive face. And she didn't look anything like the sales girls who turned up trying to sell knick-knacks.

'Come in. Sit down.'

She took off her sandals at the bottom of the steps, wiped her feet on the coir mat and climbed onto the veranda.

'You didn't say who are you . . .'

'I've come to meet Kausalya.'

His face fell.

'That's not possible.'

'Why, isn't she here?'

'No.'

'Where can I find her?'

'Molae, please forget about meeting her. Is there anything else you have to say?'

'Who are you to Kausalya?'

'Who do you think I am?'

'Husband?'

'Yes, that's right.'

She had been standing until then; she sat down now, on a chair next to his. Her legs were fatigued from all the walking and standing about in Karikkat, Moozhikkara, Kundachira.

'So, tell me, what exactly do you need? I have a lot of chores to take care of. Sweep the room, wash my clothes. When you come to Kerala, there's no time for anything else. There's no domestic help to be had in this damned place. My spine became bent from shouting slogans for the workers, but now, when I need some help, not one of them will heed my call. Why should they? They've all become tycoons.'

'You don't live here then?'

'No, I live in Ras Al Khaimah, in the Gulf. With my daughter.'

She was relieved to see that he was opening up a little.

'You have only one daughter?'

'Yeah, but she'll do for ten! She's just like her mother. Kausalya loved others more than herself. I'm lucky to have had her as my life partner.'

'I came here to ask about Unni'shnan. They're brother and sister, aren't they?'

'You can talk about anything else, just don't mention Unni'shnan. He's a crackpot.'

She had expected to extract some titbits about you and your family from him. Right at the beginning, she had only wanted to know all about your imminent death. Her plan was to scoop that story. But now, she was keen to find out everything about you, having arrived at the simple bit of logic that only by getting to know you could she understand the enigma of your death.

'His parents and sister are dead. He didn't turn up even to drop a few grains of rice in their mouths. He's a wicked man.'

'Don't say that. No one could see his side of things, or what was going on in his mind. He has suffered greatly, you know.'

Jayasheelan looked at her and asked, 'Who are you to him?'

'No one.'

'Then why are you pleading his case?'

She remained silent, then cleared her throat and asked, looking into his eyes, 'Where was Unni'shnan? Why did he run away from everyone?'

'Go and ask him yourself.'

'Why is Unni'shnan going to die on the sixteenth? How is he going to die?'

He did not understand. He knew nothing about your press conference, the announcement of the date of your death.

'Who told you he's going to die?'

'Unni'shnan himself has told everyone that.'

'Molae, you'd better leave now or you'll drive me mad.'

He went inside and closed the door. She stood there, dismayed. Why was every door she knocked on closing on her? How was it that not a single one would stay open?

She did not meet him after that. When you breathed your last, he would be in Ras Al Khaimah with his grandchild on his lap, holding his tiny hands and singing:

> *Bingo bingo Sunday*
> *What's in your kitty?*
> *A little chicken bone.*
> *What will go with the bone?*

25

YOUR DEATH AND YOUR FOREBEARS

'The sun has gone to quench its thirst.'

You recalled your mother saying that once. The sun in July and August is like that. Every now and then, it goes to drink water. It goes missing for a while, then returns after having had its fill.

The rain fell in silence, unaccompanied by wind or thunder. You stood watching it fall in an even tempo, no hissing or roaring. The dampness and shadows of July and August became entwined in your mind.

Today was the first new moon day after the autumnal equinox. The day the sun and the moon are aligned. You made preparations for the tarpanam, to propitiate the souls of your parents. You would have to remember to invoke your sister too.

When your parents died, you should have been by their side, but you weren't. You were unable to give them the ritual drops of water in their last moments. You knew that your absence would have caused them pain. How could it be that you, who ached to write a novel about those in pain, did not see the pain of your own parents? Were you so grossly selfish? Or was life only about writing and you simply failed to pay heed to the lives of others?

You continued to struggle with these thoughts. You had returned with the hope that you could live in the present and forget all about the past. However, nostalgia clung to you like an extra layer of skin.

'You're offering prayers to the departed souls? I don't believe it! Are you superstitious?'

'I don't know the difference between faith and superstition. But this appears to be the appropriate reparation for the sins I've committed.'

'What sins have you committed? You have only erred, not sinned.'

You were silent.

Balan continued, 'By leading a rational life, you can avoid a lot of complications. My life has been simple because I've avoided superstitions.'

Free consultations for patients who came to the house in the morning. Then the hospital, to look after the patients waiting there. In the evening, a bath, a change of clothes, a drink on the veranda on the first floor. Rice and fish for dinner. Reading till midnight on the sofa, in the light of the tall pedestal lamp. After that, bed, snuggled up to Kamakshi, who would have fallen asleep already. Occasionally, travel within and outside the country to speak on the subject of euthanasia . . .

Balan believed he led a very simple life.

'Bala, what trouble do I have in life? I don't think I have any,' you argued.

'Do as you please. Perform your rituals. At least a few crows will not go hungry.'

You would not listen to anyone, not even Balan. But he would not leave you in peace. He kept saying things that you disliked hearing.

'You are a scaredy cat, Unni'shna. When someone came and placed a wreath on your veranda, you trembled with fear. The howling of dogs and the hooting of owls made you flee your home. Eda, writers should not be afraid of anything. Not even guns.'

'Writers are not soldiers.'

You told Balan a few hundred times, 'For God's sake, please don't remind me of the past.'

'How is that possible? We all sit atop the mound of our memories.'

You had no desire to enter into a debate with anyone.

Today was the new moon of the month of Karkitakam. You had a ritual bath the night before and one meal of rice in the day. You could have eaten more food, as long as it didn't contain rice, but you chose to fast. You drank only water in the morning and at night. It was as good as eating something solid.

You woke up before sunrise and, braving the early morning chill, bathed in cold water. To make sure you were clean, you worked up a generous lather with the soap and washed yourself all over. Then you wore a mundu that you had washed and dried overnight and flung a wet thorthu over your shoulder.

You had arranged for an autorickshaw to take you to the beach. When you reached there with all that was required for the rituals, the sea lay in darkness. Only the silently unrolling waves flashed an occasional white tip. For the first time, you could appreciate the penumbra of a new-moon night. Your forebears dwelled on the dark side of the moon. Vendor Goyindan, Lakshmikuttyamma and Kausalya would descend from there to accept your offerings.

The place was already crowded. Women smelling of damp clothes stood among the clusters of people. The sea breeze swirled around your body, but you didn't feel the cold. A plantain leaf was placed in front of you for the oblation. And another, tender half-leaf—that was for Kausalya. All the ingredients prescribed for the ritual—balls made out of raw rice, sesame, honey, small kadali plantains and jaggery—were arranged on the leaves.

'Please forgive this son of yours,' you begged your parents.

Those doing water oblations tipped the sesame-rice balls into the sea. Those who expected souls to appear as ravens clapped their hands in invitation to the birds and waited for their dear ones to turn up.

You were happy you could offer prayers for your parents and Kausalya. Yet, the thought of your older brothers made you sad.

Where were Ramakrishnan and Shivaraman? Were they even alive?

*

'They are both doing well for themselves and have become quite wealthy,' said Choyi vaidyar.

Paru had left her home early in the morning. Despite roaming around as she had been doing these past few days, in the heat and dust, in the rain and the wind, she had not had much luck. You continued to be an enigma. Why were you going to die, and how? Why had you announced your death to the world in advance? She still had no answers to these questions. Whatever tricks she tried, whatever pressure she applied, your mouth remained shut like the door of a safe.

As the days passed, she became impatient. She was worried that she would fail the first assignment given to her by her editor. The date of your departure was fast approaching too.

Her destination today was the old Paathimukku in Karikkat, where you were born and grew up. She was hoping to find a key to your life there. She did not know that one key would not be enough.

Unable to decide where to begin her enquiries, she stood for a while on the main road. When she realised that people were watching her, she went into a teashop and sat down. Her white kurta was wrinkled. Her hair, tied in a bun at the top of her head, was dry and frizzy. Did her home lack an iron as well as oil?

'Do you want anything to eat?' She shook her head in response to the man who placed a glass of milky, oversweet tea on the table.

'Do you know Unni'shnan?' she asked him as she sipped the hot tea. It made her tongue turn red.

'Unni'ishnan? Now, which Unni'shnan would that be?'

'The youngest son of Vendor Goyindan.'

'Vendor? Who could that be?'

'He used to write deeds and sell stamp papers.'

'Ha! To have someone write up a deed, I should have at least a slice of land, right? My house is built on two cents of poramboke land.'

Were all the people of Karikkat like Unnikrishnan? Every question seemed to be met with tongue firmly in cheek.

'Vendor had two more sons. The grocer Ramakrishnan and the tailor Shivaraman. Are they here in Karikkat?'

'My dear child, I know nothing about them. Have your tea, pay up and leave. You and your vendor-kindar!'

Realising she had drawn a blank again, Paru drank half the tea and rose to her feet.

A decrepit old man seated in a corner, who had been drinking tea and listening to their exchange, raised a hand and beckoned to her.

'Come here.'

He looked on the wrong side of ninety, his scalp visible under his thinning hair. A khadi cloth was wound around his neck, and she could see a walking stick by his side.

'Where do you want to go, my child?' asked Choyi vaidyar. He must be the oldest person alive in these parts, she thought. He would know everyone here.

'Unnikrishnan's house.'

'Unnikrishnan, who worked in Velukutty's talkies . . . Vendor Goyindan's . . .'

'Exactly!'

'It's been ages since he left this place. No one has any news of him. There's talk that he's dead. Who knows what the truth is?'

'No, Unnikrishnan is not dead.'

'What?' Choyi vaidyar looked stunned. 'Where is he then?'

'I don't know. I've come here to enquire about him. I'm a journalist; I work for a newspaper. We're doing a story on him. I've come to collect details for that. Uncle, please help me.'

Choyi vaidyar took her home. Medicinal plants and herbs grew around his house. Even in his nineties, he continued to treat patients. His wife had died twenty years ago. Although he knew the *Ashtanga Hridayam* by rote, he could not save her.

In that house fragrant with herbs and decoctions, they spoke at length. No one else Paru had met knew as much as the vaidyar did.

'Why did Unni'shnan leave this place?'

'Who knows?'

'What kind of man was Unni'shnan? Was he a troublemaker?'

'He was affectionate. However, no one could tell what he was thinking. He had a complicated mind.'

She exhaled, cleared her throat, and asked the next question. 'Was he married?'

'No. Velukutty was very keen that Unnikrishnan marry his daughter, Rohini. But he wouldn't agree. I tried to counsel him, but he was adamant.'

'Where's Rohini now?'

'Not far from here.'

'Can we meet her?'

'Why not?'

'Then let's go.'

'Aiyyo! You can't leave without drinking at least a glass of water!'

Choyi vaidyar plied her with plantains and sarsaparilla juice. Afterwards, they set off for Rohini's house. Paru took his hand as he descended the steps leaning on his walking stick and didn't let go afterwards. She could see that he needed a helping hand.

'Let's take an auto.'

'No need for that. We'll walk. It's that close.'

As long as there was someone to hold his hand, he was ready to walk any distance. He started off slowly, but after a while, his steps quickened. He started to keep pace with her.

'Careful, careful . . .' she said, in spite of herself. At his age, if he were to slip and fall, he might wake up in heaven. The thought made her anxious.

'We're almost there, child.'

They could see a large concrete house at the end of the road they were on. It had high compound walls. Trees laden with flowers and fruits were visible behind them. None of the other houses in the vicinity were as big as this one. Paru gave it a good, long look before they entered.

That night, Paru stayed at Choyi vaidyar's house. He was up till midnight, talking to her about the village and its people and about your parents and siblings. He was a good storyteller. She could visualise everything he spoke of.

When Paathimukku turned into Nayanar junction, the traditional shopkeepers and tradesmen were either thrown out of business or voluntarily ceded space. Snacks such as pazhampuri, parippu vada, ela ada and sukhiyan disappeared from teashops to be replaced with cutlets, puffs, chicken curry and porotta. Then came shawarma from the Gulf.

When a supermarket opened near his shop, Ramakrishnan's grocery store had to be shut down. However, he did not give up. He went to Bahrain and started a grocery store there in partnership with a local Arab. The Arab had little interest in the trickle of profits from the sale of groceries and soap. He stopped coming to the shop. The business flourished, and Ramakrishnan became a rich man. However, your Sathiyechi continued to be barren.

And Shivaraman?

He shut down his tailoring shop and started exporting crêpe fabrics from Kannur. He too became wealthy. Vatsala had refused to have any more babies after she gave birth to a stillborn. Shivaraman, knowing who was behind the transformation of his life, from stitching loincloths to travelling in a car as big as a ship, readily agreed. They adopted a girl child.

Everyone's life had gotten somewhere. Except yours.

26

YOU AND VARIYANKUNNATH KUNJAHAMMAD HAJI

You have no doubt that the person waiting outside your locked door so early in the morning is Paru. And it is. She had come two days ago too, prattling on about things in a manner that irritated you. She is like a cat following a scent. A cat that scratches sometimes, and sometimes gives you an affectionate lick.

The last time she came, she was wearing a bright yellow-and-green saree.

'Why is there blood on your face?' she asked anxiously. There was a small cut on your chin, a speck of blood. You must have been careless while shaving. You are careless about a lot of stuff. Your mind seems to have become fickle, leaping around like a frog. It is a mind that dreams . . .

She had walked into the kitchen to make tea, as if this was her own house.

The kitchen is always spotlessly clean. No burn marks on the gas stove from spilled milk or sticky spots where the rice boiled over, nor does it smell of fried fish. Your kitchen is as clean as your bedroom.

There are three wooden shelves on the wall. Tea leaves, sugar and jaggery are kept in glass jars on the lowest shelf. The middle shelf has bottles with chilli powder, turmeric powder, coriander powder, salt, mustard and cumin seeds. Smaller bottles contain cardamoms and cloves. That's the spices section. The aluminium containers on the top shelves are filled with parboiled rice, broken rice for kanji, wheat flour, and semolina for upma. Also, lentils and oil. You use only coconut oil for cooking.

A small basket next to the gas stove holds onions, shallots, ginger and garlic. In the refrigerator in the corner are a few packets of Milma milk. The crisper at the bottom contains carrots, tomatoes, okra, aubergines and bitter gourd. You get enough drumsticks from the moringa tree in the yard to make sambar whenever you feel like it. Curry leaves and bird's eye chillies grow in the yard.

As they sit there drinking tea, Paru says, 'I met Rohini.'

'You can meet anyone you want. Why do you have to come and tell me?'

You are tired, as if you have been walking outside in the heat. You have been struggling of late. As the day of your death approaches, your breath has started to snag. Your voice cracks. Paru is unaware of any of this. You lean back, stretch your legs and sigh deeply.

'She has become a hag. Thin and withered. Her hair is completely white. I felt very sad. But they are very wealthy. Her husband owns the multiplex at Nayanar junction.'

'You've been going to Karikkat to dig up stuff, haven't you?'

'Yes, I've learnt a thing or two.'

'Did you talk to her?'

'What a question! Why else should I go to the trouble of finding her?'

You are lost in thought, your head in your hand.

'Rohini was madly in love with you.'

'Ufff! Don't you have anything else to talk about?'

You remove your hand and give her a hard stare.

'So you think you know everything about my past.'

By the time she leaves, you feel even more weighed down by your load of sorrows. She unbalances you. You feel as if one hand of the clock of your life is out of control, running back and forth.

Today, she had appeared along with the sun. How does she get here so early? Does she take the first bus? She lives at least twenty miles away. If she lived in the neighbourhood, she would have troubled you every day. You wonder how to get rid of her. You have made no attempt to conceal your displeasure. Even when you are enjoying her company, you pretend to be angry and turn her out of the house. Yet, she is back the next day, with onion vada from Kottoor Krishnan Bakery, the latest novel by some famous author, a bottle of Horlicks or Ovaltine or bun-biscuits or lotta. She knows your weaknesses.

If she has brought bun-biscuits, she goes into the kitchen and makes tea. That is the only way to have a bun-biscuit— dipped in tea. The deep-fried lotta, on the other hand, has to be eaten with care or it can crack your teeth.

Paru warns you, 'Unni'shna, be careful with the lotta. That tooth of yours, next to the left upper molar, is loose.'

That is true. But how does she know? When you ask, all she says is, 'My job is investigative journalism.'

'Unni'shna, hey Unni'shna.' Each time she knocks on your door, you pretend not to hear her. As the day of your death draws closer, you have many things to worry about. You have to pay rent until the day of your death. Your bank account has to be closed and the money donated to an orphanage. Given that you wear a fresh, starched shirt and mundu every day, you have a surfeit of clothes too, to give away.

'Unni'shna, open the door. I've brought chapatis for you, and egg curry. Open the door.'

She bangs on the door with both fists, but you continue to brush your teeth at the wash basin, as though you have not heard. You are using Binaca toothbrush and toothpaste.

Your mouth soon fills with foam. Your reflection in the mirror above the wash basin does not look like an old man's. Even at this age, your skin is taut. You need glasses only for reading, although your eyes look tired. Paru once called you a young man of seventy. Balan had also said something similar. That is because they only see your external form. They miss the age implicit in your thoughts and actions.

'Open the door or I'll kick it down.' She is using the language of men. You have never heard a girl say she will kick a door down. Not that this door can be broken by a woman. The house belongs to a wealthy Nambiar; the door is made of matured jackfruit wood. Even if ten Parus ram it, it will hold.

You do not respond or open the door. After brushing your teeth, you drink a tall glass of water and sit down on the easy chair which you drag inside at night lest some stray dog lie on it. Normally, you would be on the veranda by this time, reading the papers. But she is right outside; how will you bring the papers in?

You feel an intense loathing for Paru. 'You and your damned investigative journalism!' you shout.

There is no sound from the other side of the door. She must have got tired of waiting and left—hopefully, never to return!

You lie back in the easy chair and close your eyes.

Something lands on your lap. You are startled awake. The newspapers that you so wanted to read.

'Edi, how did you get in?'

'Magic realism.'

She entered through the kitchen door. You remember now that you forgot to lock the door the previous night. Why should you lock up anyway? What is there for burglars here except some old, faded memories? And which burglar would come looking for memories?

She looks like she hasn't had a bath. Her hair has come loose from its knot. She has a shirt on over black trousers. Her cheeks are unpowdered, her lips bare. She looks good, though.

'Let's have chapati and egg curry.'

'I don't need anything. All I want is for you to leave me in peace.'

You pick up the newspaper and scan the sheets. You are not being facetious. You have no interest in meeting or talking to anyone. In the little time that you have left, you want to do only the things you want to do.

'Edi, did you hear what I just said?'

'What? You didn't say anything.'

'Then listen. From now on, I am going to live only for myself. I am not willing to share even a moment of my life with anyone else. My time has come.'

'Unni'shna, don't lie. All these years, you've lived only for yourself. You brushed your teeth, crapped and bathed and drank tea, read the newspaper, and even this— browbeating me like you are doing—all this is for your sake. The thirty years you went away were also for you. So why sit here pretending otherwise?'

You fling the newspaper down and scream, 'You keep coming here and destroying my peace of mind. Don't you dare step into this house again! I don't want to lay eyes on you ever. If I see you again, I'll strangle you to death.'

That brings a smile to her face.

'Before you kill me, let's have chapati and egg curry. And wash it down with some hot tea.'

'Who are you to order me around? I don't want your chapati-shapati. What I want, I'll cook and eat. I don't need your help.'

You tear your eyes away from her face. You know you are lying. You don't have the strength in your hands any more to knead the dough. So you mix flour with water and salt and make dosas instead of chapatis. A dollop of ghee and some sugar sprinkled on top, that is all that is required. And that is all you want to do now: spend the rest of your days eating the food you like and doing the things you want to do.

You glare at her. 'This girl is the only obstacle in my path. I'll thrash her like a dog; I'll break her leg,' you mutter to yourself.

'Are you trying to scare me?'

You raise your hand as though to slap her.

'Oh, go away! I don't scare that easily.'

She brings two ceramic plates from the kitchen. She puts a couple of chapatis on one, ladles the curry over it and offers it to you. You look at the two eggs, the pieces of fried tomato and onion and feel your mouth water. Although close to death, your liking for food remains undiminished.

'Why aren't you eating? If you need to get angry, I'm here, get angry with me. What harm have they done to you, this chapati and curry?'

Pulling a chair close to yours, she sits down with her plate on her lap. She tears a chapati in four and starts to eat, dipping each piece in the curry. She chews with her mouth closed. You are relieved to see that. You find it repulsive when someone eats with their mouth open.

'Learn from me, Unni'shna. You'll never find me going hungry. When I feel like eating, I eat whatever comes to hand. Nobody needs to persuade me. And that's true of everything I do. What you see is what you get. You are just the opposite. You never show your real feelings. I know you are fond of me. In fact, full of love. Yet, you keep calling me names.'

Anger surges through you. You hurl your plate full of food against the wall and it crashes to the ground, scattering bits of tomato, onion and egg. The gravy splashes and stains the wall.

'What the hell have you done? I'm fed up of you.'

She is trembling with fury. Even her nose stud quivers.

Exhaling exaggeratedly, she picks up the broken pieces, sweeps up the mess on the floor and wipes the wall clean. She goes to the kitchen, makes tea and places the glass in front of you. You lie in the easy chair with your eyes closed, struggling to regain control.

'Drink!'

You open your eyes and accept the steaming glass of tea. You blow into it and take two sips. The hot tea lifts the taste of egg curry still on your tongue. You allow yourself to savour the sensation.

'Good! Behave from now on. Don't be so stubborn. That was a fine plate you destroyed.'

She gets up and takes a book from her shoulder bag. When you see the cover, you feel as if a bolt of lightning has gone through you. *Digambaran*! A naked man walking through wilted and greying foliage. You had insisted on that cover design, demanded it of Pilakkunnan. The cover is scruffy and faded; the inside pages yellowed with age, the edges frayed.

She sits down next to you.

'Where did you get that from?'

After your disappearance, there were no more reprints of *Digambaran*. There was a dispute over copyright, and Pilakkunnan died in the meantime. She must have found it in some library. Like you, it seems the book too is back after a long leave of absence.

'Now, let's have a conversation. And don't fight me, just answer my questions.'

'Who are you to give me orders?'

'Unni'shna, I'll be honest with you. At first, my editor only asked me to find out how you were going to die.

Now the man says I should write about your novel. Which means I should write about Kunjachchu Master going to Tirurangadi. It's a matter of survival for me. I have to do whatever he asks or he'll send me home. Unni'shna, please help me.'

'I can't remember anything.'

'There you go again! Can't you stop this for once, Unni'shna?'

She opens the book and riffles through the pages, her eyes skimming the text. As far as you are concerned, the book is dead. She is holding a corpse.

'I have to know a couple of things, I won't leave until then. If you don't tell me, I'll spread a mat here and stay the night. I won't even drink a drop of water. I know you said you'll die on the sixteenth. Well, I'll die before that, right here.'

She speaks gravely and in a determined voice. Her expression makes you think she might actually carry out her threat. For some reason, her words affect you.

'You can nag me only till I die. Go on, ask me whatever you want to know.'

'As soon as Kunjachchu Master landed in Tirurangadi, the Malabar Rebellion broke out. You've described it in the novel. My question is this—whose side were you on?'

You sit quietly, looking at your toenails. They are neatly cut, and there is no dirt around them.

'You've written about Variyankunnath Haji, over seven pages . . .'

She is taking you into an era that doesn't exist any longer in your memory.

'I don't remember anything.'

'Then let me remind you of what you've written. Maybe it will come back to you then.'

'No,' you plead. 'I don't want to remember anything.'

She continues as if she has not heard you, 'When the British tried to grab him, Variyankunnath Haji resisted. He had the strength and the skill to do that. For a full half hour, the white men could not lay their hands on him. He fought alone. He had the courage to do that.'

'Why are you making me remember all this?'

'It's what you've written. I learnt a few things from your book . . . Eventually, the British subdued him and put him in shackles. When he was being taken away to face the firing squad, he asked them not to blindfold him and to remove the shackles; he wanted to face the firing squad bravely and free. He died that way. The British showed no respect for his dead body. They burned it . . .'

You listen in silence.

'The British tried to destroy the peace between Hindus and Muslims. Variyankunnath mentions this in a letter he wrote to the *Hindu* newspaper. When the British filled their jails with Muslim men, their women and children were given protection by people like Vaidyarathnam P.S. Warrier. The Kizhakke Kovilakam palace was protected by Chekkutty and other Muslims. My dear Unni'shna, what you've written is deeply moving. Your craft is magical. Please tell me, whose side were you on? Were you with the Muslims or the Hindus? That's what I need to know.'

'I'm on the side of history.'

'And what does history have to say?'

'That Hindus and Muslims are two eyes on one face.'

She kneels in front of you.

'Don't ask me anything more. I'm done.'

You are no longer that Unnikrishnan. When you took a leave of absence from life and went away, your writing departed too. When you returned, your writing did not come back with you. It is still meandering in places unknown.

'Okay, I'll leave now.'

She leaves, only to return with more questions.

27

YOU AND SALMAN RUSHDIE

Your life, transplanted to Kundachira, had taken root and started to bloom.

'I like to live alone,' you would say. Many cautioned you that in a country where old men were dying in their sleep, it was not advisable for you to live alone. Your landlord was one of them. 'You should have someone sleep in the house at night,' he advised.

You were not afraid of death. But you had decided to live. And you had taken an oath to make every moment that was left to you as pleasant as possible.

Each movement of yours was planned and deliberate, like moving a piece on a chessboard. You demonstrated a discipline and tidiness that were new. You shaved in the morning and bathed twice daily. You changed your underclothes, shirt and mundu everyday. You cooked for yourself. Your favourite breakfast these days was poori and a curry made of chickpeas. You soaked the chickpeas overnight. Although you had a mixer, you used the grinding stone to prepare the masala and to grind coconut. 'If I use the mixer, the curry will lose its taste,' you would say.

After your siesta, you would make bonda or onion vada to go with your evening tea. You did not want to depend on the distant Kottoor Krishnan Bakery any more. Dinner was oats or something as light and easy on the stomach. When Kamalakshi turned up one night with biryani, not only did you not accept it, but forgetting that she was a doctor, you advised her, 'At our age, chicken biryani won't do us any good. These broiler chicken have been shot full of hormones. You must be careful, Kamalakshi; you have a liver problem.'

You started to make changes in your daily routine. You began to have a shot of vodka before setting off for a stroll by the riverside, though never before 6 p.m.. Earlier, you would have had two large drinks before leaving. Now, while walking, you took a swig of Bacardi or Smirnoff from a hip flask tucked into your mundu at the waist. But you never went beyond two large pegs. By drinking while you walked, you were able to control the level of intoxication. The high that you felt at such times could only be described as linear.

Whatever time you had left after cleaning up, cooking, buying fish at the market and doing your laundry and ironing was spent on reading and music. You were learning to identify the ragas, little by little. You could tell now that *Chithu polae muthu polae* was set in Anandabhairavi.

You also began listening to Western classical music. Maurice Ravel's *Bolero* was a composition you returned to frequently. You were not surprised when you came across this comment by Ravel: 'I've written only one masterpiece—*Bolero*. Unfortunately, it has no music in it.' It was a contradiction, but that was where its beauty lay.

There were times when you wished you had a friend to walk with, your arm around his shoulder. But you had no friends other than Balan, who was extremely busy with his practice. He was also actively engaged in raising support for euthanasia. He fought for it; he spent time on it. Nearly three decades had passed since he started the campaign. His steadfastness and staying power surprised you.

'I don't have that kind of courage,' you would tell yourself. On the rare occasions that he came to meet you, Balan spoke to you about his work. It was no longer a solitary effort. He had gathered around him a group of like-minded people from various parts of the country.

'Haven't you heard of Aruna Shanbaug? The nurse from King Edward Memorial Hospital in Bombay? She's been a vegetable for many years.'

'Who doesn't know of her?'

You remembered reading that the sweeper who had assaulted and raped the young nurse was named Sohanlal. He had nearly strangled her with a dog chain in an attempt to subdue her. Immobile, blind, deaf and mute, she lay inert, like a piece of firewood.

Balan and Kamakshi had gone to the hospital to see Aruna. She had been in that state for decades by then.

'They had cropped her hair. Her eyes were open, but she saw nothing. Her lips were parted, her teeth yellow. Her palms were both contorted,' Balan said. Aruna would never regain mobility or vision. The dog chain around her neck had cut off oxygen supply to the brain.

'Why is she being subjected to this misery? If she can never return to a normal life, shouldn't the doctors put an end to it?' you asked.

'That's why we've approached the Supreme Court. We expect a favourable judgement,' said Balan.

People feared that if euthanasia was legalised, innocent people would end up being killed. When you mentioned this, Balan retorted, 'Eda, if someone wants to kill another person, he doesn't need legalised euthanasia to do it. Those who want to kill will kill in any case. In Germany, there were many handicapped and amputee children whom Hitler ordered to be tracked down and killed. He claimed this was done for the purification of the Aryan race; there could not be any amputees or people with undeveloped or underdeveloped limbs among them. Hitler didn't wait for permission or legalise euthanasia. That's why I said that if people have to be killed, they will be killed anyway.'

You were in favour of euthanasia too. It would be deliverance for cancer patients having to live with excruciating pain and those who had suffered paralysis due to a cerebral stroke. When life is no longer liveable, it should be sloughed off.

In the beginning, though, you were conflicted about this. One must live until the last breath is taken, you thought. You had etched Salman Rushdie's words into your mind: 'You have to live until you die.' You believed that pain was also part of life. Later, your outlook changed. You were convinced that you could not love life without also loving death. After all, death was a natural phenomenon and not something to be feared. You would tell yourself that death was not the end of a journey but the beginning of a new one.

'It's been a very long time. Did you forget me?' you had asked Kamalakshi when you met her at last. Balan and she had come over and she had made herself at home, sitting on a chair with her legs crossed. She laughed at the question. She had undergone a transformation. She was no longer the antarjanam with full lips and a plump, round face. She had lost weight and her lips were dark, like a smoker's.

'She's drunk herself into this state. She's got only half a liver now. What can I do? She doesn't listen to anyone,' Balan said.

'Isn't half a liver enough? I want only half a life.'

'No one can lead a full life, Kamalakshi. Look at me. I've lived less than a full life for a very long time now.'

Yes, more than thirty years.

Whenever Balan visited, he would bring something to eat. Today there was kanji, sautéed jackfruit and lime pickle. You warmed the kanji and added grated coconut and some ghee. You fried a few pappadams. The three of you sat down at the table to eat.

'Does anyone come to meet you these days?'

'Who's there to come? Anyway, I don't want anyone to come. Living alone can be fun, Bala.'

The ship of your new life had weighed anchor and started to sail. The mind rebelled against turning or looking back. Family, job, friendships . . . everything had been left behind, too far for the eye to see.

You had heard that Ramakrishnan was visiting from Bahrain. You didn't know where he was staying, but you prayed that he would not come in search of you. It was possible that he wasn't aware of your new life in Kundachira.

As for Shivaraman, you had seen a photo of him being installed as the president of the Rotary Club of Kannur. He wore a coat and a tie. There was no trace of the erstwhile tailor from Paathimukku. The newspaper had reported that he was a leading businessman and fabric exporter. You did not discount the possibility of him landing up at your humble home in his Mercedes. You only prayed that he would not.

'On Sunday, come to our place,' Balan said.

'No, I'm not going anywhere.'

'Are Kamalakshi and I strangers to you? Would we be intruding on your solitude?'

'Don't misunderstand me. I am just loath to leave this house.'

Once upon a time, you had no hesitation stepping out and away from your own life. But no longer.

Balan had stopped asking about your life during those thirty years of absence. As far as you were concerned, that period had flashed by like a meteor in the sky, sped through space and disappeared beyond the Milky Way, never to return.

In the past, you were a regular visitor to Balan's house. The liquor library there was the chief attraction. Balan wished to turn his liquor library into a liquor museum now. He had built up a collection of two hundred different types of liquor.

'We'll sit in the yard, talk, enjoy a couple of vodkas. Like in the old days. Eda, it's not only your body but your mind that needs oxygen. As long as it's under control, alcohol can make life fun. Wasn't Old Monk your heartthrob? I have a bottle at home. Come this Sunday.'

Sunday arrived; you did not go.

You went out only to buy fish and milk, and for your evening walk in the cool breeze. You preferred to stay home and embark on mental excursions. Your solitary life had taught you how to enjoy such journeys without moving from your seat.

Although you still read widely, the one book you did not want to ever lay eyes on was the one you had written. In fact, you were adamant that no one should read it. If copies were found anywhere, you insisted they should be destroyed. One day, you secretly summoned Shailan, the youngest son of your landlord, and said, 'I'll give you a job.'

'How much will you pay me?' Shailan was at a loose end these days.

'I'll tell you. But first tell me if you can do what I want.'

'What is it?'

'I want you to go to all the bookshops and libraries around here. Ask if they have copies of a book called *Digambaran*. If they do, bring them to me.'

'Will they give me the copies?'

'If it's a book shop, buy the books. If it's a library, become a member and borrow the book. Then bring all the copies here and burn them.'

'Old man, you are mad.'

The young man in his skinny trousers and loose shirt walked away without looking back.

28

YOU AND THE DARK SPACES
OF YOUR LIFE

However hard he tried, Balan could not contain his curiosity about your time away from everyone. It became an obsession with him, perhaps because of the extreme rationality with which he himself approached things. Your oft-repeated statement of having taken a leave of absence from life just didn't make sense to him. He couldn't shake off the notion that you were hiding something from him. But he had given you his word that he would never broach the subject again with you, and he kept his word.

That didn't, however, stop him from speaking to others about it. The two people closest to him were Kamalakshi and you. When you refused to address his anxiety, he turned to her.

'Kamalakshi, I *must* know.'

Kamalakshi was busy in the kitchen, making muttamala. A delicious sweet made in Muslim homes, it was her favourite, like onion vada was yours. A terminally ill cancer patient named Raihanath had taught her how to make the sweet.

'Eda, what do you want to know?' she asked.

'You know what I mean.'

'Unni'shnan's leave of absence?'

'Yes, that.'

'Bala, how many times must I tell you? Forget it! Why do you want to poke your nose into other people's lives? Let Unni'shnan live not thirty years but a thousand years as he wishes. It's his life, his problem. We have our own problems to deal with.'

Kamalakshi arranged the muttamala on a plate and brought it to him.

'Here, eat this.'

Balan pulled up a chair. He wore a mundu and a singlet. His upper body was muscular still, despite the folds and creases that formed when he sat down. He broke off a bit of the sweet and said, 'I must know. Unni'shnan is my best friend. Why is he hiding things from me? Friends must open up to each other, or how can it be called a friendship?'

'We're oncologists. We don't have enough time even to study cancer. Why try and learn about things that don't concern us? Bala, there's no end to the knowledge available in this world. We don't have to try and get all of it. We need to know only what we need to know and stay focused. Here, have some more.'

She took another piece of the muttamala and dropped it on her husband's plate.

'But why this charade? Unni'shnan is a scoundrel. I bet he went to Fiji or Bermuda or someplace like that and made a lot of money. It's okay if he doesn't want to tell other people about it, but he should at least tell me.'

'There you go again. I don't know what to do with you. At least eat the muttamala.'

Until he gave you that oath, there had been no stopping Balan's questions. Whenever he started the inquisition, you would get up and walk away. You never submitted to the notion that others had a right to know everything about you.

One day, with Kamalakshi as your witness, you had delivered an ultimatum. 'Bala, if you keep troubling me with questions like this, I'll never meet you again. I won't open the door when you come to see me. Do you understand?'

'Eda, I have a right to know. You can't deny that.'

You walked away in a rage. You had spoken in all earnestness. If Balan carried on in this fashion, you feared that you would begin to hate him.

That night, Kamalakshi spoke to Balan as they lay in bed in their air-conditioned bedroom. Caressing his grey hair with a wrinkled hand, she said, 'There are so many things in this world that we can't even aspire to learn. Let's think about Unni'shnan's leave of absence as one such and forget about it. After this, we'll never speak about it again. Do you agree?'

'Yes, as you please.'

Kamalakshi pulled Balan down on her ageing body and pressed her lips to the sagging muscles of his neck. Balan curled up on her body like a worm. They made love, long-lasting, lingering love. When the rooster crowed at midnight, he was still awake in her arms, thinking. Not about you. He was thinking about euthanasia.

The Supreme Court order was expected soon. Balan's hopes now rested on the highest court of the land. You were also waiting for it.

*

There were some things that you did with pleasure. Cooking, listening to music, reading. You took the greatest pleasure in your evening walks, strolling along with an occasional swig from your hip flask. You would turn left after the Milma kiosk and onto a dirt track that took you to the pipal tree in front of the Annapoorneswari temple. Three or four men would be sitting under it, chatting and passing the time.

The nearly bald one with a few last grey hairs over his ears was Shreedharettan. Everyone called him that. The old man with a full head of hair was Ramadasan. He had been a clerk at Kundachira Cooperative Bank until he retired fifteen years ago. The one with hairy arms and dark patches on his face was the contractor Chathukutty Nair. And the fourth was former sub-inspector Velappan. Most people still feared him, though he had retired many years ago.

When they saw you approaching, they would say, 'Here comes our Unni'shnan.' They would invite you to sit with them beneath the pipal tree. You would refuse and continue on your walk after bestowing a broad smile on them. Each time they saw you, they wondered how you could live all alone at your age. They were all married and lived with their families.

The path in front of the Annapoorneswari temple was fringed with wild undergrowth. You would take a sip from your hip flask at this point. By the time you reached the riverbank, you would have had three swigs of vodka or rum. You made sure that no one saw you at it. Wiping your mouth with the back of your hand, you would skip along like the winter breeze skimming the trees.

The riverbank was lined with houses, an Anganwadi and a toddy shop. When you got there today, your left leg felt weak. A sudden pain made you stagger. You sat down on the trunk of a young mango tree that leaned over the water. The old mango tree had been uprooted by the previous year's monsoon winds. You decided to wait there until the pain subsided.

The water was starting to turn dark by the time you began the walk home. The men under the pipal tree had left. People were still coming to and from the kiosk, buying milk, bread and eggs. Babu, the owner, asked you, 'How is it that you have returned so early today?'

'Oh, nothing. A little pain in my leg.'

'You should apply some oil and have a hot water bath.' Babu spoke as if he were Choyi vaidyar.

Choyi vaidyar was now the oldest man in the town. His longevity should have increased the trust of his patients, but that did not happen. Most people in Karikkat had forsaken the vaidyar and Ayurveda. They had enough allopathic doctors to consult. Also, a super speciality hospital was coming up behind Nayanar junction.

The pain in your leg did not bother you. You knew that with old age, such things were to be expected. It was annoying only because it interfered with your walks. But you refused to give up. You made the daily trip to the fish market. You did not give up on your evening walk either.

Each time the pain appeared, you sat down on the mango tree and rested until you felt better.

Life in Kundachira went on thus, with your body beginning to experience all the infirmities that old age was known for.

After you held the press conference and announced your imminent death, Paru had come to meet you several times. Here is she again, today.

She gets off the bus at Kundachira, patting down her self-willed hair and looking as though she is in a hurry. Only a few days are left to the day of your death. Before that, your past has to be dug up and shared with the world. That is her mission.

She buys a packet of onion vada from Kottoor Krishnan Bakery and shows up with it and a hundred questions. But you have nothing new to tell her. You speak to her more easily these days, and candidly. But you say nothing about your death. When she tries to raise the subject, you remain silent, as though your lips have been glued together. The thought of death does not trouble you. All of your angst and anxiety are reserved for Paru.

Konnath Pappan, the owner of the daily *Aagolam*, would ask Paru every day, 'What's happened to the story on that sonofabitch?'

'I'm making enquiries.'

'How is he going to die on the sixteenth? Did you find out?'

'No, sir.'

'Have you found out why he is going to die?'

Paru stood with her head bowed.

'Which corner of hell was he hiding in for the last thirty years, do you know?'

'I'm trying to find out, sir.'

'When will your finding out come to an end? After the bastard dies and his cremation is done? Listen to me. Before that man dies, the story should be on my table. Or you're fired.'

'Sir, it's not my fault. His lips are sealed. I've been plying him with all his favourite things, but he refuses to talk. What can I do?'

'Have you done everything possible to satisfy him?'

'I believe I have.'

'No, you haven't.'

She looked anxiously at the slim, bespectacled man who was her boss. A gold ring glinted on one of his earlobes. He was infamous for his crude language. She had once heard him refer to Karl Marx as the son of a whore. She wanted to get a Godrej padlock and lock his mouth whenever he started to talk.

'Sir, what should I do now? I'm ready for anything.'

'Go and sleep with him.'

29

YOU AND THE iPHONE

One day, your older brother Ramakrishnan came to meet you. He was still a grocer, though his shop was now in Manama, not Paathimukku. You had guessed that he would turn up someday to meet you.

As the news of your return spread, people came to Kundachira in the hope of meeting you. Not everyone managed to track you down; some went back disappointed. Those who did meet you looked at you like you were a fantastical creature. You were hospitable enough to ask them to sit down, but you wouldn't speak to them. All their questions were met with a shake of the head or a nod. After some minutes of this silent treatment, they would leave.

Once word got around that you did not like entertaining visitors, people stopped coming. Only Balan, Kamalakshi and Paru visited you now.

That day, when you opened the door in response to the persistent ringing of the bell, the first thing you saw was a swanky limousine parked in front of your house. You presumed someone had lost his way and ended up here. Since you had no intention of inviting a stranger into your home, you stepped out into the yard.

'Are you Unni'shnan?'

'Which Unni'shnan?'

'Are you joking? Has it come to this, that you don't recognise your own brother?'

You were mortified.

'Come, let's sit inside,' you said with humility.

'If you don't want to meet me, I can go. I don't want to inconvenience you.'

Turned off by your cold behaviour, your brother started to walk back to the car. Just then, the door opened and a woman stepped out. She hurried towards you and enveloped you in a warm embrace, as if afraid that you might disappear again. You had no difficulty in recognising this woman in her Kanchipuram saree, as tall as you and smelling of talcum powder.

'What you did was outrageous, Unni'shna. But at least you're back now. I'm happy.'

She used a handkerchief to dab her eyes. Even at this age, she had a luxurious head of hair and thick eyelashes. She must be using an expensive dye, you thought, for her hair looked naturally black and smelled fragrant.

Ramakrishnan, potbellied and expensively dressed in a shirt and trousers, came up to the veranda. 'Even if you don't want to see us, we wanted to see you,' he said. He followed Sathi and you into the house.

'This place is suffocating. Couldn't you have found a bigger house to live in?'

Settling down on a chair, he looked around. The walls were spotless, as though white-washed just days ago. There were no photos, not even a calendar or a clock.

'You could hang up a photo of our parents, at least?'

'They are in my heart.'

'You carry everything within you. You've told no one anything. Not even me.' Sathi dabbed her eyes again.

Unable to sit down, you stood behind a chair, holding on to its back and avoiding Sathi's eyes. What was this weakness? Why did you, who held your head high in front of everyone else, lose your footing when it came to her? In your heart filled with every kind of nonsense, was she alone ever-present, like a smile that someone had left behind?

Visitors never cheered you up. Sometimes, you even resented it when Balan turned up without warning. But you felt ecstatic in this moment with Sathi here, and had to struggle to conceal your feelings. With your eyes open, you dreamed of her getting out of the car and hugging you once more. You could feel your heart beating faster, the same heart that only wished to engage with matters of real importance and which had easily buried all desires until now. You decided that your heart no longer belonged to you; it was someone else's. Or—and this was an epiphany—were you, after all, just an ordinary man?

'When Sathi heard that you were back, she jumped with joy, like a small child. She was adamant that she had to meet you immediately. We've come from Bahrain only for this. Choyi vaidyar told us that you're alive and kicking. But no one in Karikkat could tell us your address. Or your phone number.'

'I don't use a phone.'

'Is there anyone who doesn't own a mobile phone these days? Still an eccentric, I see!'

You were silent. Many had said this when they saw you, a graduate, working as a theatre manager. They said it again when you spurned Velukutty's daughter. When you disappeared for a long time, they would no doubt have echoed the same thought, unable to understand why you would do such a thing.

Ramakrishnan brought out a new mobile phone from the bag slung across his chest. 'It's an iPhone. Use it carefully. It's expensive.'

What would you do with a mobile phone? The dream product failed to excite you. But you accepted it gratefully because your older brother had brought it as a gift for you from the Gulf.

The three of you sat drinking tea and eating biscuits. As you listened to all that they had to say, you realised that although you were not interested in material wealth, you were not entirely free from a few little desires. Let them remain, you told yourself, what harm can they do?

'Did Shivaraman come to meet you?'

'No.'

'He won't. He has become a big man now. People are like that. When they come into money, they forget everyone else. Even their siblings.'

He added, 'Eda, do you know, he drives a BMW now.'

You felt a rush of happiness. How could you not be happy on hearing that a son of Vendor Goyindan, who had not even owned a bicycle, was driving around in luxury limousines? You had always hoped to see your family members—and everyone else in your village, for that matter—lead prosperous and happy lives. You might not be a communist, but that didn't stop you from wishing that all the citizens of your country could be free of exploitation and live like subjects of King Mahabali, sharing the country's wealth equally.

You sensed a note of churlishness when Ramakrishnan spoke about Shivaraman's new-found prosperity. They were both rich now. Had this made them jealous of each other?

Sathi took a tour of your house. She looked appreciatively at the clean pots and pans in the kitchen; the jars of cereals and condiments on the shelves; your books and music collection that she thumbed through and inspected approvingly. She also sat for a moment on your bed that you had covered with a freshly laundered sheet.

'This doesn't look like a bachelor's house. So neat!' she said. 'Unni'shna, you are old now. Why are you living alone like this?'

'I like living alone.'

'If you become ill or bedridden, what will you do?'

'We'll cross that bridge when we come to it,' you laughed. Sathi was relieved to see that you had not forgotten to laugh. For some reason, most people seemed to believe that you never laughed or cried or even lost your temper.

Sathi and Ramakrishnan rose to leave only when the sun started to go down.

'I'm so happy,' Sathi said.

You accompanied them to their car, which looked like a ship. Sathi's eyes as she looked at you through the car's window appeared bigger than normal. Once upon a time, when you saw a new book, your eyes would widen just like that.

*

A few days after Ramakrishnan and Sathi came to meet you, another big car drew up in front of your house. You imagined your neighbours looking at the car and then at you with a sense of wonderment. Who were these people coming to meet you in such big cars? You, who walked to the fish market every day and cut, cleaned, cooked and ate the fish by yourself?

'Eda, why don't you share your number with anyone?'

'I don't have a phone.'

'Where's the iPhone that Ramakrishnettan gave you?'

'It's here. But I haven't got a connection.'

'Do you need someone else to do that too? Unni'shna, how did you become such a useless guy?'

You had never thought of yourself as useless. You just didn't live by other people's rules or expectations.

Shivaraman did not have a paunch like Ramakrishnan. He was slim and muscular, as though he worked out every day. The moustache had disappeared. That was one of the changes you noticed. Although older than you by three years, he had less grey on his head. You remembered him as constantly fastening and refastening his mundu, the edge of which dragged along the ground, but now he was dressed in trousers and a polo T-shirt. He said his company supplied T-shirts to the Old Navy brand in the US. The American President himself wore those T-shirts for his weekend golf games.

Travelling in AC cars, sleeping in air-conditioned bedrooms and working in air-conditioned offices that were unsullied by dust and untouched by the sun, Shivaraman's face had acquired the sheen of polished marble.

'It's been a few days since Ramakrishnettan gave me your address. I had to find the time to get away, and then Vatsala said, Why should we go to Kundachira and meet him? Why can't he come here and meet us? Aren't you the older brother?'

You nodded. It was true: younger brothers ought to go and meet their older brothers. There was no need for them to come and meet you. Yet, in your heart of hearts, you were pleased. It was a while now since you had moved to Kundachira, but they had come at last.

Shivaraman sat on the same chair that Ramakrishnan had occupied. Sathi's chair remained empty.

'Vatsala has gone to Delhi to attend an AEPC meeting.'

You did not know that AEPC meant the Apparel Export Promotion Council, but you nodded as if it was a good thing that Vatsala had gone to Delhi to attend the meeting.

'She's always terribly busy. Still, one day she'll come and meet you.'

You nodded again.

'You gave all of us a lot of trouble. Do you know what people here were saying about you?'

It had been a few years since you came back. Why reopen ancient scrolls? You were fed up. Let them keep talking. One day, they too would tire of it.

'Some said you were a Naxalite and that you were hiding in the forest. Others said you had gone to Kashi. People claimed to have seen you by the Ganga, with long hair and a beard, clad in saffron clothes. You remember Koman Chettiar? His son Uthaman said he saw you in Kashi. There were other people who said you had gone to Africa to make money.'

'Umm . . .' you grunted.

'I've been sitting here for a long time, but you've said nothing. If you don't want me here, say so and I'll leave.'

'These days, I only listen.'

Shivaraman took his eyes off your face and said impatiently, 'I don't understand anything you say. Can't you talk like normal people?'

'Please forgive me, Etta.'

'We have been forgiving you all this while and that's a lot of forgiving to do. When our parents were on their deathbed, didn't it occur to you to come and see them? Do you know, Amma once said that you were born from her womb by mistake.'

You nodded.

'I'll leave then.'

'All right.'

He stood up. He didn't look like he was sweating, but he wiped his face and neck with his handkerchief and stepped out hurriedly, as if someone was calling him. Then he turned and said, 'If you need anything, tell me. Don't hesitate to ask if you need money or anything else.'

'What do I need?' you asked yourself. There was enough rice in the aluminium container to satisfy your hunger. There was coconut oil in the bathroom for your bath. There was enough Bacardi to fill the hip flask for your evening walks. There were books to read and CDs to listen to. Was this not enough for a life as simple as yours?

30

YOU AND DR KHADAR

To start with, you didn't tell anyone about the pain in your leg. It had begun as an ache when you walked in the sun or stood in one place for a long time.

Until then, you had been fairly healthy. You had never had to spend time in a hospital. In the old days, there was no hospital in Karikkat. Why have a hospital and doctors when there were no patients?

Except for one incidence of scabies on your legs and fever on two or three occasions, you were a healthy child. The fever, in fact, energised your imagination. When you lay in bed with your forehead, palms and feet on fire, images and dialogues would form before your eyes.

The pain in your leg, however, did not inspire creativity. You knew why this was so. The novelist in you had left the world long ago. You did not know if that novelist in you had given up the crown like a king, fallen like an elephant, died gloriously like a nobleman or kicked the bucket like a commoner. You knew only this—you were no longer a novelist. And you would never be one again.

'What happened to your leg?'

'Possibly a sprain.'

'The way you walk suggests there's a problem.'

'Bala, I'm past seventy. I've lived all this while without any complaints. That's good enough.'

You did not know at what age you would die. You knew only that you would. Optimist that you were, you foresaw at least twenty years of life ahead of you.

Its unpredictability was what made life interesting for you. You might pop off very soon, and it could happen like this. While taking a swig from your hip flask, enjoying the river breeze that snaked through your mundu and caressed your ankles as you walked along the riverbank. There, suddenly, in the blink of an eye, your heart would stop beating. How long had it been slogging for? Didn't it deserve to rest? The heart that beats ceaselessly, not for itself but to keep its owner alive, is a miraculous thing.

You fell face down, but the fear of death and your love for life would cause you to resist, so that with one last burst of effort you turned on your side. You would lose consciousness, but look as if you had fallen asleep in an instant.

But then, you discounted the possibility of such an end. You believed you would live another twenty years. That is, till you turned ninety. By then, you would have lost half your hair, and what was left would have turned snow white. The muscles on your face and neck would sag.

One morning, when you failed to hear the warbling of the birds leaving their nests, you would realise that you were losing your hearing. When you stopped seeing the slanted beams of light that streamed through the branches of trees at dawn, you would understand that your sense of sight was dimming. You would stop going out, afraid that you would lose your balance and fall down. You needed help to walk even inside your house. Without a wife and children, you would have to depend on the services of a home nurse. Holding your hand, the nurse would walk you through each room. As time went by, you would find yourself unable to walk even with someone else's aid. You would be entirely bedridden. That was your route map to death.

Suddenly, just like that, the ache in your leg vanished and you walked to the fish market pain-free. The mischief that one's body can play!

But it only lasted for two days. On the third day, when you woke up to pee early in the morning, the pain reappeared. You imagined that your leg was a womb and a baby was trying to emerge from it, having reached term.

'Eda, can't you take a mobile connection? Your phone will rust.' Balan had stopped briefly at your place on his way to Koothuparamba, where he was going to meet a patient.

The iPhone gifted by your brother was lying unused in the drawer. It was like a pistol with no bullets. Like the one Balan had acquired long ago.

'I don't need a phone to talk to the creator.'

It was God you conversed with the most.

'Is the pain in your leg gone?' Balan asked. He had stopped by to check on you.

'It'll go away.'

'There's a problem. I can tell from the way you walk. We'll go and see an ortho tomorrow.'

The doctor's clinic was on the way to Balan's house. You recalled seeing the name board of Dr C.P. Khadar, M.B.B.S., D.Ortho.

'It's nothing serious. It could be calcium or vitamin D deficiency. We can treat that with supplements,' Balan had told you a few days earlier.

'Why go to another doctor? You've examined me, isn't that enough?'

'Eda, I'm an oncologist.'

Currently, you had more faith in Ayurveda than in any other system of medicine. You would rather consult a vaidyar like Choyi than a doctor like Dr Khadar.

'Ayurveda is much older than your allopathy. *Charaka Samhita* was written two thousand four hundred years ago.'

'Eda, Hippocrates too lived around that time. You and your Ayurveda! Stop being silly and come with me to meet the doctor.'

'As you please.'

You thought it would be futile to consult Dr Khadar. Could he stop the process of ageing? Anyway, you were convinced that Ayurveda had the best remedies for joint pains, backache and other such problems.

Your own experience told you that physical pain was trifling when compared to mental and emotional distress. That day, when the dogs howled like wolves and the mottled wood owls called outside your window, were you not rendered incapable of writing even one sentence?

Didn't you pace the room rubbing your tummy as if you were constipated?

No, you didn't want to think about those days.

You accompanied Balan to Dr Khadar's clinic. He was a corpulent man with a raspy voice and a loud laugh. Somehow, his temperament didn't seem to match his appearance.

'My friend, Unni'shnan. We were together in school. I took up medicine. He . . .' Balan stopped abruptly. He should have said that you were the manager at Kalyani Talkies. His embarrassed look made you smile. You were quick to smile these days.

'Wait here, both of you. There's a power cut, so the AC isn't working. Sit under the ceiling fan.'

On the wall behind Dr Khadar's chair were pictures of bones and joints of the human body. Noticing that your attention was on the photos, Dr Khadar laughed.

'Patients tend to get serious when they see these. Otherwise, they won't take their medicines properly.'

You nodded.

'Would you like to have something cool, or a sulaimani maybe? Both are available. Please choose.'

'Thank you, Doctor. Nothing just now. Unni'shnan has a minor problem. If you could take a look . . .'

'Couldn't you have examined your friend?'

'Isn't it better to stick to what we know?' Balan smiled. He then explained your symptoms at length. Occasionally, Dr Khadar interrupted with a comment and a burst of raucous laughter. You showed little interest, as if they were talking about someone else. Once in a while, your eyes drifted to the pictures on the wall. Unlike the shapeless mass of muscles and tissues, the bones had a definite shape and structure. You could see the sculptor's art in those bones, unlike in the muscles and tissues.

Dr Khadar asked you to lie down on the examination table and checked both your legs. Choyi vaidyar had examined your legs long ago, when you had scabies. Since everyone in Karikkat contracted scabies as children, no one thought of it as a disease.

When Dr Khadar rang the bell on his table, a young girl in a white coat appeared.

'Molae, get an X-ray of his foot.' He scribbled something on a piece of paper and handed it to the girl. She took you to the X-ray room and helped you out of your shirt and singlet. Your chest glowed in the dark thanks to your daily oil baths.

The X-ray report was brought in after fifteen minutes. Holding it against the light, Dr Khadar scanned it and laughed loudly. The unexpected laugher jolted you.

'Forget the leg pain. Do you have any other problems?'

'No.'

'Are you sure? Think about it.'

'Well, sometimes I find it hard to chew.'

Dr Khadar nodded his head. He rose to his feet and came close to you. He moved your head up and down. Although you resented this treatment, you did not let it show. You knew that you were perfectly well.

Dr Khadar went back to his seat, thought for some time and said, 'Bala, let's get a CK test done.' He turned towards you and continued, 'I'll give you a mild painkiller for the pain. The rest we'll decide after the test.'

Balan and you spent some more time listening to him talking and laughing, then took his leave.

'Eda, what is this CK test?'

'It's just a routine test, nothing for you to worry about. Let's go home and have a drink. That'll help bring down your stress.'

You were not at all stressed. You had decided you wouldn't go back to Dr Khadar. If the pain did not reduce, you would go to Karikkat and consult Choyi vaidyar. Was he still alive? He must be. Ayurvedic vaidyars have a long life.

It was late evening. Time for your evening walk to the river, hip flask at your waist. But you found it hard to walk these days. Giving in to Balan's persuasion, you went with him to his house instead.

Kamalakshi came down from the balcony to meet you. Her health seemed to have improved. Her lips were not as unnaturally red as before. Her cheeks were brighter too. You felt happy seeing these changes in her.

You sat down on the balcony, drink in hand. The branches of a mango tree spilled over the parapet. Birds had built their nests on them. During summer, Kamalakshi left water there for thirsty birds.

'I've had enough of seeing and listening to the miseries of cancer patients. This beast has been tormenting humans for over two thousand years. I cannot die before it's tamed. If someone asks me what life is, I'd say it's about having cancer or not having cancer. That's my explication of life.'

Balan never spoke about cancer while having a drink. Death and disease were not appropriate subjects for such times. Yet, that's exactly what he had landed on today. Was it to remind you that this world was full of killer diseases and suffering?

You were drinking a blended malt whisky. IMFL. You had never understood the term 'Indian-made foreign liquor'. Liquor, to be foreign, should be made in a foreign country, shouldn't it? How could something made in India be foreign? Whoever thought up the term must have been five or six pegs down. No one in their right senses could have come up with it.

Uncharacteristically, you went beyond two pegs that night. The alcohol swung you up and down; it laid you flat and square. The swings and roundabouts took you on a wild, boozy ride.

'Enough for tonight. Get up. Let's eat something.'

'There's kanji and kadala curry. I can make a couple of chapatis too if you like,' Kamalakshi offered.

You were famished. You had dinner right there, on the balcony. As the hot kanji spread its warmth over your tipsiness, sleep overcame you. That night, you slept in Balan's house.

The next morning, Balan took you to the hospital for a creatine kinase test. He looked impatient as he waited for the result. Left to yourself, you wouldn't have waited, for you had no interest in knowing the result. There were so many other things you wanted to know, so many …

31

YOU AND YOUR BODY

Dr Khadar was a late entrant in your life. He was unlike Balan and Kamalakshi in stature and demeanour. The tiniest joke would trigger uproarious laughter. If no one else was cracking jokes, he would, before laughing loudly. He was famous as the Laughing Doctor.

He had a marked antipathy to alcohol. No drunk would go to him for a consultation, even if he had a broken bone. 'Drink more. Now only your leg is fractured. Next it will be your spine. Drink up!' he would berate anyone who turned up for treatment with alcohol on his breath.

But other patients with broken bones would come from faraway places to consult this doctor, who had over four decades of experience. Destitute patients received free treatment. Surgery, too, was free for them. As was laughter.

One day, a beat-up car came to a stop outside your house. It was groaning and wheezing like someone with broken bones. When the engine was switched off, it shuddered and shivered. The neighbours would see now that not only luxury limousines but jalopies also came to your house. With memories of your brothers' cars fresh in their mind, this would come as a revelation to them.

The knock on the door came when you were filling vodka into the hip flask in preparation for your evening walk. There had been no power the whole day, so the doorbell and the ceiling fan had been enjoying some rest. You had not heard the car being driven into your yard. Sometimes it was like that with you—although you had ears, you could not hear.

When you unlatched the door and opened it, Dr Khadar walked in, laughing, without waiting to be asked. You did not attempt to hide the bottle of vodka. Why should you? You saw nothing wrong in taking a couple of swigs during your evening walk.

'Edo, when did you start this?'

'A long time ago.'

'That is the problem with living alone. If you had a wife and kids at home, you couldn't do this.'

Dr Khadar's understanding of alcohol was only half-baked. You knew a man who used to drink at home; he had a wife and a common-law wife. After getting drunk in the night, this man from Kundachira would beat up his wife and then run to the other woman to beat her up too.

Dr Khadar picked up the bottle and examined it.

'Edo, what is this? Whisky, brandy, rum or some other arsenic?'

'It's vodka, doctor.'

'Didn't Lenin and Stalin drink this? The Soviet Union was founded by vodka quaffers. That's why it collapsed like a house of cards.'

He pulled up a chair and sat down, still laughing. You did not like the way he was trivialising such a tragic event, one that had affected the fortunes of all of humanity. You opened the bottle and gulped down two or three mouthfuls of vodka and wiped your mouth with the back of your hand. It was a challenge to the temperate, abolitionist Dr Khadar.

'Edo Unni'shna, it's not right, what you're doing. Okay, you can drink, but how much longer? You're over seventy, right? Now I understand why you and Balan are such good friends. Drunkards are like flies and dates. They get together very quickly.'

Dr Khadar's arrival at your house was typical of him. You had only met once, but here he was, acting as if you were old friends.

'Did Balan call you?'

'No.'

'He hasn't told you anything?'

'Aiyyo, I don't have a phone.'

Dr Khadar looked disbelievingly at your face, now glowing from the effects of the vodka.

'All right then. I'll tell you.'

Uninterested, you let your eyes wander outside. Across the road, on the open terrace of a house, a woman was putting out clothes for drying. A bat hung upside down from a branch of the rambutan tree in your yard. On the electric cables on this side of the road, a crow was balancing itself on one leg.

'I've got your CK test report.'

You turned to look at Dr Khadar's face, which was unusually sombre.

'The results are not too good. There's a problem there. But it's okay. We need to do more tests, then we can decide the course of treatment. Don't worry. I'll also have a word with Balan.'

'I have no worries, Doctor.'

'Good, a lot of people worry for nothing. An itch in their ass and they get tense.'

You kept quiet.

'All right, let me leave now. Take this bottle, seal it and put it away in the almirah. It's not good for you.'

You nodded. The car rattled and wheezed on its way out, just as it had on the way in.

*

'Da, did Dr Khadar come here?'

'He did. And spouted a lot of nonsense before going away.'

'Aiyyo, don't say such things. He's a good man. He talks to everyone freely, that's just how he is. Some people are like that. They speak without holding back.'

'I don't like such people. They may be world-famous doctors, but who is he to tell me not to drink?'

'So, that's the problem.' Balan laughed. 'He keeps telling me that too. In fact, he told me again, just two days ago. I don't pay any heed. He's advising us for our own good, da, we should appreciate that.'

Balan was wearing a mundu with a zari border and a full-sleeved white shirt, like a bridegroom. There was no dust on his sandals. But he hadn't shaved that morning, you could tell from the greenish tinge on his face.

Sometimes Kamalakshi accompanied Balan. She was becoming increasingly fonder of you. 'I'm trying to understand Unni'shnan. Bala, if we understand him, we'll understand life itself, to some extent,' she said to him once.

You were just as happy to meet Kamalakshi as she was to meet you.

Balan settled down on the easy chair on the veranda. You sat there every morning to read the newspapers. Two days ago, you had washed the cloth and ironed it. Even though you applied oil on your hair daily, there were no stains on the cloth.

'I need an easy chair like this. Feels so good to lie in it.'

He looked at you and said, 'I've come to tell you something important. Dr Khadar has referred you to a neurologist. I know one—Dr C.K. Unnithan. We should go and meet him soon.'

'Do you remember, a long time ago, you asked me to consult a psychiatrist. You made me into a madman. Are you turning me into a neurotic now?'

'Our job is to give patients the best treatment so they can be cured. Come with me to the neurologist and don't argue. I've got an appointment for tomorrow.'

'What is he going to do?'

'He'll examine you. If you're ill, he'll treat you. That's all.'

'What if I am not ill?'

'The doctors will decide that, not you.'

'Okay.' You nodded your assent.

The next day, Balan drove you to the appointment with Dr C.K. Unnithan. He was the opposite of Dr Khadar. Slim, soft-spoken, solemn. You noticed that sometimes, he smiled with his eyes. He was a consultant neurologist in several super-speciality hospitals. You wondered what disease you were suffering from, to have to consult such a senior doctor. You were still not convinced that you were ill.

Dr Unnithan told you to lie down so he could examine you. He asked you to hold his palm tightly. You clutched it, imagining in a sudden burst of impishness that you were holding Sathiyechi's hand.

You were then taken for a nerve conduction test by a girl in a white coat.

What was the need for such a test when all you had was a pain in the leg? Your faith in Ayurveda was reinforced. Choyi vaidyar did not ask for blood tests or scan a person's head or stomach. You decided that you should do something to popularise Ayurveda. Old Choyi vaidyar should immediately be awarded the Padma Shri and the news should travel far and wide.

You waited in the VIP lounge with Balan and Kamalakshi for the results of the test. Balan's expression was uncharacteristically grim. He sat silently, looking at his neatly trimmed toenails that were visible below his mundu.

Reluctantly, you followed Balan and Kamalakshi back into Dr Unnithan's room. He lifted his eyes from the report, looked at Balan and said, 'Let's do an MRI.'

You had heard of this test. All the impishness disappeared; your face became grim, your eyes narrowed.

'Why an MRI, doctor?'

'I have some concerns. Don't worry. There's treatment now for all kinds of diseases.'

As Balan's friend, everyone in the hospital treated you with respect. You didn't have to wait long for the MRI to be done. First, you were asked to remove all your clothes and put on a gown. You caught a reflection of yourself on the computer monitor and thought you looked like a bat in the loose gown. There was no ring or watch to take off, and you didn't have a pacemaker inside you, so you were taken directly to the MRI machine and instructed to lie still. You lay unmoving, like a corpse. Were you rehearsing your approaching death?

Balan and Kamalakshi had accompanied you to the scan centre and were waiting outside. After about an hour, Dr Unnithan summoned Balan into his room and told him, 'The prognosis is not good.'

What did he mean by that? Although he had spoken softly, you did not miss the words.

When he emerged from the room, Balan's face looked like death.

'Let's go.'

'Eda, is there a problem?'

'Don't worry. We'll talk about it when we reach home.'

Balan and Kamalakshi took you to their house, as if you had no place of your own to go to. As soon as you got there, a bottle of Old Monk was pulled out, the rum poured into three glasses, ice and water added. The three of you sat down on the balcony with your drinks.

You could see the dim coppery sunlight falling on the rambutan leaves. Your eyesight was fine. You could hear the twittering of sparrows perched on the branches above. Your sense of hearing was fine too. Your heart beat rhythmically, like a child's. All of which showed that you had not aged. Until now, you had believed that you had another twenty years to go. You wanted to continue believing that.

'Bala, I'll live till I'm ninety.'

'Very good, that's my man!'

You clinked glasses and sipped the cold rum.

32

YOU AND THE PROXIMATE YAMA

Amyotrophic lateral sclerosis.

That was the name of the disease. A name with heft, like Thaikkandi Adiyarappara Pulliyullathil Veetil Govindan Nair. You did not know the disease, but you liked the name. It had a certain gravitas. If one must catch a disease, it might as well be one with such a name. But when you realised that you were about to be consumed by something so deadly, your heart sank. Despite all its dependencies, you loved life the way lightning loves thunder. You were the lightning and your life the thunder that went with it.

You went to the market and called Balan on the phone. It was difficult to find his number. The iPhone your brother had gifted you continued to lie in the drawer like a stillborn.

'Hello.'

'Who's this?'

'Me, who else?'

'Eda, is that *you*?'

Your voice sounded different over the phone. Balan found it amusing, but only for a moment. Your voice was trembling. You had something to say, or you would not have called. In his effort to imagine what that could be, Balan's facial muscles grew taut and his face contorted. Moving the receiver from his right ear to his left, he prepared himself for whatever it was.

'I want to meet you.'

'Kamalakshi and I will come to your house.'

'What am I suffering from? Amyotrophic lateral sclerosis—what on earth is that?'

'We call it ALS.'

'Will I die?'

'You shouldn't worry. I'll tell you everything in detail. I'll be with you soon, in about half an hour.' Before he broke off, he asked, 'Should I get you something?'

'No. I have an unopened bottle at home.'

As you walked back from the phone booth along the road where autorickshaws zipped by, you felt ashamed. How could you be so rattled by the mere prospect of approaching death? Or were you always afraid of death? Had the very thought of it made irrelevant all the profound thoughts and lofty ideals you had nursed so long? You exhaled heavily, extracted a cigarette from the packet tucked into your waist and blew smoke into the air.

The distance to your house seemed to stretch. But gradually, you felt your mind growing stronger.

When Balan and Kamalakshi got out of their car with grim faces, they found you standing on the patio with a wide grin. For a moment, they wondered if they had come to the right house, if the person in front of them was indeed you. They had expected to see you weakened by fear and anxiety. But you had gathered your courage by now and invited them in warmly, as usual.

However, neither Kamalakshi nor Balan could recover their equanimity. Without reciprocating your wide smile, they entered and seated themselves, still grim-faced. You sat across from them with a burning cigarette in your right hand and an ashtray in the left.

'I was a little upset. That's why I called you.'

'Anyone would be upset in such a situation.'

Your eyes smiled at them through the cigarette smoke, adding to their confusion. Although he was your childhood friend, Balan never really understood you. At some point, he had decided that you were like Ravana's fortress and it was safer for him to stay out and look in. Kamalakshi looked at you as though she were seeing you for the first time, disquieted by the smouldering smile in your eyes.

When your disease was diagnosed, Balan and Kamalakshi had lost their peace of mind. They lost their appetite too; they barely registered their own hunger or thirst. Having worked in palliative care and euthanasia advocacy for so long, they had met innumerable patients living in misery and pain. Thanks to their efforts, euthanasia was legal now in the country. Those who lived without hope of remission could choose death.

The three of you lingered on the veranda, glasses in hand. With only half a liver, Kamalakshi now drank in moderation. But that day, she broke her own rule and drank steadily through the evening. Long after the scarlet dusk gave way to a dark night sprinkled over by white moonlight, they continued to sit there. The lights in the neighbouring houses had been switched off a long time ago. Balan was sweating despite the cool midnight breeze.

'Kamalakshi, how can I tell him this?' he had asked her the previous night.

'It's the right thing to do. Hiding it from him would be so wrong.'

'I agree. But how can I tell him?'

You had hidden many things from Balan, but he could not do the same with you. If you were an ordinary, clueless patient, Balan's job would have been easy. He could have said, 'Don't worry. Every disease can be treated now. Yours might take a little more time. But go home in peace. If you need help for the treatment, let me know.'

With the help of a few generous friends, Balan had started a fund for the treatment of indigent patients. He had helped a dozen cancer and kidney patients already. He didn't know if you had sufficient funds for your treatment. He didn't know the source of your income either. From your lifestyle, he inferred that you were not poor. A good house, clean clothes, nutritious food, a large collection of books and CDs, a daily quota of rum and vodka . . . you must have decent savings.

But it was not the money that bothered Balan. If money could cure you, he would have been at peace. If there was even a slim chance of recovery, he was willing to take you all the way to Mayo Clinic in the US.

'Kamalakshi, I'm ready to go around with a begging bowl to save Unni'shnan.' Balan's voice reflected the despondency and helplessness he felt.

'I know that. The affection between you two . . .'

Kamalakshi's heart went out to Balan. He was good at finding a logical solution to every problem and always walked with his head high and full of self-confidence. But now, as they sat talking on the balcony, he looked anxious, and there were long pauses in their conversation.

'He doesn't know how to use the Internet, or we wouldn't have to explain it to him.'

The Internet was slowly becoming popular. An Internet café had come up next to Babu's kiosk. What kind of café was that, you had asked. Was the Internet a beverage, like coffee? 'Internet café' sounded droll, like Indian-made foreign liquor. You were not good with technology. Which was why you had dumped the much-vaunted iPhone into the table drawer. You had read somewhere that Internet literacy was essential for survival in modern times. But you weren't interested only in the present—you wanted to live in all times; past, present and future.

When the cigarette between your fingers was about to die, you used its tip to light a new one and took a couple of long puffs. Balan thought it was a conscious attempt to tamp down the tension inside you.

'Kamalakshi and I have been discussing what, and how much, to tell you.'

'You can tell me anything you want.'

'We decided that it's best not to hide anything from you.'

You looked at Balan, tense and anxious.

'Yours is a very rare and unusual disease.'

'Didn't you once say that I am an unusual man?'

'Anyone who knows you or about the way you've lived your life would say this.'

You had always wanted to be an ordinary man leading an ordinary life. But when you returned from your leave of absence, you had become unusual in everyone else's eyes. And now you had an unusual disease too.

'Tell me frankly. I can handle anything.'

'This is not a disease that can be treated. A lot of research has been done, but no cure has been found.'

'So, Yama has started on his journey already, mounted on his buffalo?'

Balan swallowed hard and turned his face away, unable to look you in the eye.

'How long will I live?'

Every death warrant has an effective date. Once you knew the date, the rest of your life could be set in order. Decisions could be taken about what to do and what not to do.

Balan was silent.

'Eda, tell me.'

'A year, possibly less.'

'Meaning?'

'Around six months.'

More than enough. You had no deeds or documents to arrange, no treasury to protect. At the time of your death, you should be neatly dressed; all your clothes should be ironed and kept ready. On that last day, you should have a drink of Old Monk—a bottle would have to be acquired. Your rent would have been paid, so there would be no arrears to worry about. Your brothers in Bahrain and Kannur would have to be informed. All this could be done in a couple of days.

'Let me ask Unnithan if there's any way to delay the end. If we can have a year at least.'

'No. We should find a way to hasten the end.'

Kamalakshi stood up and came and sat next to you. She placed her hand gently on your head. Though your head had turned cottony white, the hair on your arms was still black. The veins on the back of your hand were pronounced. Your fingernails were neatly trimmed. There were no rings on your fingers, and your wrist was bare too. You were always resistant to the idea of your body being colonised by alien objects. There was a time when you had thrown out the fascism and communalism that tried to possess you. Once, long ago . . .

'Unni'shna, Balan and I are doctors. That doesn't mean we know everything. There are things beyond science. It's possible that you may get cured. You know that I too once received a death warrant. Yet, I survived. And I am still living a good life with only half a functioning liver. I sit with Balan every evening and have a couple of drinks. Therefore, you should believe. In miracles . . .'

If Balan believed in logic, Kamalakshi believed in miracles.

What kind of miracle could you expect now? Hadn't Yama the remote become Yama the proximate?

Balan opened his eyes as if waking from a deep sleep and looked at you. He shifted in his chair and cleared his throat. He had taken a decision—to tell you everything without holding anything back.

'Unni'shna, you're finding it hard to move about because of the pain in your leg. Chewing and swallowing have become difficult too. But this is only the beginning. As each day passes, your difficulties will increase, will worsen . . .'

Your face displayed neither anxiety nor trepidation. There was only curiosity there. The curiosity to know what Karikkat Bhagawathy had in store for you.

Very soon, the symptoms would start showing up. One by one, every muscle in your body would start to weaken. The weakness in your hand would make it difficult for you to lift anything. Whenever you tried to pick up something, it would fall from your hands.

When you could not walk any more, you would take refuge in a chair. Once you sat down, you would not be able to get up. With your sphincter muscles losing their strength, you would not be able to defecate. With the muscles in your throat collapsing, you would not be able to swallow even water. Your tongue would become feeble and you would lose your power of speech. Unable to ask for water, you would suffer an unquenchable thirst. You would not be able to even lift your hands to communicate in sign language.

As your neck muscles weakened, your head would droop to one side. You would be unable to open your eyes and would find darkness descending upon you. With the muscles of your lungs giving up, you would no longer be able to breathe. You would die writhing and gasping for breath.

This would be your reward for loving life like the earth loves the soil.

33

YOUR FINAL JOURNEY

'Bala . . .'

The formerly grey-bearded, now clean-shaven man looked up at you as if he was looking through you.

'Bala, it's good of you to come. I have to tell you something rather urgently. I've been thinking about it for the last two days, but my mind is made up now.'

Balan was all ears. You had never consulted him in the past while making any decision at all. Living as you were now, in the ever-growing shadow of death, what was left to be said? What could this momentous decision be?

'Eda, what is it? Tell me.'

You looked sheepish, like someone who had forgotten what he meant to say. Your tongue wouldn't obey you any longer.

'The President has given his assent to the Euthanasia Bill, right? I thank him!'

'Why are you thanking him?'

'Isn't it a good thing he's done?'

Balan nodded. He had started wearing his hair long; the grey locks fell onto his forehead.

'How many people have asked to be euthanised so far, Bala?'

'Four. Didn't you read about it in the newspaper? Two other cases are pending. All of them are from north India. From Bombay and Delhi.'

'None from Kerala?'

'No.'

'What a shame! We're ahead of everyone in everything, aren't we? We're hundred per cent literate. There are more communists here than anywhere else in the world. The maximum number of people die by suicide in our state. Then how did we become laggards in the case of euthanasia?'

'Shouldn't we be happy about it?'

You'd had no role to play in your own birth. Vendor Goyindan had fathered you and Lakshmikuttyamma had given birth to you and brought you up without consulting you on anything, not even whether you wanted to be born as a male or a female, and when. In the matter of death, however, you were unwilling to make this concession. You would decide when and how you would die.

'Bala, you need to help me.'

'What do you want me to do?'

'You must kill me.'

'Kill you? Mercy killing, you mean?'

'Yes, exactly that.'

Balan sat with his eyes closed, afraid to look at you. Was it for this that he had spent a lifetime fighting for euthanasia to be legalised? Travelling across the country and spending most of what he earned and getting cursed at by strangers, was it for this?

'Why don't you say something?'

Balan stood up. 'I'm leaving.'

'Where are you going?'

Without a word, Balan left and walked quickly towards his car. He lit a cigarette, sucked the smoke in hungrily and exhaled through his mouth and nose. The smoke billowed out, as though his insides had caught fire. He slammed the door shut and took off in a hurry, the car's wheels spinning furiously.

Kamalakshi was standing on the patio of their house, as though waiting for him. He took her wrinkled hand in his and collapsed onto a sofa. Its loose springs squeaked as it took his weight.

'What happened?'

'Unni'shnan wants to die. He says he is ready for euthanasia.'

'It was your idea, wasn't it?'

'No. It's his own decision.'

'That's good, then.'

A deep sigh escaped Kamalakshi, as if a sea trapped inside her was seeking release.

'When there's no hope, it's the best thing to do. I know that. But . . .'

'How many deaths have we witnessed, Bala? Death was deliverance for every one of them.'

'He's been my friend from childhood. How can I let death take him away?'

'Death will take him anyway.'

'Let it. I won't do it. I can't.'

Balan looked as if the disease was consuming him rather than you. The rational self he had taken pride in all his life had crumbled like a termite hill. He went into the house and returned with a glass of whisky and soda, ice cubes clinking, and sat down beside Kamalakshi. At this rate, he would drink the bar dry, she thought. But he didn't gulp the drink down as she had expected. His mouth clung to the rim of the glass like a baby sucking on a teat. Deep lines appeared on his forehead, mirroring the lines on his palm.

Slowly, he said, 'Let's do it, Kamalakshi. Let it be as he wants.'

He went in again to refill his glass.

They sat together silently. Balan was in no mood to respond to anything Kamalakshi said, so she gave up trying after a while.

The next day, they woke up late. His throat was parched, and he had a splitting headache.

'There's a lot of paperwork to be done, and quickly. At least, it will mean less suffering for him.'

He was aware that your condition was rapidly worsening.

'Let Unni'shnan leave us before the disease takes him.'

*

Paru arrives like a bird, albeit wingless. She glides rather than walks. Whether in faded jeans or a kurta with rolled-up sleeves, sometimes buttoned up wrongly, or with hair tied up in a topknot like a granny, she is always casually stylish. Today, however, she doesn't seem to have paid any attention to her appearance. With the innocence and freedom of a child, she walks into your house and sits down on your favourite easy chair. The leather shoulder bag she usually carries around, stuffed with papers, is missing.

'It's been a few days. Where have you been?'

'I was nowhere.'

She is using your words. Is she mocking you?

'I was by your side all this time. You missed me because you couldn't see me.'

Drawing up a chair, you sit down beside her. Seeing her makes you strangely happy. You tell her so.

'I've been wondering where you disappeared to.'

'So, you are no longer angry with me.'

'Why should I be angry? It just feels like the time has come for me to leave.'

There is neither fear nor anxiety on your face. Your mental fortitude surprises even you.

She still does not believe that you will die on the sixteenth. She thinks your press conference was a charade. Why would anyone call a press conference to announce his impending death? Is life a joke to you?

'Unni'shna, you are a scoundrel.'

Lying in the easy chair like a karanavar, with both her legs resting on its arms, she throws you a look. Sometimes she behaves with you the way she would with someone younger than her—why, she uses the familiar 'eda' and 'poda', unmindful of how much older you are.

She has come empty-handed, without onion vada or anything else to eat. She is making no attempt to seduce you, and this does not escape your attention. Usually, she is full of questions. Not one visit has gone by without her trying to drill you.

'You don't have any questions for me today?'

'No.'

'Then why have you come?'

You have decided that today you will answer all her questions. You are ready to speak. But she seems to have forgotten her questions.

'Unni'shna,' she says, rising from the easy chair and pulling up another chair to sit next to you, 'I've bothered you so much with my questions. But they were all for my editor's sake. Now I have no editor. I am free, I walked out of *Aagolam*.'

Like you had stopped writing novels because of mottled barn owls, she has stopped writing news stories because of Konnath Pappan.

'So, you don't want to know why I'll die on the sixteenth?'

'No. You will not die. You are pulling a fast one on all of us. I know you by now, Unni'shna, inside out.'

'You don't. Now listen carefully to what I have to say. Don't interrupt me with questions, and no crying and wailing . . .'

She looks at you anxiously.

As you speak in fits and starts, telling her about all the things she has been so curious about, surprise, anxiety, rage and pain flit over her face like changing seasons.

When you finish, she has only one question. 'Are you sad?'

'No,' you reply.

*

There is a lot of paperwork to be done. Dr Unnithan and Dr Khadar come to Balan's aid. The initial lethargy and hesitation have disappeared, and Balan is back to his rational self. He is determined that before Yama can reach you mounted on his buffalo, he will send you off to meet him.

He has also decided that not for a single day will you have to suffer being bedridden, with paralysed limbs and a lifeless tongue. Even though you are terminally ill, you shall be sent on your way without any of the attendant miseries.

It is while he is preoccupied with the paperwork that Balan hears about your press conference.

'You're crazy! Why did you do it?' he asks angrily. You are supposed to leave without anyone getting to know. There are enough groups and individuals opposing euthanasia who will grab any opportunity to stage a protest. If one of them obtains a stay order from the courts, all their plans will go awry.

'My death will be reported in the obituary columns. But only after I'm dead. I wanted to inform the world before that.'

'To what end?'

'I should say goodbye before I die, shouldn't I?'

'I don't know what to do with you!'

Balan has worked so long and so hard to make the euthanasia law possible. You want the whole world to know how proud you are of him. You want them to see that you trust your childhood friend in life and in death. All of Kerala should celebrate him, that's what you hoped for when you called the press conference.

You imagine Balan going up to receive the Padma Shri from the President of India. Yes, that too will happen.

'You have to suffer my presence for a few more days, that's all,' you say. 'After that, I won't trouble you anymore.'

Although you had set up the press conference and announced your death, none of the major dailies reported it. No placard-bearing activists turned up at Balan's house, shouting slogans. That is a relief. But Balan is on tenterhooks. He wants everything to be done as quietly as possible. Even if euthanasia has legal sanctity and backing, he is afraid that the public's overwrought emotionalism will take over and the media will fuel its flames.

Moosakutty, the Press Club secretary, has forgotten all about you and the press conference. However, Vasavan sir, the reporter-editor of the local eveninger, has not.

'Should we go to Kundachira on the sixteenth and meet that crackpot?'

'Don't waste your time, Vasavan sir. He's not going to die. He just has a screw loose, maybe several,' says Achutty Gurukkal, the reporter at the local daily.

'All the same, let's go and see.'

'I'm not coming.'

Balan hopes desperately that no one will turn up. Only after everything is done, your body cremated and the pyre calm, should people discover that you have left the world. And how you left it.

*

Balan had asked if you wanted it done at the hospital or at home. You had opted for your small, rented house in Kundachira. Two days ago, though your hands had lost their strength, you had swept and cleaned the house with the help of the maid. You removed the cobwebs on the ceiling fan and in various corners of the rooms. You mopped the floor of the living room and the bedrooms.

You took down the curtains and washed them, and the cloth of the easy chair. For your last shave, you bought a disposable razor. You bought a white cotton shirt with black buttons and kept ready a double mundu to wear for your final journey.

Dr Dattan Nampoothiri, a representative of the Euthanasia Commission, arrives from Thiruvananthapuram with a leather bag. He supervises all the arrangements. Balan and Kamalakshi follow you around like shadows. Paru is mute, sitting huddled in a chair.

'Allow me to follow protocol and ask, is there something that you want to eat or drink before the deed is done?'

'The last supper? No.'

'Old Monk. Onion vada. Anything . . .?'

'Nothing.' You shake your head with some difficulty. You had sensed the weakness in your head as soon you woke up in the morning.

'Do you want to speak to someone, tell them anything?'

'What is there to say anymore, Bala?'

'Anyone you want to see?'

You shake your head. You are on your way to meet your maker, you have no desire to meet anyone else.

'I'd like to walk for a while,' you say. You were always fond of walking.

Kamalakshi and Paru help you up. With your arms around their shoulders, you walk for some time in the yard, Kamalakshi on one side, Paru on the other.

'Mahatma Gandhi used to walk like this,' you say. Paru and Kamalakshi look at your face.

'Abha behn on one side and Manu behn on the other. Haven't you seen the photos? Both wore spectacles.'

The next morning, you wake up early. After a shave and a hot-water bath, you put on the white cotton shirt with black buttons and the double mundu. Looking into the mirror, you neatly comb what is left of your hair. Paru has made the bed with fresh sheets and pillow covers. You have breakfast, dipping the idli in coconut chutney made with bird's eye chilli and chutney powder mixed with coconut oil. After that, you read the newspaper and listen to music for a little while.

'Here, have this.' Balan offers you a glass of water and two tablets. 'Tranquillizers to calm your mind.'

You try to read, but cannot. It is a struggle to keep your eyes open. Everything around you seems to be receding. Even Balan, who stands next to you, seems to be far away. He has not bathed or shaved; his hair is dishevelled; there are black circles around his eyes.

'I must lie down. I'm exhausted,' you say to him.

Balan helps you up from the chair. Kamalakshi and Paru prop you up and walk with you to the bedroom. Before settling you down on the bed, Paru smoothes some imaginary wrinkles from the bed sheet and pats down the pillows. Slowly, you lie down on the bed.

As the ravens settle in their nests, gazing at the dusk darkened by rain clouds, Dr Dattan Nampoothiri checks each document, one by one. After making sure that you have signed in all the right places, he announces, 'I'm ready.'

He puts the papers back in his bag. He takes out a syringe and fills it with Nembutal.

'Unni'shna . . .'

You try to open your eyes and look at your childhood friend. You want to smile at him, but you can't. Your lips and face contort with the effort. Paru moves closer to the bed.

'Unni'shna, may I kiss you?'

She bends down and kisses your wrinkled forehead, your sagging cheeks, your dry, withered lips.

Dr Nampoothiri comes up to you. He straightens your drooping head and slowly buries the long needle of the syringe in your neck.

Eda Unni'shna, goodbye . . .